SUSPENSE—HIS & HERS: TALES OF LOVE AND MURDER

MAX ALLAN COLLINS
AND
BARBARA COLLINS

WOLFPACK
PUBLISHING
— EST 2013 —

WOLFPACK
PUBLISHING
— EST 2013 —

Suspense—His & Hers: Tales of Love and Murder

Paperback Edition
Copyright © 2021 (As Revised) Max Allan Collins & Barbara
Collins

Wolfpack Publishing
5130 S. Fort Apache Road, 215-380
Las Vegas, NV 89148

wolfpackpublishing.com

Paperback ISBN 978-1-64734-344-6
eBook ISBN 978-1-64734-857-1

SUSPENSE—HIS & HERS:
TALES OF LOVE AND MURDER

In memory of Barb's dad —
William L. Mull, Jr.

Contents

Contents

SUSPENSE – HIS AND HERS

An Introduction

This is a companion volume to our collection *Murder — His and Hers*. It includes stories written by Barbara Collins, others by Max Allan Collins, and a quartet by the two of us.

As a husband-and-wife writing team, we are frequently asked how we keep from killing each other or at least stay out of the divorce court. The secret of our successful collaboration is simple: we keep out of each other's way. On stories or novels that we write together, one of us gets an idea, which the two of us flesh out in several plotting sessions, often over a long lunch hour or during a lengthy road trip.

Barb then writes a first draft, usually about half to two-thirds the projected length of the finished piece. Max then does a second draft, polishing and expanding. On occasion, one of us will write a section of a story alone; but never together, looking over the other's shoulder. That way lies madness.

Gathering individual stories of ours with collaborative ones reflects our impact on each other's work. Barb has been Max's in-house editor since the beginning of his career, long before she struck out on her own as a short story writer (and, later, co-novelist with Max on *Regeneration and Bombshell* and the *Trash 'n' Treasures Antiques* series). Likewise, Max has been Barb's in-house editor from her first short story sale, and it's fair to say that almost anything by either the Barbara Collins or Max Allan Collins byline has some of both of us in it.

This collection contains both "pure" mystery/ crime stories and others that sport a supernatural, even horror element, including a vampire tale that immortalizes Barb's favorite movie star. Several of Max's series characters appear – Ms. Tree, in the Edgar-nominated "Louise," and two stories with the hitman Quarry, who generated a Cinemax TV series and a feature film.

We find that stories by either Collins seem to nestle nicely, whether crime/mystery or supernatural/horror; but we admit to learning the short-story craft as baby boomers who watched the original *Alfred Hitchcock Presents* and *Twilight Zone* (and Max includes the EC Crime and Horror comic books among his influences). So, it's not surprising that mystery and horror blur in our collective mind.

Our thanks to the publisher of this collection as well as to our much-missed friends, Ed Gorman, Marty Greenberg, as well as Max's occasional co-editor Jeff Gelb, for including these stories in various original anthologies. Thanks also to Christine Matthews and Janet Hutchings, who first published some of these tales.

Barbara and Max Allan Collins

FLYOVER COUNTRY

Barbara Collins and Max Allan Collins

Susan Parsus, a thirty-four year old book editor with long dark hair and round silver glasses, gazed out the little window of the airplane. Below, the brown and green checkerboard blanket of the Midwest extended as far as the eye could see.

Flyover country, she thought, how boring. Thank God, I don't live down there.

Not that New York was so wonderful, she admitted. Lately, the expense and the hassles and crime and just the *smell* of that city had begun to get to her, and started her thinking about moving someplace else. But, then, she was in publishing, and publishing *was* New York.

Even Los Angeles, where she'd just come from a book sellers convention, was a big disappointment: even more expensive and over-crowded, the beautiful weather she'd heard so much about covered in smog.

Wasn't there *any* place in this country worth living? Cheaply, that is.

"This is your captain speaking," a male voice crackled urgently over the intercom, interrupting Susan's thoughts. "We're having some engine trouble. Flight attendants prepare for emergency landing."

An immediate murmur spread through the cabin, more noticeably on the right side of the plane, where the passengers, Susan among them, could see thick, black smoke streaming from the engine. As the plane fell sharply, two of the flight attendants, an attractive, young blonde with terror in her eyes, and a balding middle-aged man managing to hold on to his professional demeanor, rushed up and down the aisles instructing people to put their safety belts on, tray tables away and seats in an upright position.

In the rear of the cabin a mother wailed and clutched her baby tighter to her bosom. Others hugged, some sobbing, while many more dug into pockets and purses to scribble a final farewell note to loved ones below.

Fear spread upward from Susan's stomach to her throat like a bad case of heartburn. She tensed and grabbed onto the armrests. Next to her, an older woman with gray hair and orange lipstick, who hadn't been too much of an annoyance on the trip, turned toward her for consolation, but Susan moved away. If this was going to be her last few moments alive, she wasn't about to share them with some complete stranger.

Dear Lord, Susan prayed as the airplane shimmied and shook, *if I make it through this, I promise to be a better person.*

Her thoughts turned to Steven, her fiancé, back in New York. She'd been kind of terrible to him just before she'd left. Arguing about plans for their wedding.

*A much better person. I promise, I promise...*As the plane broke through the clouds on its rapid decent, Susan could see they were over some sprawling city. Tall glass buildings sparkled as the brilliant morning sun bounced off them, and everywhere, lush green trees lined clean streets where little toy cars moved up and down them. If she hadn't been so frightened, she might have appreciated this pristine, modern city.

Susan closed her eyes tightly, because the careening silver bullet of a plane seemed much too close to the tops of the trees, and neat little houses. She hoped that in front of them was a runway or highway and not more homes.

A big jolt lifted everyone out of their seats, as wheels touched asphalt – it *was* a runway, she could see out the window – then a smaller jolt followed, and the passengers lurched forward, bracing themselves as the plane braked hard to a stop. A collective sigh of relief emanated throughout the cabin.

Twenty minutes later, Susan walked through the airport terminal on wobbly legs toward a bank of phones, her Louis Vuitton carry-on (a gift from a former lover) slung over one shoulder. She sat on one of the little round seats, smoothing her black Donna Karan dress (discounted in the district), then dug in her black leather Picasso bag (half-off at Bloomies) for her phone card.

"Steven? It's Susan."

"Where are you?"

"Des Moines fucking Iowa."

"What are you doing there?"

"The plane had engine trouble, and I'm stuck in this God-awful place because I can't get another flight to New York until tomorrow." She moaned. "Oh, *why* did I fly on the cheap? This is *your* fault!"

"My fault! It was *your* idea to cash in the first-class ticket so you could use the extra money for shopping."

"Well, you should've talked me out of it. Every time I do something on the cheap, I get into trouble." There was silence, then Steven said, "Sometimes trying to save money ends up costing you more." So, they were back to that. The argument before she left.

She said, "I just thought if we got married next Easter, we could use the church's flowers. It's being economical. What's wrong with that?"

There was silence again, and when her fiancé spoke, his voice seemed sad. "Some things are more important than saving money."

"Like what?" She couldn't imagine.

He sighed. "Call me when you get in and I'll pick you up."

"Okay," she said, "but don't park the car because it'll cost."

But he'd already hung up.

Susan picked up her carry-on and walked away from the phones. With the whole day, and night, in front of her, she might as well rent a car.

The line at the Hertz counter was short, and Susan started toward it, then stopped. They'd be the most expensive, she thought. Her eyes traveled down the line of the other car rental companies – Avis, National, Alamo, Budget – and landed on the last, U-Save. That sounded like it wouldn't cost her an arm and a leg.

A fat man in a bright yellow sports coat (why draw attention to himself?) was just stepping away from the counter when Susan came up to it, setting her bag down. Behind the counter, which came almost to Susan's chin, was a forty-ish woman with short, dull brown hair and a plain face. Susan wasn't sure if even lots of make-up would help.

"I want a car until tomorrow afternoon," Susan told the agent, "when I can get the hell out of here. What's that gonna cost me?"

The agent smiled pleasantly. "We have a luxury car for fifty-four dollars, or a mid-size for thirty-four."

"I'll take the thirty-four."

"Would you like collision insurance?"

Susan laughed. "That's just for suckers, and I'm not one of them."

"I see," the woman said, her brown eyes seeming to study Susan, the pleasant demeanor continuing. "Please sign here and here." She put the contract out on the high counter top.

Susan had to reach up to sign, and there was a plant with broad thorny leaves like a cactus in a terra-cotta pot sitting there that she shoved aside, tipping it over, spilling rich dark soil onto the counter top.

For a brief second an irritated looked flashed over the agent's face, then the professional smile returned, and the woman scooped up the dirt with her hands and put it back in the pot, setting the plant upright again.

Susan didn't apologize. The ugly thing shouldn't have been in the way in the first place.

"I'll need to see your driver's license," the woman said.

Susan dug into her purse and handed the agent her card.

The woman looked at the license and commented, "New York City, I've always wanted to go there."

"Yeah," Susan snorted, "it's a riot, literally."

The agent finished up the paperwork and handed a copy of the contract to Susan. "Just catch our shuttle bus out front," she instructed. "They'll take care of you." Then she added, "Have a nice stay in Iowa."

Susan smiled sweetly. "Is that possible?"

While the smile remained on the agent's face her eyes grew dark and cold; then suddenly they softened. The woman with the plain face leaned forward and her voice became soft and sympathetic.

"I know how you feel, stranded in a strange place, wanting to get home," the woman said. "Tell you what, I'm going to upgrade your car for nothing, because I want you to have a nice time. And, let me give you some advice on where you should go, there's a quaint little village."

The town of Prosperity, the car rental agent had told Susan, was located fifteen miles south of Des Moines. And there, she said, the newly refurbished Grand Hotel would cost her a mere fifty dollars (as compared to one hundred in the city).

Susan drove along the highway in a red Mustang convertible. She couldn't believe getting it! She could never drive anything like this in New York. With the top down, the wind blowing her long dark hair around, she felt like a teenager again.

The air was so fresh! Like a cool drink of water, and sweet, maybe from the green corn growing in the neatly tended fields along the road. She'd never thought of corn as beautiful, but it was, tall and graceful, long slender leaves bending gently in the breeze, and from the top of each stalk, yellow tassels hung like golden strands of hair. Iowa was not at all what she thought it to be, which was flat and boring. The landscape was lovely, with rolling green hills, brilliant wild flowers, and every mile or so a tidy little farm, with its own little garden, and clean clothes flapping on the line.

Susan closed her eyes, breathing in through her nose, remembering how wonderful clothes that had dried outdoors smelled back in Poughkeepsie where she was raised by her mother who had very little money. After high school, a scholarship to NYU brought her into the city and a part-time job doing clerical work at a now defunct paperback house which gave her some monetary help, that and latching onto well-heeled friends.

After graduation, she landed a job at a prestigious New York publishing house working as a copy editor. She had a good eye for detail and was smart enough to know not to meddle with the author's style and attach herself as a collaborator like some frustrated, unpublished editors she knew. This was a happy time in her life, except for still not having much money.

Soon she was promoted to senior editor and put in the uncomfortable position of deciding the fate of the hundreds of manuscripts that crossed her desk every week. She thought she'd been doing a good job selecting the list, but after a while the publisher called her into his office and told her she was within an inch of losing her job.

"Susan," the older man said, tugging at his course, gray mustache, "we're in the book turning down business, not the book buying business. Get it? Now reduce your list."

After that, she was afraid to buy anything.

Up ahead, the road narrowed to almost one lane and the tall corn fields gave way to dense forest. A fresh water stream now appeared on the left of the highway and after a curve in the road a weathered wooden covered bridge led her across the brook, reminding Susan of a bestselling novel she'd turned down a few years ago.

About a half mile across the bridge, a large painted sign depicting an exotic plant welcomed Susan to Prosperity, population 8,000. As she entered the town on a cobblestone street, she slowed the Mustang down. Grand old homes appeared on both sides of the road, and a canopy of ancient maple trees provided shade in the warm summer day.

Here and there, neighbors stood chatting while young children played, many unattended, in open yards, their bikes and toys scattered along the sidewalk. No one seemed concerned here about theft, or kidnaping or drive-by shootings.

At the end of the block Susan saw something that made her laugh out loud as she drove by: a large parcel sat on top of a blue corner mailbox, too big to fit inside, the owner just left it, without a concern that someone might take it.

The turn-of-the-century downtown buildings of Prosperity were built in a square around a small, immaculate park that had a white wooden bandstand in its center. Here and there wrought-iron park benches sat next to flower gardens of roses, geraniums, petunias, and mums. On one of those park benches sat an elderly couple, both gray-haired and bespectacled, enjoying ice cream cones, and each other.

She couldn't remember the last time she saw a happy old couple on the streets of New York. If they weren't scowling, they were in some heated argument.

Susan parked the Mustang in a diagonal spot in front of hardware store, its ancient facade freshly painted, candy-striped awning flapping gently in the breeze. As she started to get out of the car, her foot kicked something on the floorboard by the break. She reached down and picked the item up, a tan leather appointment book that must have been under the seat, sliding forward when she stopped.

Susan opened the appointment book. There was a business card tucked in a plastic see-through pouch on the left. Some woman named Madeline, representing a pharmaceutical company in Dallas. On the right was a calculator with fax-jewel pads, and in the center, in the fold, was a beautiful brown Cross pen. She'd mail it to the poor woman as soon as she could, because Susan knew how upset she herself would be to lose her own appointment book. But then, Susan thought, as she got out of the car, the woman had probably by now replaced it, and besides, *she* could use a new calculator and pen. Which Susan took and put in her purse, tossing the appointment book in a curb-side trash can.

Then she dug in her wallet for some change for the meter.

"Don't got none of them here," a friendly male voice said.

Susan looked up to see a plump man around the age of sixty, with handlebar mustache, wire-framed glasses, and mostly bald head. He was wearing a striped apron (that nearly matched the awning) over a short-sleeved blue shirt and brown pants. The man was sweeping the sidewalk with a big push broom.

"Pardon?" Susan asked.

"Why punish people who come to spend their hard-earned money by puttin' in meters?" he said with a shrug, and gave the cement walk one last sweep before turning and disappearing into the store.

Susan closed her purse. "I think I'm gonna like it here," she said with a tiny smile.

Then something in the window of the hardware store caught her eye, and she moved toward the glass.

The object of her desire in the carefully arranged display window wasn't the blue bottle of perfume called Ode to Venus, or the plant next to it with its large, thorned leaves spread open, nor even the pseudo-gold necklace carefully laid out on a piece of blue velvet. What she was gaping at was an ordinary claw hammer.

"Oh, my Gawd," she whispered, reading the price-tag sticker on its handle, her face nearly pressed up against the glass. "A dollar ninety-nine."

It had been a miserably cold, windy day last February that she had traipsed all over Manhattan to find a claw hammer because she'd loaned *hers* to a neighbor who'd never returned it before he'd left town. And the hammer that she finally did find (a cheaply made foreign one whose plastic handle fell off) cost her eighteen dollars and ninety-nine cents. Eight ninety-nine for the lousy hammer, plus ten bucks in cab fares! Sometimes, trying to find the simplest things in New York was almost impossible.

Susan rushed into the hardware store. She crossed the gleaming wooden floor and wound her way through the narrow aisles of neatly arranged items toward a large counter in the back, behind which the man in the striped apron stood, filling a glass jar with jelly beans.

"I'd like that hammer in the window," she said.

He looked up from his work. "It's a good one," he told her. "Made right here in the U.S. of A."

He came around the counter and plucked the same hammer from a pegboard on a display nearby. "And you can't beat the price," he added.

"You're tellin' me!" Susan said. "You won't believe what they cost in Manhattan."

Back behind the counter, the man wrote up a receipt on a little pad. "I bet just about everything's expensive there," he said.

"You better believe it."

The man handed a plain brown sack with the hammer inside and gave her an odd smile showing white, perfect teeth. "I hope you enjoy our little town while you're here. We try to make visitors welcome."

Susan smiled back. "Everyone does seem friendly."

She turned to leave, then turned back to ask, "Where is the Grand Hotel?"

"Directly across the square. You can't miss it."

"And a good place to eat?"

"The Venus Dinner serves up a great tenderloin."

A tenderloin! She hadn't had one of those since she was a kid on vacation in Oklahoma.

Susan thanked the man, left the store and stood

out on the sidewalk by her car in the warm summer sun, wondering which way to go to the diner, when two teenaged girls walked by her. They giggled as they passed, amused, Susan supposed, by her urban clothes. She guessed she did look a little like a witch, all in black, while they wore colorful, crisp, cotton clothes: one, a bright yellow dress with pink flowers; the other, sky blue overalls with a whiter than white blouse underneath, and sandals. Their toes painted lime and orange. How she envied them. They didn't know that in New York their bright clothing would make them stand out for an attack, and flimsy little sandals were exchanged for combat boots in order to maneuver the filthy mean streets.

A mother walked by, holding the hand of a small boy; they were in matching nautical outfits, and when the boy saw Susan he pointed. "Mommy, another funeral?"

The mother seemed embarrassed, smiled apologetically, and pulled her son along.

That did it! If there was one thing she hated, it was feeling out of place. She hurried down the street, entered a woman's clothing store she'd spotted when she drove into town and came out a half hour later in a peach rayon dress and brown sandals.

Her long dark hair was braided loosely down her back and held at the end with a peach floral clasp. She felt euphoric, so feminine, like a college student again. And the best part was she got the whole outfit half-price, and it wasn't even on sale, because the owner, a nice woman in her forties, wanted Susan to "have a good time," in Prosperity. Boy, was she beginning to love this town!

The Venus diner, two doors down from the clothing store, was a turn of the century ice cream parlor that had stayed in one family for three generations. Susan read this on the back of the menu as she sat on a stool at the counter, hungrily eating a huge tenderloin with ketchup and pickle, washing it down with a lime phosphate. The owners, Mr. and Mrs. Satariano, a friendly couple in their sixties, ran the establishment together. Right now, Mr. Satariano, a slight man with thinning gray hair and a bulbous nose, was fixing Susan the house specialty, coffee ice cream topped with gooey marshmallow and Spanish peanuts. He set the dessert down in front of her with a wink. "That's on us," he said.

Susan's mouth dropped open, from both the kind gesture and the sight of the heavenly concoction. "Really?"

"Enjoy yourself."

"How sweet!"

And it was. She eagerly dug into the ice cream, the combination tasting so delicious. In between bites she asked, "Was this place always called the Venus Diner?"

Mrs. Satariano, a tall, still handsome woman, who was washing a glass in a small stainless-steel sink behind the counter, answered Susan. "No, the original name was the Candy Kitchen. But we changed it a few years back."

"How come?"

The woman and her husband exchanged glances. Mr. Satariano, wiping the counter around Susan, stopped. "Prosperity wasn't always so prosperous," he explained. "As a matter of fact, seven or eight

years ago the town went bankrupt along with half
its citizens."

Susan set her spoon down. "My goodness. What
happened?"

"A couple bad years for the corn crops. First
a flood, then a drought. That's all it took to put
everybody under."

"But the town seems to be doing fine, now."

Mr. Satariano nodded. "Thanks to that," he said,
gesturing to a thorny plant sitting in a terra-cotta pot
by the cash register.

"What *is* it?" Susan asked, intrigued. "I've been
seeing that plant in all the shop windows."

Mrs. Satariano smiled proudly, like a pleased
grandparent. "It's a Venus flytrap," she pronounced.

Susan leaned forward and looked closer at the
plant. This one was about a foot tall, much bigger than
the others she'd seen. Out of its center rose a stalk
bearing a cluster of tiny white flowers, and around the
stalk were leaves about six inches in length. Each of
the kidney-shaped leaves lay like a partially opened
book and was fringed with long stiff bristles.

"For heaven's sake," Susan murmured. "I didn't
know the Venus flytrap could grow here. You mean,
that saved the town?"

Husband and wife nodded together.

"But *how*?"

The screen door of the shop opened with a creak,
then banged shut.

Mrs. Satariano looked toward the door and threw
up her hands. "Johnny! How is my boy today?"

Susan swiveled on the stool, also looking toward
the door, where a young sandy-haired man stood,

wearing jeans and a faded blue short-sleeve work shirt. The sun, shinning in behind him, enveloped him like a god. Then he walked out of the light toward the counter, with a shy little smile, his head tilted slightly.

"'lo Mom, Pop," he said, taking a seat one away from Susan at the counter.

Susan looked from Mrs. Satariano to Mr. Satariano to the young man, whom she guessed, now that he was closer, to be in his late twenties. She couldn't imagine that they were related, with the Satarianos so dark complexioned (like her) and the young man so fair.

Mr. Satariano, with the rag still in his hands, must have read Susan's thoughts, because he said, "Johnny's not our son, but you might say we think of him as one, ever since his folks died a few years back."

Susan turned toward Johnny. "Oh, I'm so sorry."

For a second, sadness flashed over the man's rugged face, then the cheerful but shy manner returned, and he said to Susan without looking at her, "That's all right. I'm doing fine, but, of course, Mom and Pop here think I can't tie my own shoes without their help."

Mrs. Satariano set one of the heavy ice cream glasses down on the counter with a loud noise. "Is that so? When have we ever stuck our noses in your business?" she asked with mock anger. "We just give you a little friendly advice on how to run the farm, and other things." She looked at her husband. "Isn't that right, Papa?"

"That's right, Mama," he agreed. "Only a little advice." And he winked at Susan.

"You can see I'm outnumbered," Johnny said, swiveling on his seat so that he faced Susan.

He was handsome, by any woman's standards, but not like a slick male model. While his body was muscular, deltoids and biceps tugging at his chambray shirt, they were muscles obtain from *real* work, not a workout, and his bronze tan came from laboring in the sun, not relaxing in a tanning bed. He was the real thing, not contrived, which made him so much more exciting.

And there was something else that aroused Susan, the scent coming off him, a combination of honest sweat and fresh country air an intoxicating drink, that made Susan both high and dizzy.

"Be careful," he warned Susan, his bedroom brown eyes playful, "or they'll start running your life."

She looked down at her High School Special and felt herself blush (when had she last done that?). The ice cream was a melted puddle, just like her heart.

"Mom, a cherry Coke, please," Johnny said, and slid off the stool. Then to Susan he asked, "Would you like to join me in a booth?"

Now it was she who smiled shyly. "Okay."

"And bring her one, too," he told Mrs. Satariano.

The booth Johnny led her to was against the back wall of the long, narrow room, giving them some privacy. The benches were dark mahogany, as was the lower half of the wall. The upper half was a mirror on which were written menu items in some kind of white paint. Above them a wooden fan hung from the high tin ceiling, churning slowly, providing a soothing breeze. It was all very quaint and charming.

"You're not from around here, are you?" Johnny asked.

"No, out east."

"I thought as such." He paused. "From your accent, I mean." Then he added, "Anyhow, I sure would have remembered you." He said this with a drop of his head, and a small one-sided smile.

She studied his face, so open and honest, and thought of all the pick-up lines in sleazy bars from sleazy men she'd ever heard, and this approach was so sincere.

Mrs. Satariano appeared with the Cokes and Johnny dug in his front pocket. Susan reached for her purse.

"I'll get mine," she said.

"You will not," Johnny said firmly. "You're my guest here. When I come to New York, you can buy me a Coke."

"Fair enough," she said, then thought wryly, *Johnny in New York. There'd be a fish out of water, susceptible to all kinds of pitfalls and traps.*

The next hour passed quickly for Susan, as she and Johnny talked about everything under the sun, their conversation punctuated with laughter. She found herself telling him things, personal things, that she'd never told close friends or even her fiancé, Steven. Which reminded her of him. And suddenly, impulsively, her hands went in her lap, beneath the table, as she removed the engagement ring and tucked it in her purse.

She returned her attention to Johnny. What she loved most about him, apart from his good looks, was the way every single thought registered on his face. With him, she would always know *exactly* where she stood. Imagine that advantage! No more evasive looks or cold silences, while she wondered what she'd done or didn't do.

Susan looked at her watch and sighed. "I'm afraid I'm keeping you from your work."

"On the farm, you mean?" Johnny asked. He was leaning back comfortably in the booth, biting on the plastic straw, as if it were a real piece of hay. "Chores are done," he said, "except for the Venus plants, and I do need to water them."

Susan leaned forward in the booth, elbows on the table. "Mrs. Satariano said growing them saved the town's economy," she said. "Tell me about the plants. I want to know all about them."

He straightened; brow furrowed. "Well, there's not much to tell."

"Are they female?" she asked. "Or male?"

Now he leaned forward, his elbows on the table. "Would you like to see?" His brown eyes were eager, like a cocker spaniel's, hopeful for a treat.

"Sure!" she said.

"Then let's blow this pop stand!" He grinned and tossed a crumpled dollar bill on the table.

Behind the wheel of the red Mustang, she followed Johnny in his blue Ford truck, through gently rolling green Grant Wood hills. About three miles outside of Prosperity he turned off the blacktop onto a gravel road.

Even with the car's top down, Susan didn't mind the dust. It seemed so clean and natural! Ashes to ashes, dust to dust. She felt good being this close to nature.

After another mile or so, Johnny's truck slowed down and turned into a short lane that led to a pictur- esque farm. To the right sat a white two-story house with green shutters and a large porch with thick white pillars. A porch swing hung by chains from the ceiling swinging gently to and fro in the warm summer breeze. The front door to the house was old and beautifully refinished, with an oval window in etched glass. It led her to believe that antique furniture might be inside.

Behind the house, to the left, was a big red barn that looked freshly painted. A black wrought iron weather vane of a rooster perched proudly on its roof. The summer sky above was a bright blue, and clouds, like dollops of whipped cream, drifted slowly by. The sun, beginning its decent in the late afternoon, made everything cast long shadows over the farmyard, bringing all its colors to a brilliant hue.

Susan parked her car behind Johnny's truck, in the large driveway that separated the house from a cornfield, and got out. Even the grass was picture-postcard perfect, freshly mowed, not an unsightly weed anywhere.

Johnny approached her, with a big grin on his face. "Well, what'd'ya think of the old homestead?"

Susan took a deep breath. "It's so beautiful," she said. "So peaceful." It would be wonderful to live here, she thought.

"The greenhouse is around back," he told her, and led the way.

They stood just inside the screen door of the green-house, which was a long, narrow building. Unlike the other structures on the farm, this one was new, with a curved, Plexiglas roof to let the sun come through.

Wooden tables ran the length of the building, with narrow paths in-between. And on those tables were hundreds, maybe thousands, of tiny green plants in black plastic trays.

"You wanted to know about the Dionaea," he said, gesturing to a nearby table. "That's the scientific name of the Venus flytrap."

"But they're so tiny," she said, moving to the table, taking closer look at the little green sprouts.

"That's because this is a brand-new crop," Johnny explained. "I start one each month." He gestured again to the plants. "These will be transplanted to the back field, where we're harvesting the crop planted last month."

Susan shook her head. "How on earth did you get the idea to grow them? I thought the Venus Flytrap was some kind of tropical plant."

"No. They're found in the bogs of North Carolina," he told her. "The soil there lacks certain nitrites." He picked up one of the plastic trays holding about a dozen plants and looked at them.

"Seven or eight years ago," he went on, "you wouldn't have recognized this farm. It looked like something during the depression, the land fallow, soil robbed of nutrients that would take years to replace." He was staring now, at the tray in his hands, like it was a crystal ball he was using to look back into the past.

"At that time," he continued, "I was in high school, and we were studying about these plants. And I thought, hey, that was one thing that would grow in the soil."

He looked at Susan. "And it did, with the help of some special plant food. And we made a bundle. Then the whole town, because they were in trouble just like us, started to grow the plants, and we sold them all over the world."

Johnny set the tray of little plants down on the table.

"Since then," he continued, "the corn crops have made a comeback, and folks have stopped growing Dionaea, except for me, on the back forty. And everybody helps with the harvest and the proceeds go to better the community."

Susan was so touched by his story, and generosity, that she felt tears forming in her eyes.

Johnny's stomach growled. "Sorry," he said. "Except for that Coke, I haven't had anything since early morning." His face brightened. "Would you join me for dinner? I have some left-over fried chicken and corn from the garden."

She touched his upper arm; his bicep was hard as a rock. "I'd love to," she smiled.

In the cozy kitchen of the farmhouse, they sat at a round oak table. Before them, lay a feast of fried chicken, sweet corn, and garden vegetables. The meal was simple, but delicious. Just like Johnny.

As they ate, he told her about taking over the farm the summer after graduating from high school, when his parents both died in a freak combine accident. And how hard he worked to keep the place going, fixing it up, little by little, even buying back family heirlooms, piece by piece, that had been sold to an antique dealer when times were hard.

And she told him about growing up poor, never having any money, and how she hated her job and New York. But that the past hours she'd spent with him were the happiest she been in a long, long while.

To that he replied, "More than anything right now, I want you to be happy."

Later, after the dishes were washed and dried, they went out on the front porch, and sat in the swing, eating vanilla ice cream covered with fresh strawberries, watching the purple-pink sunset, saying very little. And still later, when the fireflies came out, and a chill in the air drove them inside, they sat on a couch in the parlor, in front of a fireplace with a walnut mantle, sipping red wine, and watching the flames hypnotically.

They started to kiss (she wasn't sure who made the first move, which was how it should be) and never before had any man made her feel the way she did.

"I should go," she said after a while, pulling away. Her face felt hot, flushed. "I need to get a room in town."

"You can if you want to," he said softly, "but the guest room upstairs is free." He kissed her, and she kissed back, wrapping her arms tightly around him, pushing him back on the couch as the flames danced seductively before them.

Susan woke in the morning in the four-poster bed in Johnny's room. The early morning sun streamed in a nearby window and a cool breeze, with just a hint of the warm day to come, softly rustled the white cotton curtains.

She stretched. Never before had she slept so well! The night sounds of the farm were a soothing symphony in her ears each time she woke and went back to sleep. Not to mention Johnny's tender lovemaking, first on the couch in front of the fire, and later during the night, in the four-poster bed. He hadn't tried to impress her, like other men she'd been with, Steven included. Johnny was so completely at ease with the act, that it put her at ease.

Then sometime very early in the morning, he kissed her cheek, told her he had to get up for chores, and she should go back to sleep. Which she did. Perhaps, after they were married, she would get up to help him.

Susan got out of bed and padded across the braided rug to her suitcase that lay on the floor, getting what she needed for the bathroom. Through the open window she could hear Johnny out the in greenhouse, whistling, as he tended to the plants.

A half hour later, she emerged from the bathroom and stopped in front of a hall phone on a small half-circle table against the wall. Not impulsively, for she'd been thinking during her bath just what she would say, she called Steven's number at their apartment, knowing he'd be at work, and informed him she wasn't coming back, and he should pack her things, which she'd send for later.

Then wearing the same floral dress that she'd bought (she didn't want to scare Johnny with all that black), she skipped down the stairs to the front hallway and went back to the kitchen. There on the table was a glass of orange juice, and some muffins on a plate and a note saying there was coffee on the counter. Wasn't he thoughtful? She drank the orange juice, took one bite of a muffin, then hurried out the back door to the greenhouse.

When she got there, though, the greenhouse was empty. He was probably off to get something, and would be back soon, she thought. Smiling, she began to walk down one of the narrow paths between the tables. The little green shoots coming out of the black dirt looked like rolled green dollar bills, or fifties. That's what he told her they sold for last night.

She stopped, noticing that there was a little metal plaque on the side of the table which held a white card with a name and date. The card seemed to identify the month the seeds were started.

She moved along to the next table which had a similar plaque. But this one read "Heather, May." The other had been "Jill, April." She continued to the last table, where rows of trays sat empty. Her eyes went to the plaque, its paper whiter, newer than the others. It said, "Susan, July."

Her mouth fell open with delight. Johnny was going to name some plants after her! How romantic. She touched the card and another one, which had been stuck behind it, slid out the bottom of the holder onto the floor. She bent down and picked up the weathered piece of paper, which must have been in there a long, long time because the paper was brown and stained. It seemed to say "Mother" and the date was gone.

The screen door of the greenhouse banging shut made her look up to see Johnny standing in the doorway, in faded jeans and a white t-shirt.

She let the old piece of paper fall from her hands and she hurried toward him.

"Did you sleep well?" he asked.

She was a little out of breath when she reached him. "Oh, yes! And thank you for the breakfast." She pointed to the back of the greenhouse. "I noticed that the last table had a card that said "Susan"...Does that mean those plants will be named after me?"

"Uh-huh."

She squealed and threw her arms around his neck, and kissed him, but he didn't return the kiss. She brought her arms down slowly, and looked at his face, which wore a peculiar expression.

"I want you to know about the others," he said.

Was that all? she thought and breathed a sigh of relief. She'd thought something was *really* wrong. "It doesn't matter," she said. "I've been no angel."

He shook his head. "But you have a right to know. Just like the others."

She started to say something dismissive, but he continued, looking intently at her. "In April, there was Jill. In May there was Heather. In June there was Madeline...now you...and that's just this year..."

Madeline? She remembered the appointment book she'd found in the car...hadn't that woman's name been Madeline?

"You see it all started seven years ago with Mother."

"Your *mother*?" she said, completely befuddled.

He moved forward, pinning her against the table, his expression now cold, sinister.

"You see," he explained, "the Dionaea can only survive in dry Iowa soil if it's first been given a nutritious start in soil high in nitrates, human nitrates with estrogen."

A chill ran up her spine. Was this why everyone was so nice to her, Johnny included, wanting her to have a good time, as if it was her last day on earth?

She tried to escape, but Johnny's strong arms closed around her, and flailing away with her fists was like hitting a stone statue.

"Why me?" she asked, terrified.

His smile was sickening, evil. "U-Save Car Rental sends me their rudest customers, women so nasty they won't be missed." And his hands went around her throat.

"But I've *changed!*" she managed to rasp. Johnny shook his head, tightening his grip. "People don't change," he said. "I know because I never could."

And his hands squeezed tighter, like the leaf of the Venus flytrap when a victim haplessly enters its lair.

The Dionaea plant sat on a windowsill in an apartment on Seventy-third and Central Park West, warming itself in the late afternoon sun. It didn't even care if some dumb old fly or other idiotic insect came by and landed on one of its many thorned leaves, triggering that leaf to clamp shut, beginning the slow process of digestion, because earlier in the day that nice woman who lived here alone, fed it the special plant food from Iowa, making it feel big and strong.

It missed the farm. But across the street was a really big park and maybe someday, when it got too big for the little apartment, the nice lady would transplant it over there. There was always some activity going on in the park, although some of it was not very nice.

There was a knock at the front door, and the woman went to answer it. The plant liked the woman; it felt like she was a sister.

"Steven!" the woman said to a tall, dark man who entered. "Thank you so much for the plant. Come and see it."

The man came over and bent his head down toward the plant. It didn't like him. It didn't know why.

"What in the world?" he asked. "I just told the florist to send something exotic."

"It's a Venus flytrap," the woman said excitedly.

"Wow. I've never seen one." His face came closer and the plant wanted so badly to clamp down on his nose.

"From the Susan series," he read from a little card that lay next to the plant. He made a disgusted sound with his lips.

"What's the matter?" the woman asked.

"That's the name of that bitch who dumped me by leaving a message on the answer machine. I wonder what became of her."

Then they left the apartment, off to eat at some expensive restaurant, and the plant sat alone, basking in the last rays of the late afternoon sun.

LOUISE

A Ms. Tree story
Max Allan Collins

Her face was pretty and hard. Her eyes were pretty and soft.

She was a waif in a yellow and white peasant dress. A Keane painting child grown up; oval freckled face framed by sweeping blond arcs. She wore quite a bit of make-up, but the effect was that of a schoolgirl who'd gotten into mommy's things. She stood with her purse held shyly before her, a guilty Eve with a brown patent leather fig leaf.

"Miss Tree?" she asked tentatively, only half-stepping inside my private office, despite the fact my assistant had already bid her enter.

I stood, paying her back the respect she was showing, and tried to put her at ease with a smile. "I prefer 'Ms.,'" I told her, sitting back down, and gestured toward the chair opposite me.

She settled gradually into the chair and straightened her skirt primly, though her manner was at odds with the scoop neck that showed more bosom than modesty would allow. "I never been to an office on Michigan Avenue before," she said, her big blue eyes taking in the stark lines of my spacious but austere inner chamber. "You sure have a nice one."

"Thank you, Miss Evans."

Pretty as she was, she had the sort of countenance that wore more suffering than even heavy make-up could hide; so, it was kind of a shock when her face brightened with a smile.

"Louise," she said, and she extended her tiny hand across the desk, with a deliberation that revealed the courage she'd had to summon to behave so boldly, "call me Louise. Please."·

"My assistant tells me you were quite insistent about seeing me personally."

She nodded and lowered her head. "Yes. I'm sorry."

"Don't be sorry, Miss Evans."

"It's Mrs. Evans. Excepting, I'd like you to call me Louise. I need us to be friends."

"All right," I said. This wasn't going to be easy, was it? "You said this is about your daughter. That your daughter is in trouble."

I was too busy for this, with Gold Coast divorce cases, legal work, and corporate accounts, but it hadn't been the kind of plea you could turn down.

"Terrible trouble," she said, and her lower lip trembled; the blue eyes were filling up. "My husband, I'm afraid of what he might..."

Then she began to weep.

I got up, came around and knelt beside her as she dug embarrassedly for Kleenex in her purse. She was so much smaller than me, I felt like an adult comforting a child as I slipped an arm around her.

"You can tell me," I said. "It'll be all right."

"She's gone," she said. "He took her."

"Your husband took your daughter?"

"Months ago. Months ago. God knows what he done to her, by this time."

"Tell me about it. Start at the beginning. Start anywhere."

But she didn't start. She grabbed my arm and her tiny fist gripped me hard. As hard as the life that had made the sweet features of her young face so old.

"I wish I was like you," she said. Her voice had an edge.

"Louise..."

"I've read about you, Ms. Tree. You're a strong woman. Nobody messes with you. Nobody pushes you around."

"Please..."

"You're big. You killed bad men before."

That was me, a cross between King Kong and the Lone Ranger, in a dress. Frankly, this petite if buxom woman did make me feel "big"; at five ten, one hundred forty pounds, I sure wasn't small. My tombstone would likely read: "Here Lies Michael Tree - She Never Did Lose That Ten Pounds."

And so, I was to be Louise's savior, her avenger. I sighed, smiled and said, "You really should tell me about your daughter, Louise, and your husband."

"That's why I come here. I need somebody like you to go get Maggie back. He took her, and the law can't do nothing."

I got a chair and sat next to her, where I could pat

her reassuringly when necessary, and, finally, she told me her story.

Her husband Joe was "a good man, in lots of ways," a worker in a steel mill in Hammond. They met when she was working in a MacDonald's in South Chicago, and they'd been married six years. That was how old Maggie, their only child, was.

"Joey's a good provider," she said, "but he...gets rough sometimes."

"He beat you?"

She looked away, nodded. Battered women feel ashamed, even guilty, oftentimes; it makes no logical sense, but then neither does a man beating on a woman.

"Has he beaten your daughter, too?"

She nodded. And she started to weep again.

She was out of Kleenex; I got up and got her some.

"But that...that's not the worst part," she said, sniffling. "Maggie is a pretty little girl. She got blonde hair, just like mine. And Joey was looking at her... you know. *That* way. The way my daddy done me."

"Do you think your husband ever...?"

"Not while I was around. But since he runned off with her, that's what I'm afraid of most."

I was a little confused; I had been assuming that this was a child custody situation. That the divorced husband had taken advantage of his visitation rights to disappear with his daughter.

"You haven't said anything about divorce," I said. "You and your husband *are* divorced?"

"No. We was talking about it. I think that's why he done it the way he done."

"What do you mean, Louise?"

"He knew that that if we was divorced, the courts'd give Maggie to me. And he didn't want me to have her. Ms. Tree, when I was Maggie's age, my daddy beat on me. And he done other things to me. You know what kind of things."

I nodded.

"Ms. Tree, will you take my case? All I got is two hundred dollars I saved. Is that going to be enough?"

"It's going to be like MacDonald's, Louise," I said.

"Huh?"

"You're going to get back some change."

Louise had reported her husband's disappearance to the police, but in the five months since Joey Evans and his daughter vanished, there had been little done. My contact at the police department confirmed this.

"The Missing Persons Bureau did what they could," Rafe Valer said, sitting on the edge of his desk in his small, cluttered office at Homicide.

"Which is what, exactly?"

Rafe shrugged. Darkly handsome describes him, but considering he's black, saying so may be in poor taste. Thirty, quietly ambitious and as dependable as a pizza at Gino's, Lt. Valer had been my late husband Mike's partner, before Mike went private.

"Which is," he said, "they asked around Hammond, and South Chicago, talking to his relatives and friends. They found that one day, five months ago, Joe Evans quit his job, sold his car for cash, packed his things and left."

"With his six-year-old daughter."

"With his six-year-old daughter. The assumption is, Evans has skipped the state."

I almost shouted. "Then this is an FBI matter!"

"Michael," Rafe's said, calmly, smoothly, brushing the air with a gentle hand as if stroking an unruly pet, "it isn't kidnapping when a natural parent takes a child along when they take off."

"This is a case of child abuse, Rafe. Possibly sexual abuse!"

"I understand that," Rafe said, his voice tightly patient, "but Louise Evans never filed charges of any kind against her husband, before or after he ran off. Nor has she filed for divorce."

"Goddamnit. So, what does that leave her with?"

"You," Rafe said.

As if I were dealing a hand of cards, I tossed a photo of rugged, weak-jawed Joe Evans onto the conference room table; then a photo of blond little Maggie, her mother's cute clone; then another of the family together, in what seemed happier times, unless you looked close and saw the strain in the faces of both adults.

"Sweet-looking child," Dan Green said, softly, prayerfully.

Dan, not yet thirty, was the younger of my two partners, a blond, mustached, good-looking kid whose regular features were slightly scarred from a fire an arsonist left him to die in. He'd lost an eye in that fire, too, and a hand; a glass eye and a hook took their place.

"Right now," I said, "she's very likely enduring hell on earth."

"Sexual abuse at any age is a tragedy," Roger Freemont said, taking Maggie's photo from Dan. His deep voice was hollow. "At this age, no word covers it."

Roger, balding, bespectacled, with a fullback's shoulders, was the rock of Tree Investigations, Inc. He'd been my husband's partner in the business; like Rafe Valer, Roger had worked with Mike in the Detective Bureau.

"I accepted a retainer of fifty dollars from Louise Evans," I said.

The two men gave me quick, searching looks, then shrugged and gave their attention back to the photos spread before them.

"Of course, I did that for the sake of her self-respect," I said. "She works at a White Castle. She had two hundred bucks she'd saved and wanted to give it all to me."

"Fifty bucks will cover it," Roger said.

"Easily," Dan said. "So, where do we start?"

"They've been gone five months," Roger said, "and that's in our favor."

"Why?" Dan asked.

Roger shrugged. "He's settled in to his new life. Enough time has passed for him to think he's gotten away with something. So, he gets careless. Enough time has passed for him to start seriously missing family and friends. So, he makes phone calls. Writes letters."

Dan was drinking this in.

"Evans has a big family," I said, referring to my notes from several conversations with Louise. "They're a tight-knit working-class bunch. Two brothers and three sisters, all grown adults like Joey. One brother and two of the sisters live in the area - Hammond, Gary, South Chicago. Another brother lives in Dallas."

"*That* sounds like a good bet," Dan said. "I bet Joey's deep in the heart of you-know-where."

"Maybe. He also has a sister in Davenport, Iowa."

Roger perked up. "What is that? A three-hour drive?"

"Around," I said.

"Close to home," Roger said, eyes narrowing, "but far enough away."

"Where do we start?" Dan asked.

"You're going to go by the book, Dan. And Roger, you aren't."

Dan said, "Huh?" while Roger only nodded.

I assigned Dan to check up on Evans' last place of employment, the steel mill, to see if Evans used the place as a reference for a new job; ditto Evans' union – that union card would be necessary for Evans to get a similar job elsewhere.

"If Evans wanted to drop out," Dan said, "he wouldn't have used the mill as a reference or maintained his union card."

"Right," I said. "But we can't assume that. He may not be using an assumed name. Maybe he's still living as Joe Evans, just somewhere else. Also, Dan I want you to go over Louise Evans' phone bills for the six months prior to her husband leaving. Find out what, if any, out-of-town calls he was making."

Dan nodded.

"Any credit card trail?" Roger asked.

I shook my head no. "The only credit card the Evans' had was an oil company card, and Louise received no bills incurred by her husband after he took off."

"Any medical problems, for either the father or child?" Roger asked.

"No."

"Damn," Roger said.

"Why 'damn'?" Dan asked him.

"Prescription medicine would give us a trail," Roger said. "And we could check the hospitals and clinics in areas where we suspect they might be staying."

"They're both in fine health," I said. "Except, of course, for whatever physical and mental traumas the son of a bitch is inflicting on that child."

The two men shook their heads glumly.

"Roger," I said, "you talk to Evans' family members - his father's deceased, but mother's still alive. She may be the best bet. Anyway, after you've talked to them all, keep ma under surveillance. Go through all their trash, of course, phone bills, letters."

Roger nodded, smiled a little. This was old hat to him, but Dan was learning.

"Better cook up some jive cover story, for when you talk to the family," Dan advised him. "Don't tell them you're a detective."

Roger smirked at him. But he let him down easy, "Good idea, kid." There was no sarcasm in his voice. He liked Dan. "I'll tell 'em I'm trying to track Joey down for a credit union refund. They'll want to help him get his money."

Dan grinned. "I like that."

"Make it fifty-dollar refund check," I said.

"I like that figure, too," Roger said.

Dan made it unanimous.

Three days later, we had something.

It hadn't come from Dan, not much of it anyway. The by-the-book route had only confirmed what Missing Persons found: one day, Joe Evans quit and took off, abandoning, if not quite burning, all his bridges behind him. His boss at the steel mill had not been called upon for a reference, nor had his union card been kept active. And his friends at the mill claimed not to have heard from him.

"None of his pals saw it coming," Dan said. "Or so they say."

"What about the phone records Louise provided?"

Dan checked his notes. "Joey talked to both his brother in Dallas and his sister in Davenport, a number of times in the six months prior to his disappearance. They're a close family."

"Which sibling got the most attention? Texas or Iowa?"

"Iowa. That's where little sister is. Agnes, her name is. He must've called her twenty times in those six months."

Roger fleshed out the picture.

"They're a close family, all right," he said. "Even when a business-like stranger comes around with fifty bucks for their brother, they clam up. Nobody wanted the refund check except the gal in charge - Loretta Evans, the matriarch, a tough old cookie who could put the battle in battle-axe. Come to think of it, she could put the axe in, too."

"She took the check?"

"She did. And she mailed it out the same day. I saw her do it. Speaking of mail, I checked trashcans all over Indiana, feels like. I got to know the Evanses better than the Evanses know the Evanses I could save 'em some money."

"How's that?"

"They should share a copy of the National Enquirer. Just pass one around, instead of all picking it up."

"Speaking of inquiring minds, what did yours find out?"

"Exactly what it wanted to know," Roger said. "The family seems close in general, but in particular, they seem to want to keep in touch with Agnes."

"Joe's sister."

"His baby sister. She's only twenty-two. Anyway, they been calling her a lot. All of 'em."

"Interesting."

"There's also a bar in Davenport, called Bill's Golden Nugget, where they call from time to time. Maybe she works there."

"It's a lead, anyway," I said. "Damn, I wish I knew where that letter Loretta Evans mailed went to."

"It went to Agnes," Roger said. He was smiling smugly.

"How do you know?"

"Because I waited around on the corner where she mailed it till a postman came around to empty the box and told him I slipped an important letter in that I thought I forgot to put a stamp on. I had a hysterical expression on my face and a stamp ready in my hand, and the bastard took pity on me and let me sort through looking for my letter."

"And you found one addressed to Agnes Evans."

"Sure."

"What did you do with it?"

"Left it right there," he said. "You don't think I'd

tamper with the U.S. Mail, do you?"

A foul, pungent odor from Oscar Mayer permeated the working-class neighborhood the massive plant bordered; but nobody seemed to notice on this sunny June afternoon, or anyway care. Ragamuffin kids played in the streets and on the sidewalks, wearing dirt-smudged cheeks that knew no era, and house-wives hung wash on lines strung across porches, apparently enjoying a breeze that to me only emphasized the slaughterhouse stench.

The address I had for Agnes Evans was 714 1/2 Wundrum; it turned out to be a paint-peeling clapboard duplex in the middle of a crowded block.

My Buick was dirty enough to be at home in the neighborhood, and in my plaid shirt, tied into a halter top, and snug blue jeans, I fit in, too. I felt pretty much at home, actually, with a cop for a father, I had grown up in neighborhoods only a small step up from this - minus the slaughterhouse scent, thankfully.

I knocked at 714 1/2 and then knocked again. The door opened cautiously and a round-faced woman in her early twenties peeked out at me. She had permed dishwater-blond hair, suspicious eyes, and her brother's weak jaw.

"Yeah?"

Pleasant, not at all pushy, I said, "I'm looking for Doris Wannamaker."

"No Doris anybody here," Agnes Evans said. She eased the door open somewhat; not all the way, but I could get a better look at her. She wore tight jeans with fashion-statement holes in the knees and a blue tee-shirt with "QUAD CITIES USA" in flowing white letters. She was slim, attractive and wore no make-up.

I said, "Isn't this 714 1/2?"

"Yeah."

I could hear a TV inside, a cartoon show.

"Wundrum Street?"

"That's right."

I sighed. "She's gone, huh. I guess that's the way it goes these days. Wonder how much I missed her by."

"I've lived here six months," she said. "I don't know who lived here before me."

I shrugged, smiled. "We were in beauty school together, Doris and me. I was just passing through town and wanted to surprise her. Sorry to bother."

Agnes Evans finally smiled. It was an attractive smile. "I went to beauty school. At Regent."

Of course, I'd known that.

I said, "I went to the University of Beauty Science in Cedar Falls."

"Supposed to be a good school," Agnes allowed. "I graduated, Regent. I didn't keep my certificate up, though."

"Me neither," I said.

The door was open wider. I could see the little girl, wearing a red tee-shirt and underpants, sitting like an Indian in front of the TV, watching Tom bash Jerry with a skillet.

"Sure, sorry I bothered you," I said.

"No problem."

"Look, uh...is there any chance I could use your phone? I want to try to catch my boyfriend at the motel, before he goes out."

"Well..."

"I thought I was going to have the afternoon filled

with seeing Doris and talking old times, but now...
could I impose?"

She shrugged, smiled tightly, but opened the screen
and said, "Come on in."

The house was neat as pin; neater. The furniture
was the kind you rented to own, but it was maintained
as if owning it was the plan. The TV was a big portable on a stand, and there was a Holiday Inn-type
landscape over the plastic-covered sofa. A window
air-conditioner chugged, and the place was almost
chilly, and the smell of whatever-goes-into-weenies
wasn't making it inside.

"Hi, honey," I said, stopping near the little girl.

She didn't look up at me; she was watching Jerry
hit Tom with a toaster. "Hi," she said.

Maggie looked older than her picture, but not
much. A little child with almost white blonde hair,
and a lot of it, a frizzy frame around a cameo face that
was blank with TV concentration.

I pretended to use the phone in the kitchen, which
was tidy and smelled of macaroni and cheese, while
Agnes stood with her arms folded and studied me
as she smoked a cigarette. She was still just a little
suspicious.

"I'll see you later, then," I told the dial tone,
and hung up and smiled at Agnes and shrugged.
"Men," I said.

She smirked and blew smoke and nodded in mutual understanding.

As I walked out, she followed. I said, "So you're
not in hair anymore?"

"No. My boyfriend Billy runs a bar. I work there
most evenings."

"Really? Who looks after your little girl?"

"That's not my little girl. Cindy is, uh, a friend of mine's kid. I look after her, days."

"Sweet little girl," I said.

"She's a honey," Agnes said.

I left them there, in the neat house in the foul-smelling neighborhood. I wasn't worried about leaving Maggie in Agnes' care. It was someone else's care I was worried about.

The someone who was with Maggie, nights.

Bill's Golden Nugget was a country-western bar on Harrison, a one-way whose glory days, at least along this saloon-choked stretch, were long gone. I parked on a side street, in front of a natural-food co-op inhabited by hippies who hadn't noticed the sixties were over. The Nugget was between a pawn shop and a heavy-metal bar.

It was mid-afternoon and the long, narrow saloon was sparsely populated: a few out-of-work blue-collar urban cowboys were playing pool; a would-be biker played the Elvira pinball machine and a couple of guys in jeans and work shirts were at the bar, having an argument about baseball. Just enough patrons to keep the air smoky and stale. A Johnny Paycheck song worked at blowing out the jukebox speakers. The room's sole lighting seemed to be the neon and/or lit-up plastic signs bearing images of beer, Marlboro men and *Sports Illustrated* swimsuit models, none of which had the slightest thing to do with the Nugget, except for the beer.

A heavy-set, bearded, balding blond man in his late

twenties was behind the bar. He wore a plaid shirt that clashed with mine and red suspenders that clashed with his. I heard somebody call him Bill.

He seemed pleasant enough, but he was watching me warily. I was new, and maybe I was a hooker.

I took a stool.

"What'll it be, sweet thing?" he said. There was nothing menacing about it, not even anything condescending. But he was eyeing me carefully. Just a good on-top-of-it bar owner who was probably his own bouncer.

"What have you got on tap that I'd like, big guy?"

"Coors," he said, and it was sort of a question.

"You kidding, Bill? Drinking that stuff is like makin' love in a boat."

"Huh?"

"Fucking close to water," I said, and I grinned at him.

He liked that.

"I also got Bud," he said.

"Bodacious," I said.

He went away smiling, convinced I was not a hooker, just available. Even a guy with a good-looking girl like Agnes at home has his weaknesses.

I milked the Bud for fifteen minutes, tapping my toes to the country music, some of which was pretty good. That Carlene Carter could sing. Nobody hit on me, not even Bill, and that was fine. I just wanted to fit in.

There was a room in back that was at least as big as the front, with tables and a dance floor and a stage for a band and a second bar. It wasn't in use right now, but some beer-ad lighting was on and somebody was back there working, loading in boxes of booze or whatever, through the alley door.

When the guy finished, he came up front; he was in a White Sox sweatshirt with cut-off sleeves and blue jeans. He was a brawny character, maybe twenty-five, good-looking except for a weak chin.

He was Joey Evans.

I had a second Bud and eavesdropped as Evans, whose voice was high-pitched and husky, not suited to his rather brutish build, asked if he could take a break.

"Sure, Freddy," Bill said. "Take five, but then I need you with me behind the bar. It's damn near happy hour, kid."

Freddy/Joey went behind the bar and got himself a can of Diet Coke. He went to a table, away from any patrons, and sat quietly sipping.

I went over to him. "You look like you could use some company. Hard day?"

"Hard enough," he said. He took my figure in, trying to be subtle; it was about as successful as McGovern's run at the Presidency.

"Have a seat," he said, and stood, and pushed out a chair.

I sat. "Hope you don't mind my being so forward. I'm Becky Lewis." I stuck out my hand. We shook; his grip was gentle. Right.

"You're from Chicago, aren't you, Becky?" he said. He smiled boyishly; his eyes were light faded blue, like stonewashed denims.

I was supposed to be the detective. "How did you gather that?"

"The accent," he said. "I'd know that flat nasal tone anywhere."

He should; he had it himself.

"I figured you for Chicago, too. South Side?"

"Close," he said. "How...?"

"You're not wearing a Cubbies sweatshirt, now, are ya?"

He grinned. "Hell, no! Screw them and their Yuppie fans."

"You got that right. Let me buy you a beer... Freddy, is it?"

"Freddy," he said. "No thanks. I'm workin'. But I'll buy you one."

"I already got one. Let's just get to know each other a little."

There was not much to know, he said. He was fairly new to the area, working as a bartender for Bill, who was a friend of a friend.

"You got strong hands, Freddy," I said, stroking one. "Working hands, steel-mill hands."

His eyes flared. Maybe I'd gone too far.

"I...I got tired of factory life. Just too damn hard. I need to be sharp, not wasted, when I spend time with my kid. I'm a single parent, you know. I'm trying for that quality time thing, you know."

I bet he was.

"How many kids you got, Freddy?"

"Just the one. Sweet little girl. Cindy. Starts first grade next year. You got any kids?"

"I'm divorced, but I never had any kids. Didn't think I was cut out for it."

"Oh, you should reconsider. There's nothing like it. Being a parent, it's the best thing that ever happened to me."

Really.

"I don't know," I said, "I'm afraid I might lose my temper around 'em or something."

"That can be a problem," he admitted. "But I'd never lay a hand on Cindy. Never."

"Spare the rod and spoil the child, Clyde."

His brow knit. "I don't believe in that shit. Look, I used to have a bad temper. I'll be honest with you, Becky. I used to...well, I used to get a little rough with the ladies sometimes."

I stroked his hand, and almost purred: "I like it a little rough."

Gag me, as they say, with a spoon.

"I don't mean that. I don't mean horseplay or nothing. I mean, I hit women before. Okay? See this Diet Coke? It's not just 'cause I'm workin'. I don't drink anymore. I get nasty when I drink, so I don't drink."

"It's a little rough, being a recovering alcoholic, isn't it, working in a bar?"

"Being somebody who don't drink is a valuable commodity when you work in a bar-type situation. That's what Bill likes about me."

"You're not...tempted?"

"No. I haven't had a drink in five years."

"Five years?" Was he lying, or crazy? Or both? Was this a trick question?

He swirled the Diet Coke in the can. "Five years sober. Five years dry. Besides, Becky, this job was all I could get."

"A strapping boy like you?"

His expression darkened. "I got my reasons. If you want to be my friend, you got to respect my privacy, okay?"

Funny, coming from a guy I just met who already

had admitted he was a reformed drunk and supposedly reformed woman-beater. Was there something psychotic in those spooky faded blue eyes?

"Sure, honey," I said, "I'll respect your privacy. If, you respect me in the morning."

He grinned again, shyly. "I got to get behind the bar, 'fore Bill tears me a new you-know-what."

"Can we get together after you get off work?"

"I got to spend the evening with my little girl."

"Right. Quality time."

"That's it. But I ought to have her in bed by nine o'clock."

I bet.

"You could stop over after that," he said. "I can give you the address..."

Louise sat next to me in the front seat. She wore the same peasant dress she'd worn to my office; clutched the same patent leather purse. Her heavy make-up, in the darkness as we sat in the car at the curb, gave her a Kabuki-like visage.

I had phoned her long distance, right after my encounter with Joey at the Nugget. She'd been standing by for my call, as I'd primed her that if I found Maggie, I'd need her to come immediately. I couldn't take Maggie without Louise present, and not just because the child would rightfully resist going with a stranger.

The fact was, with Louise along, taking Maggie would not be kidnapping. Without her, it would be.

"Are you all right, Louise?"

She nodded. We were in my Buick. We had left her Datsun in a motel parking lot near the Interstate. That's where we had met, after she made the three-hour drive in two and a half hours. It was now approaching nine-thirty and the sky was a brilliant dark blue with more stars than any child could ever hope to dream upon. Moving clouds seemed to rise cotton-candy-like, but it was only smoke from Oscar Mayer.

We were several blocks from Agnes Evans' duplex, but the meat-packing smell still scorched the air. Joey Evans and his daughter lived in a single-family, single-story clapboard, smaller and newer than his sister's place. Built in the fifties sometime. I lived in a house like this when I was six.

"He's expecting me," I told her. I'd already told her this, but I'd been telling her a lot of things and I wasn't sure anything was sticking.

She nodded.

"I'll go up, and knock, and after he lets me in, I'll excuse myself to go to the restroom, I'll find the back door, unlock it, and you come in and I'll keep him busy while you find your way to Maggie's room."

She nodded.

"Then you slip out the back door with her. When you're in the car with her, safe, honk twice. Short honks. Then I'll get out of there on some excuse, and we're outa here. You girls will be on your way home."

She smiled wanly. "Ms. Tree, thank you. Thank you so very much. I knew you could do it. I knew you could."

"I haven't done it yet. *We* haven't. Now, you need to have a clear head about you, Louise. I want to get you in and out, with Maggie, without him knowing till we're tail-lights. I don't want any violence going down, that husband of yours looks like he could bench-press a grand piano."

She nodded.

"Wait five minutes after I go to the door; then go around behind the house and find the back door. How long?"

"Five minutes."

"When you're safe in the car, how many times will you honk?"

She raised two fingers, as if making the peace sign. "Short honks."

"Good, Louise." I patted her shoulder. I felt confident about this. About as confident as you feel when you make your first dental visit in five years.

He answered my first knock. He was wearing a blue-and-white checked sport shirt and jeans; he looked nice. He asked me to come in, and I did. He smelled like Canoe cologne; I didn't even know they still made that stuff.

"It's not much, Becky," he said, gesturing about, "but it's enough for Cindy and me."

Whether he and his sister had similar decorating styles, or whether one of them had done the other's home, I couldn't say; but it was the same rent-to-buy decor, just a tad sparser than sis's place. The TV was a console, apparently an old used model, with a Nintendo unit on the floor in front representing the only visible extravagance. Over the couch was another discount-store oil painting, this one a sad-eyed Gacy-like clown handing a red balloon to a little girl who looked disturbingly like Maggie.

"You really keep the place neat," I said, sitting on the couch.

"Cindy helps me. She's really the strong one in the family."

"I'd love to meet her."

"Maybe next time. She's asleep. Besides, I don't like her to see me with other ladies."

"Other ladies?"

"Other than her mommy."

"But you're divorced."

"I know. But she's only six. She doesn't understand stuff like that. Of course, then, neither do I."

What sort of sick relationship did this son of a bitch have with little Maggie? Had he turned her into a "wife"? A six-year old wife? This guy was lucky I wasn't armed.

"Look," I said, smiling, trying to maintain the pretense of warmth, "I need to use the little girl's room. Where...?"

He pointed the way. It was through a neat compact kitchen, which connected to a hall off of which was Maggie's room. Or, Cindy's room. At least she didn't sleep with her daddy.

She sure looked angelic right now, blonde hair haloing her sweet face on the overstuffed pillow. Her room was the only one that wasn't sparse; even in the meager glow of the night light, I could see the zoo of stuffed animals, the clown and circus posters, the dolls and their little dresses. Daddy gave her everything.

The sick bastard.

When I returned, having flushed a toilet I really had had to use, I left the back door, off the kitchen, unlocked.

I sat down next to Joey, keeping in mind I needed to call him Freddy, and he said, "I can get you a beer, if you like."

The last thing in the world I wanted was for him

to go traipsing through the kitchen while Louise was sneaking in.

"No thanks, I'm fine. I just got *rid* of a beer, honey."

He laughed embarrassedly.

I nudged him with an elbow, gently. "What are you doing with beer in the house, anyway? You haven't had a drink in five years, right?"

A smile creased his pleasant face. "You're sure a suspicious girl. I keep a few brews in the fridge for company."

"You entertain a lot?"

"Not much. My sis..."

He started to say *sister*, I think, then shifted gears.

"My friends, Bill and Agnes, both like their beer. In fact, Bill sometimes likes it too much." He shook his head. "A guy who runs a bar shouldn't drink up the profits."

"He's lucky to have you around."

"Actually, he is. I only hope he can stay in business. I sure need this job."

The child's scream shook the house.

Evans and I both bolted off the couch, and then, framed in the archway of the hall leading to the kitchen, there was Louise, pulling the unwilling little girl by the arm. The child, wearing an oversize, man's white tee-shirt with Bart Simpson on it, was screaming.

Louise, her eyes crazed, her Kabuki face frozen with rage, slapped the little girl savagely; it rang like a gunshot off the swirl-plaster walls.

That silenced the little girl's screams, but tears and whimpering took their place.

"Louise!" Evans said, face as white as a fish's

underbelly. "What..."

Her purse had been tucked under one arm. Now, still clinging to the little girl with one hand, she dug her other hand into the brown patent leather bag and came back with a snout-nosed black revolver.

"You bastard," she said, "you sick bastard..."

Those had been my thoughts, exactly, earlier, but now I was having new thoughts...

"Louise," I said, stepping forward. "Put the gun down."

"You did it to her, didn't you?" she said to him. "You did it to her! You fucked her! You've been fucking her!"

The little girl was confused and crying.

Evans stepped forward, carefully; he was patting the air gently. "Louise, just because your father..."

"Shut-up!" she said, and she shot at him. He danced out of the way as the shot rang and echoed in the confined space, the couch taking the slug.

I wasn't waiting to see who or what took the next one. I moved in and slapped the gun out of her hand; then I slapped her face, hard.

I had a feeling I wasn't the first one to do that to Louise.

She crumpled to the floor and she wept quietly, huddling fetally; her little girl sat down close to her, stroking her mother's blond hair.

"Mommy," Maggie said. "Don't cry, Mommy. Don't cry."

I picked up the gun.

Evans was standing looking down at his wife and child. He looked at me sharply, accusingly.

"I'm a private detective," I explained. "She hired

me to get Maggie back."

"She told you I beat Maggie, right?" he snapped. "And worse?"

I nodded.

"Why the hell do you think I ran from her?" he said, plaintively; his face was haunted, his eyes welling. "*I* wasn't the one beating Maggie! But the courts would've given Maggie to her mommy. They would never have believed me over her. How *else* could I have stopped this?"

I didn't have an answer for him; he wasn't necessarily right – the courts might have realized Louise was the abusing parent. But they might not have. I sure hadn't.

He knelt beside his wife; the little girl was on one side of her, and he was on the other. They were mostly in the kitchen. Louise didn't seem to notice them, but they tried to soothe her just the same.

"Her father did terrible things to her," he said softly. "She got me all confused with him. Looked at me and saw her daddy, thought I'd do the same things to Maggie he done to her."

"But the only one imitating her father," I said, "was Louise."

"Mommy doesn't mean to hurt me," the little girl said. "She loves me." It was almost a question.

Sirens were cutting the air, responding to the gunshot.

"I was wrong," he said, looking at me with eyes that wanted absolution. "I shouldn't have run. I should have stayed and tried to fix things."

Who could blame him, really?

Something in Louise had been broken so very

long ago.

But as I watched them there, the little family huddling on the cold linoleum, I had to hope that something, at long last, could start being mended.

DARK SIDE OF THE MOON
Barbara Collins

Harriett Gipple clutched the silk, black, crotchless panties tightly to her chest, her eyes squeezed shut, an expression of pain etched on her pasty, lumpy face.

She sat that way, in a frumpy brown dress, on the edge of a pink satin bed, in a room that seemed designed more for sex than sleep, for nearly a full minute. Then she sighed, letting the panties fall down onto her protruding stomach.

To Jack Lawson, who stood by quietly, the sixty-plus year-old woman with her slight balding spot and facial hair, appeared about as out of place, and uncomfortable, as a nun in a cathouse.

It just wasn't like her.

He went to the woman, squatted down next to the bed, and put one hand tentatively on her knee. "Maybe something in the closet...?" he asked anxiously.

"No," she said firmly, shaking her head, looking at

him with her only redeeming feature: a pair of shockingly beautiful green eyes. God mercifully must have given them to her, Lawson supposed, to keep people from running away.

Lawson stood up, and now he sighed. He was baffled by Harriett's lack of response, which, as long as he'd known her, had never before happened. And even more disturbing was his own reaction: beads of sweat were forming on his brow.

Had he come to need this woman so much, that, without her, he couldn't function? As he stood looking down at Harriett, he suddenly wished she'd never come into his life at all.

It was two years ago, April to be exact, when Roy Kautz, C.E.O. of a multi-billion-dollar chemical plant, became a victim of corporate kidnapping. He was snatched, appropriately enough, while visiting his mistress. The unfortunate woman was killed. A ransom note, sent to the company, demanded a mere five million.

Jack Lawson, then new to the force, was at the station, working into the night, when the woman named Harriett Gipple came in. She started babbling about having an autographed copy of the industrialist's best-selling book, *How to Get Ahead and Climb to the Top*. And, when she heard Kautz was missing, she had gotten out the book. That's when she "saw" him buried in a coffin, equipped with some water and a hose for air.

She thought he was alive. She thought she could find him.

Lawson thought she was nuts.

Back in Chicago, he'd dealt with psychics before:

a bunch of self-professed, self-serving, egotistical misfits who would, dollars to donuts, send him scurrying off in the wrong direction every time. Like when the DA turned up missing, her car abandoned in an empty lot, court papers and briefs thrown to the wind. Yes, they were eventually called in, to give their pronouncements of "lake" and "train trestle" and in the case of one that needed interpretation, "frisbee." And all the while, the DA was at the bottom of a dumpster just fifty feet away.

The skepticism must have showed on Lawson's face because Harriett Gipple had reached out across the desk, taken his coffee cup, closed her eyes, then opened them and said, "Prostate problems in a man of your youth are unusual."

With the help of Harriett Gipple, Lawson found Kautz, buried in a cornfield in a wooden box. Though the executive was alive, physically, the traumatic experience rendered him dead, mentally.

As Roy Kautz's brilliant career went nova, Lawson's lackluster one began to shine.

"We're all done out here, Lieutenant," said a sergeant who stood in the bedroom doorway.

Lawson looked at Harriett, who was rising up from the bed and avoiding his stare.

"I guess we are too," he said, picking up the black panties that had fallen onto the floor. He went over to a dresser, its top covered with perfume bottles and make-up, and put them away in the drawer where he'd found them.

"Probable homicide, Lieutenant?" asked the sergeant.

"Missing person," responded Lawson. "Until we

find a body."

Lawson followed Harriett out into the living room, which was as blandly decorated as a second-rate furniture store display room. The beige carpet looked new, spotless, except for the thin trail of blood leading off to the bathroom.

Lawson and Harriett left out the back, down a short flight of steps, and into the alley behind the house. The night was lit by a ghostly white moon, shapeless black clouds floating across it, spirits from another world.

The late fall wind sent dry leaves and debris dancing and swirling around their legs as they walked quickly along. At the mouth of the alley, a cat digging in garbage, saw them, arched its back and hissed.

Around the corner, Harriett's car was parked at the curb. They stopped on the sidewalk a few feet from it.

"What happened?" asked Lawson quietly, as he faced the woman. "Why didn't you see her?"

Harriett was silent for a moment before she spoke. "I didn't say I didn't."

"Then what? Is it so horrible...?"

Harriett shook her head.

"Tell me!" said Lawson, putting his hands on her shoulders. "Where *is* she?"

Harriett looked up, toward the source of the light. "She's there."

"Where?"

"There. On the moon."

The women stood motionless, all in a row, their clothes splotched red, their hands bound in front, slashes of gray duct tape covering their mouths.

In spite of thick ropes that looped around their hands, many held sticks. And at the end of those sticks were signs that read: STOP VIOLENCE AGAINST WOMEN!

Jane Yeoman squinted against the brilliant autumn-day sun as she watched Jack Lawson enter the police station just across the street. She put down her sign, shook off the ropes, untaped her mouth, and said to the woman standing next to her, "I'll be back."

Then she picked up her bag from the sidewalk, and started across the street, weaving in and out of the traffic that had slowed to a crawl as drivers and passengers gawked at the demonstrators.

Once in the building, she hunted for him, her ketchup stained corduroy skirt swishing, brown loafers slapping the tiles as she walked. On the third floor she found him, bent over a water fountain.

"Mr. Lawson," she said, approaching the sandy-haired man of average build, who she guessed was in his early thirties.

He stopped drinking and straightened up. Water dripped from his unshaven chin and he wiped it away with the back of one hand. His white long-sleeved shirt and black trousers looked slept in.

"Ms. Yeoman," he said with a smile she didn't believe for a moment.

"Why haven't you found Rita Cato?" Yeoman demanded.

Lawson's smile turned patronizing. "We're working around the clock," he said. "Now, if you don't mind, I'm very busy."

He turned away from her, walking on.

"I see," said Yeoman, standing her ground by the

water fountain. "Of course, you found Roy Kautz in twenty-four hours. But then, he was an important citizen, not an insignificant housewife. He was a man, not a woman."

Lawson stopped in his tracks, looked back at her with what she thought was amused disgust. He started to say something but thought better of it. Then, he continued down the hall disappearing into a room.

"And, I'd like to know," asked Yeoman, now standing in the doorway of his office, "why that husband of hers isn't in jail!"

Lawson, seated behind his desk, shuffling papers, didn't bother to look at her. "I'm not at liberty to discuss the case with you," he said flatly.

Yeoman moved in front of the desk. "You know she's been murdered, from the rope and the tape and the blood in the bathroom! *And, he did it!*"

Now Lawson looked up. "Ms. Yeoman, we're pursuing every available avenue to solve this thing. But there'll be no arrest until we have proper evidence."

Yeoman rummaged around in her bag, pulled out a video tape and place it on the desk. "Then perhaps," she said, "*this* might help."

Lawson looked at the black cassette, then back at her.

"It 'stars' Rita Cato," Yeoman explained. "She came to see me last month at the Women's Resource Center."

Lawson leaned back in his chair. "Do you always video tape your clients?" he asked.

"No," she said. "But if they've been battered, like Rita, I do. In case, they change their mind and want to file charges." She paused. "They're aware I do it," she added.

Lawson reached out, picked up the tape, turning it over, like he'd never seen one before.

"Well?" Yeoman said, after a moment. "Shouldn't we look at it?"

"'We'?" He used the work disdainfully. "*I'll* look at it when I get around to it. Now, why don't you be a good girl and run along, back to your little group."

"Disturbing you, are we?" Yeoman sneered.

"Can I give you some advice?"

"What? Not 'friendly' advice?" she smirked.

"If I were you, I'd be careful about picking a team mascot until I found out the score."

What the hell did that mean? "If you were me," she snapped, "you wouldn't be a condescending sexist jerk."

His smile was typically smug. "Wouldn't I?" he asked.

She grunted, threw her bag onto her shoulder, and stormed out.

On the front steps of the police station, Yeoman spotted a TV crew across the street, filming the bound and gagged women, and her frown disappeared.

"Jane!" called out the perky, petite newscaster Yeoman recognized as Heather Hart, co-anchor of the local Channel 8 News.

"Could you answer a question for our six o'clock edition?" she asked the approaching Yeoman, then laughed, "No one else here seems to be able to talk!"

"Certainly," said Yeoman, business-like.

Heather gave her long blonde hair a toss and licked her pink lips as the cameraman with mini-cam stood nearby, ready to roll.

Then she pointedly asked Yeoman, into the microphone, "Just how *long* do you plan on keeping up this vigil?"

Yeoman looked into the camera. "The Women's Resource Center, along with friends and concerned citizens of Rita Cato, will keep up our vigil, here in front of the police station, until *they* find her, and the *man* responsible for this horrible atrocity is brought to justice."

Yeoman went on. "Nearly every ten seconds a woman becomes the victim of a brutal crime and..."

"Thank you, Jane Yeoman. Founder of the Women's Resource Center. This is Heather Hart, Channel 8 Eye-witness News."

"Sorry, Jane," said Heather after a moment, when the cameraman stopped filming. "We need sound-bites."

As the young woman walked away, Yeoman pursed her lips and glared. "Airhead," she said, under her breath. "How's that for a sound-bite?"

She was the worst, thought Yeoman, watching Heather leave in the news van. The real lack of support for women's rights didn't come from men, who could be made to feel guilty; it came from the white-collar women, who saw their suffering sisters as just less competition.

"I'm going home," Yeoman said, disgruntled, to the woman she'd talked to earlier when she'd spotted Lawson. "Can you handle the second shift?"

The silent, muzzled woman nodded.

"I'll see you in the morning."

Yeoman walked to her car, which was parked on the street a block away. She got in and started the engine.

"Hey! There's that women's libber!" she heard a bystander say as she drove off.

How Yeoman hated that label. But there were worse ones like troublemaker, lesbian, and PMSer. Men who fought injustice received distinguished titles like "advocate," and "protector of consumer affairs." Hell, even comic book superheroes got more respect. There was no "Justice League of America" for those who fought the feminist battle.

But Yeoman hadn't planned on becoming a feminist.

As a little girl growing up in a small town in Iowa in the 1960s, the heyday of the women's movement, Jane didn't even know what a feminist was. The third child born to Elizabeth and John Yeoman, she remembered being told more than once that her arrival "wasn't planned."

Her mother, a cold and calculating social climber, and father, a never-at-home auto parts salesman, paid little attention to the girl. Jane spent her childhood starved for affection. Though she had older twin brothers, they teased her relentlessly, nicknaming her "Clarabell the Clown" because of her thick red hair. When the boys went off to college, her father saw his responsibility as done and moved out.

But there were a few bright spots in Jane Yeoman's life. In high school, with the help of a kind drama teacher, she excelled in theater. A shy, quiet introvert, she blossomed when performing on the stage. Then, an unexpected scholarship let her escape to the University of Colorado.

It was there, on a ski-slope in Boulder during Christmas break, that she ran into Bob. Literally. She tripped him, coming down a run, and they landed in a twisted pile, him hurting his shoulder and her an ankle. They hobbled back to the lodge, where, as an apology, she bought him a drink. As they sat in front of a crackling fire, she couldn't believe how funny and attentive he was. Tall and muscular, dark and handsome, he was a Prince Charming if ever there was one. And they found an immediate common ground: both hadn't gone home for the holidays because they hated their families.

After a short, whirlwind, passionate courtship, they drove off to Las Vegas and got married. And she happily sacrificed her scholarship to go to work in a bank in Boulder so Bob could continue his studies. But then, just a few months into the marriage, Jane began to discover that her Prince was really a toad.

It began in the form of what he called "constructive criticism," but really was vindictive brow-beating, designed (she felt) to undermine her assertiveness and chop away at her new-found self-esteem. At first, she complied with his wishes and tried not to "be so selfish," thinking, because of her upbringing, she just didn't know what it took to make a good marriage.

But then, nothing she seemed to do was right, and he would fly off the handle, throwing and breaking things. If she threatened to walk out, he would cry and promise her the moon. So, they would make up, and he would be nice, for a while, but pretty soon it would start all over again.

It was such a shame, Jane had thought, because Bob was so good in bed!

When he broke her nose, though, she moved out, taking the cat, to an apartment of her own. That's when he started in with the threats and harassment that sent her into a tailspin of fear. He began following her, and phoning at all hours and hanging up. Once, when she went out to her car, it was covered with raw eggs. Another time, her tires had been slashed. But the final blow came when she arrived home from work and could tell someone had been in her apartment. The place wasn't ransacked, but drawers had been gone through, and a bottle of what used to be their favorite wine had been left, empty, by the sink as a calling card. And, the cat was missing.

The next day, putting groceries away, she found the cat. In the freezer. She sat hysterically crying, holding her dead pet, until the poor thing thawed out. Then a calmness settled over her. Something had to be done.

That night she waited in the darkness, behind the wheel of her Cherokee Jeep, in the parking lot of a bar outside Boulder on Shadow Mountain. When Bob came out with a slut on his arm, Jane slumped down in her seat and watched as they got drunkenly into his Pinto. They made out for a few minutes before Bob started the car and eased it out, heading down the winding hill. Jane followed, lights out.

On a particularly treacherous stretch of road, she floored her accelerator and rammed into him, hard. To her amazement, the rear of the Pinto burst into flames and the tremendous jolt caused the car to crash through a guardrail, where it sailed over the edge.

Jane, unhurt, pulled her scorched Cherokee over, jumped out and looked down at the burning car which was flipping ass over tea-kettle down the mountain-side.

She hadn't meant for him to die, exactly. But, as she stood staring at the crimson flames, it reminded her of the beginning of their fireside romance; and she was as happy as she was back then.

With a large check from an insurance policy Bob had taken out on himself shortly after they were married, Jane returned to college, but back in her home state, at the University of Iowa. On campus she was active in school politics; off campus she worked for the passage of the Equal Rights Amendment and was instrumental in bringing to the public's attention the dangerous rear-end collision problem of the Pinto. Eventually, she changed her major to Political Science.

After graduation, with the help of state and local funds, along with the last of the insurance money, she started the Women's Resource Center in Iowa City. She wanted to help other women who had been abused like herself.

But as of late, the center had fallen on hard times. The recession had put a stranglehold on community donations, and the government dropped its funding. If something didn't happen soon, the facility would go under.

The high profile the center was now attracting, however, by rallying around Rita Cato, was beginning to help.

Yeoman pulled her car into the driveway of her rustic A-frame condominium on the outskirts of the city and got out. She walked up the wooden flight of steps and around the tree-lined deck where yellow and orange mums, along with other potted plants, sat like patio guests, whispering in the cool breeze. Wind chimes dangled from the overhang, twisting, singing their monotonous tunes.

She unlocked the back door and let herself in.

Gloria, her calico cat, greeted her, weaving in and out of her master's legs. Yeoman bent over and petted it. Then, she threw her bag on a chair and went to the kitchen to pour herself a drink. She took the glass of wine to the couch, where she flopped down, kicking off her shoes.

She sat there, sipping her drink, staring into space, recharging herself, until at last she focused on a video tape on top of the TV. The tape was a dub of the one she'd given Lawson. She got up, turned on the set and put the cassette in the VCR.

She'd never actually viewed the tape of her meeting with Rita; after all, she'd *been* there, and had only partially screened it, to make sure the tape wasn't defective before copying it.

Yeoman returned to the couch to watch.

The woman filled the screen, from the waist up. She was lovely, beautiful really, despite her bruised face and distraught expression. She had long, raven hair, a delicately turned-up nose, and full, round lips. She spoke softly, hesitantly, like a little lost girl. She said her husband abused her.

Yeoman leaned forward; eyes glued to the set. Even though her senses were dulled from the wine, something suddenly seemed wrong. She was reminded of a performance she had given in a high school play. She thought she had been good, but later, watching a tape that a friend had made, she looked bad, stilted, over-rehearsed. Like Rita.

Now the woman was emptying her purse into her lap, looking for a kleenex, and Yeoman saw something that made her drop down off the couch, onto her knees, and crawl like a baby toward the screen to see better.

Then Yeoman got up, grabbed her bag and coat, and ran out to her car.

Rita Cato floated, dreamily, inside the tiny crater, its hot, bubbling liquid soothing her naked, voluptuous body. She looked upward. The earth, brown with swirling blue and white masses, seemed so very far away. Lazily, she turned her head, smiling at the sight of the silver space capsule which rose phallically off the floor just a few yards away.

She drifted, self-absorbed, until a rap-rap-rapping in the distance brought her back to reality.

"Who's there?" she called out.

"Room service!"

Rita got out of the hot tub, reached for a white towel resting among man-made moon rocks, wrapped herself up, and answered the door.

"Hello, Jamie," she smiled to the young dark man standing with a covered tray in his hands. "Come on in. There's a beautiful earth out tonight."

She blocked the doorway provocatively, forcing him to squeeze by her. About her height, he was real Chippendale material, in spite of his crater-like acne.

She closed the door.

"Where...where do you want it?" he stammered, then seemed to get flustered by his phrasing.

She smiled, amused, undulating past him, letting the towel fall open to reveal the perfect full moon of her ass. "Why, over here," she purred, pointing to the round white bed in the bottom of the open capsule, "where you put it yesterday."

He took the tray to the bed and bent over, leaning in the hatch door. Rita reached out and ran her hand along his cute butt, and down between his legs.

He jumped, surprised, hitting his head on the metal frame, spilling the food from the tray.

She laughed.

"No," he said, pulling her hand away. "I don't want to lose my job!"

"But, you'll come back later?" she asked with an exaggerated pout, pressing forward. "To turn down the bed?"

He sidestepped her, to make his escape.

She waited until he reached the door before calling out, "Hey! I forgot to give you a tip!"

He stopped and looked back.

"Bring some inner-galactic condoms!" she said, then howled with laughter.

When he had gone, she discarded the towel and climbed inside the capsule, on to the bed. She poured herself another Scotch on the rocks from the small bar hidden behind a fake control panel and chugged the booze down.

"He'll be back," she smirked, running a long, red-nailed finger around the rim of the glass.

She leaned against the pillows. *What a great place*, she thought. And what a great idea! A hotel designed to fulfill your every fantasy.

She saw the Minneapolis playground advertised in the Iowa City newspaper. Wouldn't it be fun to go there, she had thought – of course, not with her husband.

And that had given her a wicked little idea.

What if she just disappeared? That would fix him.

She would teach that bastard never to bat her around. So, what if she started the fight by clobbering him with the clock radio? It was *his* turn to take out the garbage. He shouldn't have then hit her.

She was a *woman,* wasn't she?

Vindictively, she'd gone to the Women's Resource Center, to get him into trouble. But when the lady there wanted her to go to the police, she thought she'd better back off.

Then a day later, while shaving her legs, she sliced her ankle; she hadn't realized she'd done it until she saw all the blood on the carpet.

Here was her chance...

She planted the duct tape and rope in the bathroom, got her secret stash of cash, then caught a bus for Minnesota, leaving her purse and i.d. behind.

When she arrived after a six-hour ride, the hotel was nearly booked. She had wanted to be Cleopatra in the ruins of Rome, but the only beds left were the space capsule, or a '57 Chevy.

She took the capsule; she'd done enough screwing in a car.

And, was she ever thrilled with her choice! When the anti-gravity force was simulated, making love in the capsule was a cosmic blast! It gave the Big Bang Theory new credence.

There was a knock at the door.

Rita put on her robe and answered it, eagerly, expecting Jamie.

But instead, it was that woman, Jane Yeoman, from the Resource Center!

"Hello, Rita," she smiled.

Rita was so startled she didn't know what to say,

caught with her pants down, if she'd been wearing any.

"May I come in?" the woman asked.

Rita hesitated, then stepped aside.

Jane Yeoman, in a black coat, her red hair pulled back from a tired face, stood for a moment taking in the lunar decor.

"Tasteful," she finally said.

"How did you find me?" Rita asked, pulling the robe more securely around herself.

The woman walked further into the room, then stopped and bent over to pick up a stray moon rock in her path. "I saw you at the ice machine a little while ago."

"But how the hell did you know I was *here*?" Rita demanded.

"From the video tape," Yeoman answered as she walked to the whirlpool, where she stood, turning the rock in her hands, looking down at the now still water. "The advertisement fell out of your purse."

Rita thought for a second, then grunted, realizing her mistake. She went to the woman, faced her and said, "So what! Since when is it a crime to take a vacation?

"Rita," Yeoman said as if trying to make a naughty child feel bad, "I don't think you realize the magnitude of the trouble you've caused."

"Like what?" Rita asked, hands on hips.

"Everyone thought you were dead. The police have worked hundreds of hours trying to locate you. Concerned citizens raised thousands of dollars on your behalf. We held daily vigils for you. I put my reputation, and the future of the Women's Resource Center, on the line for you. I trusted you, and you used me. And you used our cause to get back at that misogynist husband of yours."

Now the bitch was starting to irritate Rita. "Look," she snapped, "he really did slap me around! And I just wanted to get the bastard in a little hot water – not that it's any of your goddamn business!"

Yeoman nodded understandingly, then gave Rita a nasty, conspiratorial smile. "I think you can do better where your 'better half' is concerned."

"What do you mean?"

"Why don't you *leave* him in the hot water, to boil?"

Rita narrowed her eyes. "How? I don't understand."

"It's easy," the woman said. "But first, you need to do me a little favor."

"Such as?"

"Really die."

And Jane Yeoman swung the rock in a savage arc.

Yeoman checked the hallway to see if it was clear.

She looked back at Rita, submerged lifelessly in the pool, the bottom half of her robe floating peacefully on the water's crimson surface.

She tucked the bloody rock wrapped in a towel under her coat, and slipped out. The rock would disappear out her car window somewhere between here and home. She followed the red-carpeted corridor to the nearest exit.

Outside, a fierce northern wind slapped her around, waking her up from the numbness she felt.

Disposing of Rita was not a task Yeoman enjoyed; but it was a responsibility she had had to face. In a war, soldiers died. This time a deserter would be seen as a valiant martyr. But sometimes the truth, like Rita Cato, had to be sacrificed. It meant the survival of the Resource Center and the future well-being of their sisters.

Yeoman vowed to make it up to Rita. She would give her a unique life after death.

With yearly vigils and charity events commemorating her violent disappearance, there could be a new facility, the Rita Cato Women's Resource Foundation.

And, with a little luck, Rita's misogynist husband might get tried for her disappearance. Yeoman would work toward that end. That wife-battering son of a bitch had it coming.

As for the unidentified dead woman found in the pool, that would, if there were any justice, be written off as the work of some unknown male assailant. If Rita had been spending her vacation in and out of bed with the likes of that busboy Yeoman spotted coming out the room, then some innocent man might find himself in hot water, too. But, so be it. After all, in this male-dominated society, what man was truly "innocent," anyway?

Yeoman smiled, feeling better.

At her car, she looked in her purse for her keys, using the light of the silvery moon.

She had the keys in her hand.

"Leaving so soon?" a voice asked.

Yeoman spun around, keys flying. She saw someone standing between two parked cars, a man.

He moved toward her, out of the shadows, and Yeoman was horrified.

Jack Lawson.

Quickly, she took the defensive. "You scared me to death! What the hell are you doing here?"

"I was just going to ask you that," he said, coming closer.

Now Yeoman noticed that Lawson wasn't alone. A figure, a witchy old woman, emerged from the shadows behind him. She bent down and picked up Yeoman's keys on the ground.

Lawson must have also seen the newspaper ad on the tape! Yeoman commanded herself to be calm.

"I thought Rita might be here," she said matter-of-factly. "But I checked at the desk and there's no one registered under that name."

"Ah," said the old woman, "but she *is*." She turned to Lawson. "Rita Cato is as I first saw her. But dead, killed by this woman." She pointed a knobby, accusing finger.

Yeoman's mouth fell open, and before she had a chance to speak or move, Lawson was in front of her, patting her down.

Finding the moon rock.

And inside Yeoman's head, the Resource Center came crumbling down.

She had to admit, as he almost gently held her by the arm, helping her walk back to the hotel, that no matter how much she hated him, he was conducting himself professionally. He didn't smirk, or gloat, or look condescendingly at her.

And she was thankful for that.

Then his professional mask slipped as he guided her up the winding stone stairway to the hotel.

"Watch your step," he said. "You might stumble – it's just one small step for a man, you know, but a large step, for womankind."

His irony was not lost on her, but it held no sting. She was too busy crossing over to the dark side of the moon.

GUEST SERVICE
A Quarry Story
Max Allan Collins

An American flag flapped lazily on its silver pole, against a sky, so washed-out a blue, the handful of clouds were barely discernible. The red, white and blue of it were garishly out of place against the brilliant greens and muted blues of the Minnesota landscape, pines shimmering vividly in late morning sunlight, the surface of gray-blue Sylvan Lake glistening with sun, and rippling with gentle waves. The rails of the grayish brown deck beyond my quarters were like half-hearted prison bars that I peeked through as I did my morning sit-ups on the other side of the triple glass doors of my well-appointed guest suite.

I was not a guest of Sylvan Lodge, however; I ran the place. Once upon a time I had owned a resort in Wisconsin not unlike this, not near the acreage, of course, and not near the occupancy; but I had *owned* the place, whereas here I was just the manager.

Not that I had anything to complain about; I was lucky to have the job. When I ran into Gary Petersen in Milwaukee, where he was attending a convention and I was making a one-night stopover to remove some emergency funds from several bank deposit boxes, I was at the loosest of loose ends. The name I'd lived under for over a decade was unusable, my past had caught up with me back at the other place, and I'd lost everything in a near instant. My business yanked from under me, my wife (who'd had not a clue of my prior existence) murdered in her sleep.

Gary, however, had recognized me in the hotel bar and used a name I hadn't used since the early '70s: my real name.

"Jack!" he said, only that wasn't the name he used. For the purposes of this narrative, however, we'll say my real name is Jack Keller.

"Gary," I said, surprised by the warmth creeping into my voice. "You son of a bitch. You're still alive."

Gary was a huge man, six-six, weighing in at somewhere between three hundred pounds and a ton. His face was masked in a bristly brown beard, his skull exposed by hair loss, his dark eyes bright, his smile friendly, in a goofy, almost child-like way.

"Thanks to you, asshole," he said.

We'd been in Vietnam together.

"What the hell have you been doing all these years, Jack?"

"Mostly killing people."

He boomed a laugh. "Yeah, right!"

"Don't believe me, then." I was, incidentally, pretty drunk. I don't drink often, but I'd been through the mill lately.

"Are you crying, Jack?"

"Fuck no," I said. But I was.

Gary slipped his arm around my shoulder; it was like getting cuddled by God. "Bro - what's the deal? What shit have you been through?"

"They killed my wife," I said, and cried drunkenly into his shoulder.

"Jesus, Jack - who...?"

"Fucking assholes...fucking assholes..."

We went to his suite. He was supposed to play poker with some buddies, but he called it off.

I was very drunk and very morose, and Gary was, at one time anyway, my closest friend during the most desperate of days.

I told him everything. I told him how after I got back from Nam, I found my wife, my first wife, shacked up with some guy, some fucking auto mechanic, who was working under a car when I found him and kicked the jack out. The jury let me off, but I was finished in my hometown, and I drifted until the Broker found me. The Broker, who gave me the name Quarry, was the conduit through whom the murder for hire contracts came, and, what? Ten years later, the Broker was dead, by my hand, and I was out of the killing business, took my savings, and went to Paradise Lake in Wisconsin, where, eventually, I met a pleasant, attractive, not terribly bright woman and she and I were in the lodge business until the past came looking for me, and, suddenly, she was dead and I was without a life or even identity. I had managed to kill the fuckers responsible for my wife's killing, but otherwise I had nothing. Nothing left but some money stashed away, that I was now retrieving.

I told Gary all this, through the night, in considerably more detail, though probably even less coherently, although coherently enough that when I woke up the next morning, where Gary had laid me out on the extra bed, I knew I'd told him too much.

He was asleep, too. Like me, he was in the same clothes we'd worn to that bar. Like me, he smelled of booze, only he also reeked of cigarette smoke. I did a little, too, but it was Gary's smoke. I never picked up the habit. Bad for you.

He looked like a big dead animal, except for his barrel-like chest heaving with breath. I looked at this man; like me, he was somewhere between forty and fifty now, not the kids we'd been before the war made us worse than just men.

I still had liquor in me, but I was sober now. Too deadly fucking sober. I studied my best friend of long ago and wondered if I had to kill him.

I was standing over him, staring down at him, mulling that over, when his eyes opened suddenly, like a timer turning on the lights in a house to fend off burglars. He smiled a little, then it faded, then his eyes narrowed, and he said, "Morning, Jack."

"Morning, Gary."

"You've got that look."

"What look is that?"

"The cold one. The one I first saw a long time ago."

I swallowed and looked away from him, sat on the edge of the bed across from him and rubbed my eyes with the heels of my hands.

He sat across from me with his big hands on his big knees and said, "How the hell d'you manage it?"

"What?"

"Hauling my fat ass into that Medivac."

I grunted a laugh. "The same way a little mother lifts a Buick off her baby."

"In my case, you lifted the Buick onto the baby. Let me buy you breakfast."

"Okay."

In the hotel coffee shop, he said, "Funny, what you told me last night, about the business you used to be in?"

I sipped my coffee; I didn't look at him - didn't show him my eyes. "Yeah?"

"I'm in the same game."

Now I looked at him; I winced with disbelief. "What...?"

He corrected my initial thought. "The tourist game, I mean. I run a lodge near Brainerd."

"No kidding."

"That's what this convention is, Northern Resort Owners Association."

"I heard of it," I said, nodding. "Never bothered to join, myself."

"I'm a past president. Anyway, I run a place called Sylvan Lodge. My third and current, and I swear to God ever-lasting wife, Ruth Ann, inherited it from her late parents, rest their hardworking souls."

None of this came as a surprise to me. Grizzly bear Gary had always drawn women like a great big magnet, usually good-looking little women who wanted a father figure, Papa Bear variety. Even in Bangkok on R & R, Gary never had to pay for pussy, as we used to delicately phrase it.

"I'm happy for you. I always figured you'd manage

to marry for money."

"My ass! I really love Ruth Ann. You should see the knockers on the child."

"A touching testimonial if ever I heard one. Listen, about that bullshit I was spouting last night..."

His dark eyes became slits, the smile in his brushy face disappeared. "We'll never speak of that again. Understood? Never."

He reached out and squeezed my forearm.

I sighed in relief and smiled tightly and nodded, relieved. Killing Gary would have been no fun at all.

He continued, though. "My sorry fat ass wouldn't even be on this planet, if it wasn't for you. I owe you big-time."

"Bullshit," I said, but not very convincingly.

"I've had a good life, at least the last ten years or so, since I met Ruthie. You've been swimming in Shit River long enough. Let me help you."

"Gary, I..."

"Actually, I want you to help me."

"Help *you*?"

Gary's business was such a thriving one that he had recently invested in a second lodge, one across the way from his Sylvan Lake resort. He couldn't run both places himself, at least not "without running my fat ass off." He offered me the job of managing Sylvan.

"We'll start you at 5Ok, with free housing. You can make a tidy buck with no overhead to speak of, and you can tap into at least one of your marketable skills, and at the same time be out of the way. Keep as low a profile as you like. You don't even have to deal with the tourists, to speak of – we have a social director for that. You just keep the boat afloat. Okay?"

"Okay," I said, and we shook hands. Goddamn I was glad I hadn't killed him.

Now, a little more than six months into the job, and a month into the first summer season, I was settled in and damn near happy. My quarters, despite the rustic trappings of the cabin-like exterior, were modern, pine paneling skirting the room with pale yellow pastel walls rising to a high pointed ceiling. It was just one room with bath and kitchenette, but it was a big room, facing the lake, which was a mere hundred yards from the deck that was my back porch. Couch, cable TV, plenty of closet space, a comfortable wall bed; I didn't need anything more.

During off-season, I could move into more spacious digs if I liked, but I didn't figure I'd bother. Just a short jog across the way was an indoor swimming pool with hot tub and sauna, plus a tennis court; a golf course, shared with Gary's other lodge, was nearby. My duties were constant, but mostly consisted of delegating authority, and the gay chef of our gourmet restaurant made sure I ate well and free, and I'd been banging Nikki, the college girl who had the social director position for the summer, so my staff relations were solid.

I took a shower after my push-ups and got into the usual gray Sylvan Lodge t-shirt, black shorts, and gray and black Reebox, to take a stroll around the grounds, and check up on the staff. I was sitting on the couch tying my tennies, with a good view of the patch of green and slice of sand below my deck, when I heard an unpleasant, gravelly male voice tearing somebody a new asshole.

"Why the fuck *didn't* you rent the boat in advance, Mindy?"

"I'm sorry, Dick."

"Jesus fucking Christ, woman, you think I want to come to a goddamn lake without a goddamn boat?"

His voice carried into my living room with utter clarity, borne by the wind coming across the lake.

I looked up. He was big, not as big as my friend Gary, but big enough. He wore green-and-red plaid shorts and a lime-green golf shirt and a straw pork-pie hat with a wide leather band; he was as white as the underbelly of a crocodile, except for his face, which was a bloodshot red. Even at this distance, I could see the white tufts of eyebrows over narrow-set eyes and a bulbous nose.

He was probably fifty, or maybe more. His wife was an attractive blonde, much younger, possibly thir-ty-five. She wore a denim shorts outfit that revealed an almost plump but considerably shapely figure, nicely top-heavy. Her hair was too platinum for her age, and too big for her face, a huge hair-sprayed construction with a childishly incongruous pink bow in it.

Her pretty face, even from where I sat on my couch, was tired-looking, puffy. But she'd been beautiful, once, an actress or a dancer or something. And even now, even with the too big, too platinum hair, she made a man's head turn, except maybe for my chef.

"But I thought you'd use your brother's boat."

"He's in fucking Europe, woman!"

"I know, but you said we were going to use Jim's boat."

"Well, that fell through! He loaned his place *and*

his boat to some fucker from Duluth he wanted to impress! Putting business before his own goddamn brother."

"But I didn't know that."

He grabbed her arm; hard. "You should've made it your business *to* know! *You* were supposed to make the vacation arrangements. God knows you have little enough to do otherwise. I have a fucking living to make for us. You should've got off your fat ass and..."

"Let's talk to Guest Services," his wife said, desperately. "Maybe they can help us rent a boat somewhere in the area."

"Excuse me!" I called from the deck.

Still holding onto the woman's arm, the aptly named Dick scowled my way. "What do you want? Who the hell are you?"

I was leaning over the rail. "I'm the manager here, Jack Keller. Can I be of any help?"

He let go of her arm and the plump, pretty blonde moved toward me, looking up at me with a look that strained to be pleasant. "I called both numbers your brochure lists and wasn't able to rent a boat."

"It's a busy time," I said. "Let me look into it for you."

"We're only going to be here a week," Dick said. "I hate to waste a goddamn day!"

She touched his arm, gently. "We wanted to golf while we here. We did bring the clubs. We could do that today."

He brushed her hand away like it was a bug. "Probably have to call ahead for that, too."

"I'll call over for you," I said. "You are...?"

"The Waltons," he said.

"Excuse me?"

"We're the fucking Waltons! Dick and Mindy."

The Waltons. Okay...

"Dick, I'll make the call. After lunch, around one-thirty a suitable tee time?"

"Good," Dick said, pacified. "Thanks for your help."

"That's what I'm here for," I said.

"Thank you," Mindy said, and smiled at me, and looped her arm in his, and he allowed her to, as he walked her over to the restaurant.

I called over to the golf course and got the Waltons a tee time and called Gary over at Gull Lake Lodge to see about a boat.

"They should've called ahead," Gary said. "Why do you want to help these people? Friends of yours?"

"Hardly. The husband's an obnoxious cocksucker who'll browbeat his wife into a nervous breakdown, if I don't bail her out."

"Oh, the Waltons."

"Addams Family is more like it. So, you know them?"

"They were at Sylvan the last two seasons. Dick Walton is a real pain in the ass and an ugly drunk."

"Maybe we don't want his business."

"Trouble is, he's as rich as he is obnoxious. He's from Minneapolis, runs used car lots all over the Cities. Big fucking ego, does his own commercials. 'Big Deals with Big Dick' is his motto."

"Catchy."

"It's been popular with Twin Cities school kids for a couple decades. He's worth several mil. And he brings his sales staff up for conferences in the off-season."

"So, we cater to him."

"Yeah, within reason. If he starts busting up the bar or something, cut him off and toss his ass out. When he starts spoiling things for our other guests, then fuck him."

"I like your attitude, Gary. But what about a boat?"

"He can use mine for the week. It's down at dock nine."

"That's generous."

"Generous my ass. Charge him double the going rate."

The restaurant at Sylvan's is four-star, and it's a real asset for the business, but it's the only thing Gary and I ever really disagreed about. Dinner was by reservation only and those reservations filled up quick, and the prices were more New York than mid-west.

"The goddamn restaurant's a real calling card for us," Gary would say. "Brings in people staying at other lodges and gives 'em a look at ours."

"But we're not serving our own guests," I'd say. "We're a hotel at heart, Gary, and our clientele shouldn't have to mortgage the farm to buy supper, and they shouldn't get turned away 'cause they don't have reservations."

"I appreciate your dedication to the guests, Jack. But that restaurant brings in about a third of our income, so fuckin' forget it, okay?"

But, of course, I didn't. We had this same argument at least twice a month.

That particular evening, I was having the house specialty - pan-fried walleye, and enjoying the way the moon looked reflected on the silvery lake when I heard the gravel-edged sound of Dick Walton's voice, singing a familiar tune.

"You're a stupid cunt!" he was telling her.

They had a table in the corner, but the long, rather narrow dining room, with its windows on the lake, didn't allow anyone much privacy. Even approaching nine-thirty, the restaurant was full, older couples, families, a honeymooning couple, all turned their eyes to the asshole in the lime sport coat and green-and-white plaid pants who was verbally abusing the blonde woman in the green-and-white floral sundress.

She was crying. Digging a Kleenex into eyes where the mascara was already smeared. When she got up from the table to rush out, she looked like an embarrassed, haunted raccoon.

He shouted something unintelligible at her, and sneered, and returned to his big fat rare steak.

The restaurant manager, a guy in his late twenties who probably figured his business degree would get him a better gig than this, came over to my table and leaned in. He was thin, sandy-haired, pockmarked; he wore a pale-yellow sweater over a shirt and tie.

"Mr. Keller," he said, "what should I do about Mr. Walton?"

"Leave him alone, Rick. Without his wife to yell at, I doubt he'll make much more fuss."

"Should I cut him off with the bar?"

"No."

He gave me a doubtful expression, one eyebrow arching. "Personally, I..."

"Just leave it alone. If he passes out, he won't

bother his wife or anybody, and that would probably be ideal."

Rick sighed, he didn't like me much, knowing that I was lobbying to have his four-star restaurant turned into a cafeteria, but he nodded in acceptance of my ruling, and padded off.

I finished my walleye, touched a napkin to my lips and headed over to Walton's table.

"You got my message about the boat?" I asked.

His grin was tobacco-stained; the tufts of white eyebrow raised so high they might have been trying to crawl off his face. "Yeah! That was white of you, Jack! You're okay. Sit down, I'll buy you one."

I sat, where his wife had been (her own walleye practically untouched on the plate before me), but said, "I had enough for tonight. I know my limit."

"So, do I, buddy boy," He pointed a steak knife at me and winked. "It's when the fuckin' *lights* go out."

I laughed. "Say, what was the little woman riding you about? If you don't mind my asking."

His face balled up like a fist. "Bitch. Lousy little cunt. She fucked up royal this afternoon."

"Oh?"

"Yeah, fuck her. We're playing with another couple, the Goldstein's, from Des Moines. He's a dentist. Those docs are loaded, you know, particularly the Hebrew ones."

"Up the wazoo," I affirmed.

"Anyway, Mindy is a decent little golfer, usually. Shoots a 19 handicap on the country club course back home, but this afternoon she didn't shoot for shit. I lost a hundred bucks because of her!"

"Well, hell, Dick, everybody has a bad afternoon

once in a while."

His aftershave wafted across the table to tickle my nose, a grotesque parody of the pine scent that nature routinely provided us here.

"I think she did it just to *spite* me. I'd swear she muffed some of those shots just to get my fuckin' goat."

His speech was pretty slurred.

"That sounds like a woman," I said.

He looked me with as steady a gaze as he could muster. "Jack, I like you."

"I like you, Dick. You're a real man's man."

I offered him my water glass for him to clink his tumbler of Scotch on the rocks against.

"I'll have to sneak away from the little woman," he said, winking again, "so we can spend some *quality* time together."

"Let's do that," I said. "You going fishing tomorrow?"

He was lighting up an unfiltered cigarette; it took a lot of effort. "Yeah, me and that kike dentist. Wanna come along?"

"Got to work, Dick. Check in with me later, though. Maybe we can take in one of the casinos."

"One of the ones those Injuns run?"

Gambling having been ruled legal on reservation land; casinos run by Native Americans were a big tourist draw in our neck of the woods.

"That's right, Dick. A whole tribe of Tontos looking to fleece the Lone Ranger."

"Hah! How 'bout tomorrow night?"

"We'll see. If you're getting up early tomorrow morning, Dick, to fish, maybe you ought to hit the sack."

He guzzled at his drink. "I ought to hit that fuckin' cunt I'm married to, is what I oughta hit."

"Take it easy. It's a hell of a thing, but a man can get in trouble for hitting a woman, these days."

"Hell of a thing, ain't it, Jack? Hell of a thing."

I walked out with him; he shambled along, slipping an arm around me, cigarette trailing ash.

"You're a hell of a guy," he told me, almost crying. "Hell of a guy."

"So are you, Dick," I said.

Outside the real pines were almost enough to cancel the room-freshener cologne he was wearing.

Almost.

I was sitting in the dark, in my underwear, sipping a Coke in the glow of the portable television, watching a Randolph Scott western from the 1950s. I kept the sound low, because I had the doors to the deck pushed open, to enjoy the lake breeze, and I didn't want my movie-watching to disturb any of the guests who might be strolling along the beach, enjoying the night.

Something about the acoustics of the lake made her crying seem to echo, as if carried on the wind from a great distance, though she was at my feet, really, stumbling across the grass beneath my deck.

Underwear or not, I went out to check on her, because the crying sounded like more than just emotions – there was physical pain in it, too.

"Mrs. Walton," I called, recognizing her. She still wore the flowered sundress, the scoop top of it displaying the swell of her swell bosom. "Are you all right?"

She nodded, stumbling. "Just need a drink, need

a drink..."

"The bar's closed. Why don't you step up here, and I'll get you a beer or something."

"No, no..."She shook her head and then I saw it, the puffiness of the left side of her face, eye swollen shut, the flesh already blackening.

I ran down the little wooden stairs; if somebody complained to the manager about the man running around in his underwear, well fuck 'em, *I* was the manager. I took her by the arm and walked her up onto the deck and inside, where I deposited her on the couch in front of the TV, where Randolph Scott was shooting Lee Van Cleef.

"Just let me get dressed," I said, and I returned with pants on and a beer in hand, which I held out to her. "It's all I have, I'm afraid," I said.

She took it and held it in her hands like something precious, sipped it like a child taking first communion.

I got her a washcloth with some ice in it.

"He's hit you before, hasn't he?" I said, sitting beside her.

She nodded, tears trickled from the good eye. Her pink-bowed platinum blonde hair wasn't mussed, too heavily sprayed for that.

"How often?" I asked.

"All...all the time."

"Why don't you leave the son of a bitch?"

"He says...he says he'll kill me."

"Probably just talk. Turn him in for beating you. They go hard on guys who do that, nowadays, and then it'll be harder for him to do it again."

"No, he would kill me. Or have somebody do it. He has the kind of connections where you can get somebody killed, if you want. And it'll just be written off as an accident. I bet you find that hard to believe, don't you?"

"Yeah." I sipped my Coke. "Sounds utterly fantastic."

"Well, it's true."

"Are you sure you're not staying 'cause of the prenup?"

She sighed, nodded slowly, the hand with the ice in the washcloth moving with her head. "There is a prenuptial agreement. I wouldn't get a thing. Well, ten thousand, I think."

"But you're not staying 'cause of the money."

"No! I don't care about the money, exactly. I got family I take care of. A younger sister who's going to college, mom's got heart trouble and no insurance."

"So, it is about money."

The good eye winced. "No! No, it was about money. That's why I married Dick. I was...I was trash. A waitress. Topless dancer, for a while. Anything to make a buck, but never hooking. Never!"

"Where did you meet Dick?"

"In a titty bar a friend of his used to run. I wasn't dancing, then, I was a waitress. Tips in a topless place are always incredible."

"So I hear."

"This was, I don't know, over ten years ago."

"You been taking this shit all that time?"

"No. He was sweet, at first. But he didn't drink as much in those days. The more he drank, the worse it got. He calls me stupid. He can't have kids, his sperm count is lower than he is. But he calls me 'barren' and hits me, says I'm fat. Do you think I'm fat?"

I'd been looking down the front of her sundress at the time, and swallowed, and said, "Uh, no. I don't like these skinny girls they're pushing on us, these days."

"Fake tits and boy's butts, all of them." Her lips were trembling; her voice sounded bitter. "He has a girlfriend, she works in a titty bar, too. A different joint, this is one that he's got money in. She's like that, skinny little thing, and a plastic chest and a flat little ass."

"You should leave him. Forget his threats. Forget the money."

"I can't. I...I wish he was dead. Just fucking dead."

"Don't talk that way."

Her whole body was trembling; she hugged herself with one arm, as if very, very cold. "I need a miracle. I need a goddamn miracle."

"Well, here's a suggestion."

"Yes?"

"Say your prayers tonight. Maybe God'll straighten it all out."

"With a miracle?"

"Or something," I said.

"Hop in," he said.

He was behind the wheel of a red-bodied, white-topped Cadillac, his bloodshot face split in a shit-eating grin as he leaned over to open the door on the rider's side. He was wearing a green-and-orange plaid sport coat - it was like a Scotsman had puked on him, and orange trousers and lots of clunky gold jewelry.

I slipped inside the spacious car. "Didn't have any trouble getting away?"

"Naw! That little bitch doesn't dare give me any

lip. I'd just knock some *more* sense in her! Anybody see you go?"

"No. I think we're all right."

I'd had him pick me up at the edge of the road, half a mile from the resort, in darkness. I said I was on call tonight and wasn't supposed to be away.

"You tell your wife where you were going, and who with?"

"Hell no! None of her goddamn business! I tell you, Jack, I should never have married that lowlife cunt. She's got a family like something out of *Deliverance*. Poor white trash, pure and simple. No fuckin' class at all."

"Why don't you dump her, then?"

"I just might! You know what a prenuptial agreement is, don't you, Jack?"

"Got a vague idea."

"Well, my lawyer assures me I don't have to give her jack shit. She's out in the cold on her flabby ass, soon as I give the say so."

"Why don't you, then?"

"I might. I might...but it could be bad for business. I use her in some of my commercials, and she's kinda popular. Or anyway, her big ol' titties are, pardon my French."

"She helps you put up a good front."

"Hah! Yeah, that's a good one, Jack...that's a good one."

The drive to the casino was about an hour, winding through tall pines and little bump-in-the-road towns. The night was clear, the moon full again, the world bathed in an unreal, and lovely, silver. I studied the idyllic landscape, pretending to listen to Walton blather on about his accomplishments in the used car game, cracking the window to let some fresh air cancel out his Pinesol aftershave and cigarette smoke.

It was midweek, but the casino looked busy, just a sprawling one-story prefabricated building, looking about as exotic as a mobile home, but for the huge LAKEVIEW CASINO neon. The term "Lakeview" was cosmetic, as the nearest lake was a mile away. Some construction, some expansion, was going on, and the front parking lot was a mess.

He pulled around back, as I instructed; a couple of uniformed security guards with guns, Indians, like most of the employees here, were stationed in front. None were in back. A man and a woman, both weaving with drink, were wandering out to their car as Walton found a place to park.

"No limit here, right?" he asked.

"Right. You bring a pretty good roll?"

"Couple grand. I got unlimited cash access on my Gold card, too."

The car with the couple in it pulled out and drove unsurely around the building. Once their car lights were gone, it was as dark as the inside of cow back here. I got out of the Cad.

"If you need a couple bucks, Jack, just ask."

He had his back to me, as we walked toward the casino. When my arm slipped around him, it startled him, but he didn't have much time to react, the knife had pierced his windpipe by then.

When I withdrew the hunting knife, a scarlet geyser sprayed the night, but away from me. He fell like a pine tree, flopping forward, but the sound was just a little slap against the cement. The knife made more noise as it clattered against the pavement; I kicked it under a nearby pick-up. He gurgled a while but that stopped soon.

Yanking him by the ankles, I dragged him between his Caddy and the dumpster he'd parked next to, a slim trail of blood glistening in the moonlight, but otherwise he was out of sight. So was I. I bent over him, using the same flesh-colored, rubber-gloved hand that had held the knife, and stripped him of his gaudy gold jewelry and lifted his fat wallet from his hip pocket, the sucker pocket the dips call it. I removed the wad of hundreds and tossed the wallet in the dumpster.

The jewelry was a bit of a problem: if somebody stopped me to talk to me about the dead man in the parking lot, I could be found with it on me. But a thief wouldn't leave it behind, so I had to take it, stuffing it in my jacket pockets. Tomorrow I would toss it in Sylvan Lake.

Right now, with my couple of thousand bucks, I walked around the front of the casino, said, "Nice night, fellas," to the Indian security guards, who grunted polite responses to the paleface.

Inside, the pinball-machine-like sound of gambling fought with piped-in country western; the redskins seemed to favor cowboy music. I found Nikki where I knew she'd be, at the nickel poker machines. The slender girl had a bright-eyed, pixie face and a cap of brown curls.

"Jack! I'm doing *fantastic*. I'm up four dollars!"

"Sounds like you're making a killing."

"How about you?"

"Same."

I had told Nikki I'd meet her here, we usually took

separate cars when we went out, since the manager and his social director weren't supposed to fraternize.

She moved up to the quarter poker machines, at my urging, and ended up winning about thirty bucks. Before long, I was up two hundred bucks on black-jack. If somebody found the body while I was there, things could get interesting. I'd have to dump that jewelry somewhere.

But I didn't think anybody would be using that dumpster tonight and I knew nobody would use the Caddy. Leaving too soon would be suspicious. So I stayed a couple hours.

"Jeez," I said, as we were heading out finally, her arm in mine, my hand on my head. "I think I drank a little too much."

"That's not like you, Jack."

"I know. But you better drive me home."

"What about your car?"

My car was back at the resort, of course, parked where Nikki wouldn't see it when she went to her own cabin.

"I'll have Gary drive me up for it tomorrow."

"Okay," she said, and she steadied me as we walked back around to the parking lot in the rear.

It was still dark back there and quiet. Very quiet. I could barely make out a dried dark streak on the pavement, over by the Caddy, but nothing glistened in the moonlight, now.

First thing the next morning, the police came around to see me, Gary was with them, a pair of uniformed state patrolmen. It seemed, around sun-up, that one of our guests had been found dead in the parking lot at the Lakeview Casino. His wallet, emptied of money, had been found nearby.

"Mr. Walton wore a lot of jewelry," I said. "The gold kind."

"Asking for trouble," said one of the cops, a kid in his mid-twenties.

Gary, wearing a gray jogging suit, wasn't saying anything. He was standing behind them like a mute grizzly, his eyes a little glazed.

"That casino's probably gonna get sued," the other, slightly older cop said. "Bad lighting in the parking lot back behind there. Just asking for it."

"Both Walton *and* that casino," the young one said.

I agreed with them, said sympathetic things, and pointed them to the cabin where they could find - and inform - the new widow.

Gary stayed behind.

"You know," he said quietly, scratching his beard, "I'm glad that bastard didn't get killed on our grounds. We might be the ones getting sued."

"Right. But that's not going to happen around here."

"Oh?"

"Don't worry, Gary." I put a hand on his shoulder; had to reach up to do it. "*We* have adequate lighting."

He looked at me kind of funny, with narrowed eyes. He seemed about to ask me something, but thought better of it, waved limply, and wandered off.

I was doing my morning sit-ups when she walked up on my deck, looking dazed, her perfect, bullet-proof platinum hair wearing the girlish pink bow, her voluptuous body tied into a dark pink dressing gown. She stood looking through the cross-hatch of screen door, asking if she could come in.

"Of course," I said, sliding the door open, and took her to the couch where she'd sat two nights before. "You heard about Dick?" she said, in small voice. She seemed numb.

"Yes. I'm sorry."

"You...you won't say anything, will you?"

"About what?"

"Those...terrible things I said about him." Her eyes got very wide; she seemed frightened, suddenly, but not of me. Exactly. "You don't think...you don't think I..."

"No. I don't think you did it, Mrs. Walton."

"Or...or hired somebody...I mean, I was saying some crazy things the other night."

"Forget it."

"And if the police knew about Dick hitting me..."

"Your face looks pretty good today. I don't think they'll pursue that angle."

She swallowed, stared into nothing. "I don't know what to do."

"Why don't you just lean back and wait to inherit Dick's estate? You can do those TV commercials solo, now."

She turned to look at me and the faintest suspicion seemed etched around her eyes. "You've been...very kind, Mr. Keller."

"Make it Jack."

"Is there anything I can do to...repay your kindnesses?"

"Well...you can keep coming to Sylvan Lodge, despite the bad memories. We could sure use your business, for those sales conferences and all."

She touched my hand. "I can promise you that. Maybe we could...get to know each other better. Under better circumstances."

"That would be nice."

"Could I just...sit here for a while? I don't really want to go back to the cabin. It still...still smells of Dick. That awful cologne of his."

Here all you could smell was the lake and the pines, real pines; the soothing touch of a breeze rolled over us.

"Stay as long as you like," I said. "Here at Sylvan Lodge, we strive to make our guests' stay as pleasant as possible."

FATHER, SON AND HOLY GHOST

Barbara Collins

My Sunday afternoons are sacred. Hubby is glued to his easy chair, watching football. The kids are down in the rec room, playing video games, out of my hair. And I'm cloistered in the bedroom, under the rumpled sheets, enjoying an old movie on the VCR, and eating a box of sinful chocolates I keep hidden in my underwear drawer.

But sometimes my sacred Sundays get ruined.

My name is Joan Munday. I'm one of six detectives on the Port City Police Department, in a town with a population of about twenty-five thousand, give or take a soul.

It was 2:33 p.m., October 25, when the phone rang on the nightstand by the bed. I knew it was Captain Velez, because even my own mother knows better than to bother me on a Sunday afternoon. The captain told me to call my partner, Frank Lausen, and get over to St. Mark's Church right away. He said Father

O'Brien had called the station, very upset. The priest was claiming his church had been possessed by a ghost, and not the holy kind.

I hung up, then dialed Frank, and ruined *his* Sunday. I told him I'd be by to pick him up in a few minutes.

Frank lived in a split-level home in a new addition not far from our old two-story clapboard. He was twenty-eight years old, a decade younger than me, and had a wife, who taught elementary school, and two small children.

He was buttoning up a wrinkled white shirt beneath a navy jacket when he came out of his house, red tie hanging loose around his neck like a noose. His thick, sandy hair was tousled, his face unshaven.

He grunted a greeting as he got into the car. Quickly, he reached for the dial on the radio, turning it on, and tuning it in to the Hawkeye-Buckeye football game he'd been watching.

I looked in the rear-view mirror, catching my own image, and cringed a little as I pulled away from the curb; with my own hastily made-up face and brown hair in need of a coif, we looked like a couple that really tied one on the night before.

Port City was beautiful in the fall. Nestled on the Mississippi River among rolling hills, the town was blessed with many trees, vibrant with color now, reds as red as blood, oranges as orange as the pumpkins sitting on porches of houses that we sped by on our way to the church. Halloween was making a big comeback here, after a slow couple of years, following some treaters getting cyanide-laced tricks. Black cats and witches clung to doors and windows, while white sheet ghosts hung twisting by their necks from trees.

I turned my car into a cobblestone drive that lead up a narrow winding road to St. Mark's Church. The huge gothic building, pale gray granite trimmed in carved limestone, looked down ominously at us, and the rest of the city, from its hilltop perch. I thought the old Protestant church I attended was austere; this looming edifice was downright intimidating. I parked the car in the lot and we got out.

Father O'Brien stood waiting for us at the front door of the rectory, a simple gray three-story building next door. He wasn't at all the jolly Friar Tuck-type I had naively imagined. Tall, bear-like, he was an imposing figure in all black, except for the traditional white collar. His dark hair was carefully combed, the grey at his temples hinted of middle-age. While his facial features seemed benevolently boyish, a square jaw and jutting chin gave the impression he was no pushover.

Outwardly the priest looked composed, but his eyes betrayed something else. Frank and I approached.

"Father O'Brien," I said, "I'm Joan Munday and this is Frank Lausen, from the Police Department."

"Thank you for coming," he said solemnly. "And I'm sorry to take you away from your families on a Sunday afternoon."

I smiled. "I don't think they'll miss me," I admitted. I couldn't lie to a priest.

"What's this about a ghost, Father?" Frank asked.

Father O'Brien gestured toward the doorway. "We'll talk inside," he said.

We followed Father O'Brien into the rectory,

down a dark, drafty hallway lined with portraits of priests. Who they were, I couldn't say, but one of them reminded me uncomfortably of that old *Saturday Night Live* character, Father Guido Sarducci.

Father O'Brien led us into what I assumed was his office. It was cozy and comfortable. There was a large oak desk, a file cabinet, a picture of Pope John Paul II on the wall, and two chairs. Occupying the chairs was another priest and a woman. The priest, also dressed in black slacks and jacket, rose as we entered. He was older than Father O'Brien, tall and slender, with a handsome but world-weary face.

The woman, who remained seated, was about my age. She had short, straight brown hair, and wore little make-up on her plain but not unattractive face. Her burgundy blouse and skirt were at least ten years out of style. She looked at me with apprehension.

"This is Elizabeth Keyes," Father O'Brien said, making the introductions. "She's church organist, and also helps out in the office."

Frank and I nodded at her.

"And this is Father Hanson," Father O'Brien continued. "He gives the early morning mass."

"Would you like to sit down?" Father Hanson asked. He gestured to his empty chair. "I can get another."

"We'll stand, if you don't mind," Frank answered, almost curtly. "Now, who wants to tell us about this 'ghost'?" Frank wasn't usually so brusque. He just wanted to get home in time for the second half.

Father O'Brien moved behind his desk. "It began about three weeks ago," he said, sitting down, the chair creaking beneath his weight.

His put his elbows on the desk and pressed his

hands together, prayer-like. The Pope peeked over his shoulder. "October sixth. I remember because the day before was a funeral for one of our parishioners. Afterward, the family donated the flowers to the church, for mass the next morning."

He paused. We waited.

"But when I went into the church that Sunday morning," he continued, "something was terribly wrong with the flowers – all of them were wilting, and dying."

There was silence. Then Frank said, "That's it? Dead flowers?"

I gave Frank a wilting look, his rudeness to these men of the cloth surprising me. But then, they had interrupted *his* religion, football.

"Father O'Brien," I said. "Have you had any trouble with flowers since?"

"Oh, yes," the Priest said, and sighed. "We've finally resorted to using artificial ones."

"What else can you tell us?" I asked.

"There's an odor," he said. "A smell, a *stench* really, so unpleasant I have to open every window to get rid of it."

"Do you recognize this odor?" I asked. "Or can you describe it?"

Father O'Brien furrowed his brow. "No," he said slowly, thinking. "I can't."

"Maybe it's just a dead, decaying rat," Frank offered. "I mean, you probably have a few in an old building like this!" Frank was in rare form today.

Father Hanson spoke. "It's not a dead, decaying rat," he said politely. "Many of us have encountered this odor, and in different places in the church. It's like walking into a fog, that's how I would describe it."

Elizabeth Keyes, who was nodding in agreement, leaned toward Father O'Brien. "Tell them about the music," she said, conspiratorially.

"Our 'ghost' plays the organ," he said, "and quite well. Father Hanson and I can hear it at night from our rooms here in the rectory."

"The organ," I said to Elizabeth, "*can* it play by itself?"

"No," she said almost huffily. "It's a pipe organ, not a synthesizer."

"Just what kind of music does this ghost like to play?" Frank asked, smirking. "*The Monster Mash*?"

"Hymns," Elizabeth Keyes answered, tersely.

"Any *particular* hymns?" I asked.

The two priests and organist exchanged glances. Then Father O'Brien said, "It seems to favor 'Ave Maria.'"

Frank snorted. "Look, somebody's just pulling your chain. Your flock's got a disgruntled sheep, is all this is. Or a neighborhood kid playing a Halloween prank. And if that's the case, we'll catch him." Frank raised an eyebrow. "But if this *is* some ghost, some spirit of the other world...well, why don't you just *exorcise* it?"

Patient until now, Father O'Brien stood up, face flushed, and leaned with both hands on the desk.

"Mr. Lausen," he said angrily, obviously frustrated, "this isn't some Hollywood horror show. Father Hanson's mass this morning was interrupted by screams so blood-curdling it cleared the congregation out of the church! Whatever it is *has* to *stop!*"

A strained silence fell over the room. I shifted

uncomfortably from one foot to the other. I looked at Frank. "We could stake out the church next week," I offered.

Frank sighed, nodded. Then he looked at the priests. "I've got no experience in the ghost-busting business," he said, "but I'm willing to give it a try... if one of you can tell me who or *what* I'm expected to bust."

"*I* can tell you," Elizabeth Keyes said, her voice strange, eyes haunted. "I've *seen* her." "Her?" Frank and I said.

"Rebecca Madden."

"Now I'm confused," I admitted, looking from Father Hanson to Elizabeth to Father O'Brien. "If you know who it is why don't you...?"

"You don't understand," Father O'Brien said softly. "Rebecca Madden was murdered in the woods behind this church ten years ago."

It was 4:45 p.m. when I dropped Frank off at his house. We decided to alternate nights at the church; the priests could keep an eye on things during the day. I thought it was sweet of Frank to offer to take the first watch, so I could have Sunday evening with my family. Then I figured out he wanted tomorrow night off so he could watch Monday Night Football.

I drove over to the station and pulled the folder on Rebecca Madden; it was still in the active file.

The manila envelope was thick with papers and notes and newspaper clippings. It had all the ear-markings of an officer obsessed with a case. The name of Sergeant Richard Lynn was printed in ink on the outside of the envelope. I'd heard he left us for the Chicago PD a few years back, before I arrived.

I looked at the autopsy report. It said the thirty-three-year-old, female Caucasian died from strangulation. The only evidence gathered at the scene, a quarter-inch thick brown rope, four and a half feet long, was listed in the evidence locker, number JW714. The woman had not been sexually molested.

Among the clippings was Rebecca Madden's obit from the local newspaper, dated October 10, with accompanying photo.

Long tresses, that looked like Angel's Hair, encircled her head like a huge halo. Her delicate features, eyes large and demanding, were that of a porcelain doll. She was smiling, but it somehow seemed sad. A hauntingly beautiful woman...

The obit read like a pitch for sainthood: assistant organist at St. Mark's Church, part-time Catholic elementary school teacher, charity work that would have made Mother Theresa proud. She left behind both parents, who at that time were still living in town, and a ten-year-old son. She was preceded in death by her husband.

I leafed back through the file and noticed Sergeant Lynn had kept track of the family. Rebecca's parents had moved to Naples, Florida, three years ago. The son, Chris, enrolled at the University of Iowa, in Iowa City. If the boy was still in college, he would be a junior today.

That night I couldn't sleep. I lay in bed next to my husband, thinking about that poor woman, and that sad little boy. I got up and put on my white robe stained with bacon grease and tiptoed in to my sleeping kids and kissed their faces. Then I went downstairs to watch TV. Sometime around three, I fell asleep for what seemed like a second, when the shrill ring of the phone woke me.

It was Frank.

"What time is it?" I asked, groggily.

"Six forty-five," he answered, sounding the same.

"Anything happen?"

"Yes."

That woke me up. "What?"

"I hurt my back, that's what happened," he said crossly. "Here's a piece of advice – never sleep on a goddamn church pew."

The phone clicked in my ear.

I got up and showered and dressed and got my kids off to school. Then I kissed my husband good-bye and wished him a good day at the bank.

I went out to my car.

The drive to Iowa City, which was forty-five miles north of Port City, was as refreshing as a cool drink of water. I cracked a window and let in the crisp fall air. Farm fields were brown with ripened corn, ready for harvesting, and the colorful trees, bathed in the morning sun, glistened like an artist's lovely landscape not yet fully dried.

I loved the energy of a college town and envied the students in their new coats and sweaters, faces flushed, rushing to and from class with the knowledge that their whole lives lay ahead of them.

Obtaining Chris Madden's class schedule from the Dean of Admissions was easy enough, but I did have some trouble finding the Arts Building where Chris was supposed to be. Locating a parking place was the hard part. After circling the packed lot a few times, I invented a spot. What were those campus rent-a-cops going to do, arrest me?

Chris was in the theater, backstage, painting a prop, brush in one hand. There were other students around, working on the sets, but I easily picked him out. He was of average height, slender, but muscular in a blue t-shirt and black jeans. His tan tennis shoes were splotched with the green paint he was using. He had mop of thick curly brown hair and a small mustache. The ten-year-old boy was now a twenty-year-old man. He must have sensed me watching him from the wings, because he turned and looked at me with his mother's eyes.

"Something?" he asked politely, but with an edge that said, "I'm busy."

I crossed the stage, shoes echoing off the floor-boards, and told him who I was.

He set the brush down on the top of the paint can.

"This is about my mother, isn't it?" he asked, but it was more like a statement than a question.

I nodded.

"Somehow I knew it," he said.

"Could we go somewhere and talk?"

He gestured toward the prop tree he was painting. "I've got to finish this," he said. "But I could meet you in the cafeteria, around noon."

"How about Bushnell's Turtle?" I suggested.

"Fine," he said.

I turned and left the stage, feeling his eyes on my back. I went outside to my car, where a fifteen-dollar parking ticket was pinned under a wiper. I guess that answered my question about what the rent-a-cops could do to me.

Bushnell's Turtle was famous for its sub sandwiches. The restaurant got its name from the man who invented the first submarine, so the card on the table said. Established in the early 1970s, the eatery had something most other hippie-era restaurants didn't have, great food.

The place was packed right now. I grabbed a wooden booth in the back, along a wall of framed photos of dogs playing cards, leaving my jacket to claim the booth before going back up to the counter to order.

At 12:13, Chris came in the front door. I waved to him as he stood in line to get his food. I had already gotten mine: carrot soup, a veggie salad with peppercorn dressing, a super sub deluxe, and chocolate cake. I had given up losing those ten pounds a long time ago. After a few minutes, Chris came back with his lunch, a bottle of "natural" soda. He slid into the booth across from me.

"I don't have much time," he said apologetically. He took a sip of the pop, then ran one finger over his mustache.

I put down my super sub deluxe and told him about the strange things that Father O'Brien had said had been happening at St. Mark's Church. I told him Elizabeth Keyes claimed to have seen his mother, in a pink floral dress, standing in the balcony of the sanctuary one night.

A peculiar look came over his face. "You don't know how relieved I am to hear this," he said softly, "because I thought *I* was going crazy."

I waited for him to explain.

He looked up at me with tortured eyes. "You see," he said, "I've seen my mother, too."

I leaned forward. "Where?"

"In my dreams," he said. "Although lately I can sort of sense her..."He ran one hand through his hair."...I can't exactly explain it, but it's *more* than a feeling."

"Tell me about the dreams."

He leaned toward me and lowered his voice. "She's floating above me, in a white robe, not a pink floral dress. She's trying to tell me something, her lips are moving, but I can't tell what she's saying. Then I wake up, drenched in sweat."

I studied his face. Then I asked, "What can you tell me about Elizabeth Keyes?"

He shrugged, took another drink of his soda. "Not much," he said. "I haven't seen her for years. But I remember that she and my mother were very close, almost like sisters. She was always over at our house, and she was very kind to me after my mother died."

"And Father O'Brien and Father Hanson? Do you see them often?"

"Father Hanson will drop by my dorm whenever he's in town. He comes up to visit parish members who are at the University Hospital." He paused. "I haven't seen Father O'Brien in quite some time. But both Father Hanson and Father O'Brien were responsible for me getting that church scholarship to go to college here."

"I see," I said.

Chris pushed his now empty pop bottle away. "Look," he said, his eyes searching my face, "I don't know what's going on, but I think someone at that church knows something about my mother's death."

"What makes you think that?" I asked.

He shrugged again. "Why else would she be haunting it?"

I didn't have an answer for him.

I finished my food, and we left the booth and went outside. The sky had clouded over, and the chill in the air was a promise of winter, or maybe a threat.

"I'll be in touch," I told him.

Chris took a few steps from me, then stopped and looked back over his shoulder. "Oh, one thing," he said. "That pink floral dress Elizabeth saw my mother wearing?"

"Yes?"

"That was the dress she was buried in."

He walked away, down the street, a solitary figure among the crowd. I watched him until I couldn't see him anymore.

Sitting in the dark in St. Mark's Church, I wished I was anyplace else. My rear end hurt from the hard-wooden pew I'd been planted on for the past four hours, having positioned myself in the back row by the double doors that lead out into the vestibule. I'd brought along a flashlight, a Thermos of strong coffee, and my .38 snubnose.

It was 1:58 a.m., and I was cold and tired. Outside the wind picked up, rattling the stained-glass windows, making it even more drafty inside. The light of the moon, filtering in through the windows, cast long, distorting shadows, making everything look like a potential ghost. It gave me the creeps to be here. I tried not to think of that woman. I was afraid if I did, she might suddenly materialize, her mouth moving silently, just like Chris had said, in a desperate attempt to tell me who her murderer was.

But wasn't that what I wanted? For our "ghost" to make an appearance? I was a cop. I didn't believe in apparitions or the supernatural or any such nonsense. Or did I? God! This dark cavern of a church was driving me crazy!

I stood up and stretched, then walked along the outside of the pews, down toward the sanctuary. I stopped and looked up at a statue of the Madonna and Child. The sculpture was recessed into the wall, in a small alcove. Moonlight fell on her face, which had the expression of both joy and sadness. It was the joy a mother feels having a child, and the sadness of knowing that that child could be taken away.

I peered closer. A tear seemed to trickle down her cheek.

My mouth fell open in a gasp, and I backed up into the side of a pew, lost my footing and sat down hard on the seat.

Somewhere a door slammed. I jumped up and raced to the back and got my gun and flashlight. Quickly, I crouched down against the wall by the double doors.

I held my breath and commanded my heart to stop thumping.

Seconds seemed like minutes. Then slowly one of the doors began to open.

I rose, planting my feet, aiming the gun in one hand, the flashlight in the other.

A dark, formless figure emerged.

I said, "Hold it right there," and clicked on the light.

Father Hanson's hands flew up to his face. "It's just me!" he said, shielding his eyes from the glare.

"Don't shoot!"

"Father!" I said, relieved, lowering the gun. I directed the flashlight's beam off his face. "You could've been hurt."

"I'm...I'm sorry," Father Hanson said, "I wasn't thinking. I just came to tell you I'd turned up the heat."

"It *is* cold in here," I admitted. Wasn't that why I was shivering?

There was an awkward silence. Then Father Hanson said, "Nothing yet?"

"Nothing yet."

"And I don't suppose there *will* be after my little entrance."

I smiled. "That's okay," I said. "I think if anything was going to happen, it would have by now."

We fell silent again, and when he made no move to leave, I said, "I have some coffee. Will you join me?"

"Yes, yes I will. I can't seem to sleep."

We moved to the pew where I'd left the Thermos and sat down. I poured some coffee into the lid, and handed it to the priest.

"Father," I said, "I was looking at the Madonna. I could swear she was crying."

In the semi-darkness Father Hanson smiled a little. "Many people say that," he said. He took a sip of the hot coffee.

"Is it real or my imagination?"

He stared at the coffee he held in both hands, warming them. "Who can say for sure?" he asked softly, then added, "But I rather think that the sculptor intended it to appear that way."

I nodded and took a drink from the Thermos. The coffee tasted bitter. We sat for a while without saying anything.

"Father," I finally said, "what happens if a Catholic dies before she, or he, gets the Last Rites?"

"In the first place," Father Hanson replied, "it's not called 'The Last Rites.' You've been watching too much television." His tone was not condescending, merely informative. He went on to explain. "The Sacrament of the Sick is intended to be given to the seriously ill while they are able to spiritually benefit from it, not a last-minute prayer to console relatives, or a ticket to heaven, if that's what you're getting at."

"Oh."

We fell back into silence. I felt slightly embarrassed.

"Father," I said again, "if you believed in spirits, how might a soul get caught in limbo? I mean, not go to heaven, or hell, for that matter."

He took a deep breath, and his first few words came out a sigh, as if he were tired. "As far as the Church is concerned, the concept of limbo has pretty much gone out the window. It was something thought up because St. Augustine was willing to permit unbaptized babies to go to Hell. People didn't much like that. And so, Purgatory was kind of a compromise."

"I thought Purgatory *was* Hell."

"No. There is a difference. Purgatory is a place where we can 'catch up,' so to speak, on our growing, on the preparation we didn't get a chance to do on earth."

"I see," I said. "Sort of a detention room." I paused. "But I can't imagine a person with the pristine background of Rebecca Madden being condemned to Purgatory. It's not her fault she was brutally murdered. And if the absence of the Last Rites, excuse me, Sacrament of the Sick has no bearing on her entry to heaven...well, then, I just don't get it."

He turned to look at me. "I don't know why you seem so convinced Catholic theology holds the answer to this problem." There was an edge to his voice.

"I just want to understand it," I said. "Is there something wrong with that?"

He said nothing.

I pressed on. "She went regularly to confession?"

"Sacrament of Reconciliation."

"Sacrament of Reconciliation," I repeated.

He nodded.

I thought for a while. "What if," I asked, "a Catholic took his life? That's a mortal sin, isn't it? A sin he couldn't very well ask for forgiveness for after it was done."

The priest nodded slowly.

"But what if he asked for forgiveness *before*...?"

Father Hanson turned his face toward me. "That's a very interesting question," he commented. "But one I'm not sure I can answer."

I looked toward the front of the church, where Christ hung on the cross, his thorned head bowed.

"Many questions," I whispered, "but no real answers."

"I must go now," Father Hanson said abruptly.

He rose to leave, and that's when I said, "Chris has seen his mother, too."

Father Hanson's face turned white as a ghost.

"I visited him today," I explained. Then, not wanting to give the priest anything further, I said, "Good night, Father Hanson."

He hesitated, just for a moment, then left. I heard the door close quietly behind me.

Sunday, 10:15 a.m. I was attending my second mass of the morning - my second mass ever, for that matter. The eight o'clock mass, given by Father Hanson, went without a hitch. Frank covered the back, while I sat down in front. We'd had an uneventful week of surveillance at the church.

Now Father O'Brien, in white vestment, stood at the pulpit, while an assistant organist, a female college student, had replaced Elizabeth Keyes at the organ. Elizabeth Keyes and Father Hanson had returned to the rectory.

I found the service majestic but mysterious, comforting but confusing. We were into the Liturgy, the reading of the Scriptures, when I felt the hair stand up on the back of my neck.

A foul odor wafted across me, permeating the air.

Somewhere in the bowels of the church a loud moan could be heard. Everyone in the church seemed to freeze. Father O'Brien stopped in mid-sentence, one hand up in a gesture, suspended in the air. As the moan built to a muffled scream, I looked back at Frank. He was already heading out the back-double doors.

I jumped up and ran through the front of the sanctuary and into the sacristy, where the robes and other religious objects were kept. A door at the other end of the open-beamed room was open. It led out to a hallway, where stairs rose to rooms above.

An altar boy of perhaps ten, in white robe, stood plastered against the door jamb, his brown eyes as big as the collection plate he was holding. He pointed a quavering finger down the hall.

"The ghost went that way!" he shouted. "It came up from the basement!"

I ran past the boy and down the narrow hall and up the steps. As I came to the top, I drew my gun.

It was dark and cold up there. Another hallway stretched before me. The only source of light came from small open rooms that yawned off the hall. A door slammed at the other end.

Oh, Christ! I thought. *Don't go up to the bell tower! Vertigo* wasn't just a Hitchcock film where I was concerned.

I sprinted down the hallway, and opened the door to another set of stairs, just in time to see a pink floral dress, white legs and tennis shoes disappear at the top. The tennis shoes were splotched with green paint.

"I'm not coming up after you!" I shouted. "Chris!" I waited in the awful silence.

Then the tennis shoes appeared, and the pale legs, and pink floral dress, and Rebecca's face, ghostly white, eyes ringed in black, mouth painted red, blonde hair long and wild. The apparition seemed to float down the steps.

"Up against the wall," I said, gesturing with the gun.

I patted him down. No weapon. I read him his rights. Then I put my gun away and said, "Nice ensemble."

He relaxed and put his hands down from the wall. "Thank you," he said.

"The dead flowers?"

"Herbicide."

"And the odor?"

"Something a friend cooked up in Chemistry lab."

"I suppose your mustache was of the spirit gum

variety."

He nodded smugly. "After I shaved my real one off for this 'role,' it was. What now? Are you going to book me?"

"That depends," I answered. "But first I thought we might have a chat with some people – that's what you *really* want, isn't it?"

"Yes." He raised one hand to remove the wig, like a gentleman about to remove his hat.

I reached out and stopped him. "No, don't," I said, smiling wickedly. "Leave it on."

Frank cleared out the church, sending the parishioners on their bewildered way home. Only a few of the die-hard curious were left loitering on the lawn, staring and whispering among themselves, as I led Chris, dressed as his late mother, into the rectory.

I instructed Frank that just Fathers O'Brien and Hanson and Elizabeth Keyes were invited to our little party.

In Father O'Brien's office, Chris sat in a chair. To the others, the sight of him must have been unnerving. Anyway, that's what I was counting on.

The two priests and the organist took their turns in expressing to Chris their indignation over his "inex-cusable actions." I let them have at him a few minutes, then told them all to shut up.

"Let's hear what Chris has to say," I said.

"I want to know what really happened to my mother!" he demanded.

You could have heard a perfect-attendance pin drop.

Father O'Brien cleared his throat and began with

some compassion. "Chris, we understand your feelings. Perhaps certain...details were kept from you. After all, you were just a child of..."

"Bullshit!" Chris snapped. He reached under the dress into the pocket of a pair of cut-off jeans, and pulled out a piece of folded white paper. Carefully he opened it. With liquid eyes, Chris passed the paper to me.

"I found it the day after she died. I didn't show it to anybody...it was all I had of her, to hold onto."

It was a letter to him from his mother. In it she wrote of her love for him. But she also wrote of another love. A forbidden one.

Frank, who had moved behind me, read it over my shoulder.

"It's a suicide note," Frank said flatly.

Chris nodded. "I didn't realize it then," he said, his masculine voice now sounding small and child-like. "After all, everyone said she was murdered. And I didn't show the letter to anyone because I was afraid that for some reason, they would take it away from me."

He looked up at me earnestly.

"But what I told you was true," he said. "A few weeks ago, my mother *did* appear to me in a dream. She was holding the letter. I woke up and jumped out of bed and re-read it. That's when it became clear to me."

"That she wasn't strangled," I said. "That she hanged herself."

Father O'Brien and Elizabeth Keyes had stunned looks on their faces, but Father Hanson buried his in his hands and began to weep.

"I took her down," the Father sobbed, "from the sacristy where I found her. I moved her into the woods, to protect her, because I was afraid of how it would look in the eyes of the Church."

"You mean you were afraid your affair with my mother would be found out!" Chris accused.

Father Hanson wiped one hand across his wet face. "Yes," he admitted, "that, too." Then he said to Chris, beseeching him, "Don't you think I regret what I did? Don't you think I've asked for forgiveness a million times?"

Chris had only hatred in his eyes.

Father Hanson looked at me. "To answer your question, Officer Munday, you don't have to die to go to Purgatory. You can find it right here on earth."

"Rebecca wanted you to marry her," Frank said.

"Yes," Father Hanson replied, "and at first, I thought I could, because I did love her. But in the end, I loved the church more. As the years went by, she became more and more unhappy, because you see, we had a nine-year-old son."

Chris rose from his chair, astonished.

Father Hanson told him, "About a year before you were born, your mother came to me for counseling. Her husband was abusive, and she wanted my help to secure an annulment, sanctioned by the church. Instead, we became...involved. Then her husband was killed in that drunken car accident and she found herself pregnant, and alone. Everyone just assumed the child was his..."

"Why didn't you tell me!" Chris said in anguish. "All these years...all these years..."

"I wanted to, believe me, but I was afraid. I looked after you the best I could."

Father O'Brien stepped out from behind his desk. "What's going to happen now?" he asked

Frank and myself.

"In the eyes of the law, you mean?" I said. "Well, Chris' crime is minor, a misdemeanor at worst, and I doubt any court would convict him anyway, due to the extenuating circumstances."

I looked at Father Hanson. "The statute of limitations makes your activities non-prosecutable."

I looked at Frank and we exchanged glances, our work here done.

As we were leaving, I heard Father Hanson ask his son for forgiveness.

Whether he would get it or not, I didn't know, nor could I say what would happen between the priest and the church. Rebecca had asked for forgiveness in her letter. Had she been granted it?

Frank and I walked out into the crisp autumn day.

"That wraps it up, then," Frank said.

"Except for tracking down Sergeant Lynn in Chicago, to let him know how his case came out."

"I'll leave that to you," Frank called from across the lot. "Game starts in fifteen minutes!"

I shook my head, laughed a little, and got in my car. As I drove down the cobblestone drive, I caught a glimpse of St. Mark's in the rear-view mirror, standing forlornly on the hill.

My husband and kids weren't going to be happy when I got home and pulled the plug on the video game and turned off the TV set, but even if I got yelled at, I desperately needed us to do something together, as a family.

AUTHOR'S NOTE: I wish to acknowledge the non-fiction works of Father Andrew Greeley.

THE CABINET OF WILLIAM HENRY HARRISON

Barbara Collins and Max Allan Collins

From up ahead the voice of the tour guide echoed back to them: "...saved by Dolly Madison from the White House fire of 1814 was the portrait of George Washington, painted by Gilbert Stuart in 1805, that hangs over the..."

The thirty-something couple at the rear of the little group was paying scant attention to these or other tidbits of White House lore.

The woman, her mousy brown hair in a short serviceable cut, her gray sweater and slacks casual but not sloppy, wore a look of intense concentration; but the tour guide's words had nothing to do with it.

"I don't know what I'm going to do, Steve," she whispered. Her rather pleasant face, which seemed plain only for its lack of make-up, was contorted with worry.

Her husband, his handsome, if horsey, face drawn with concern, had wheat-colored hair tied back in a small ponytail, his plaid shirt and chinos making him look more like a college student than a vacationing math professor.

"Darling," he whispered, "we've been over all that. Can't we please just enjoy this? Not everybody gets honored with a VIP tour like this."

But his words made no more impact than the tour guide's. She said, "Can't you see I'm *drowning*? Like a damn bubble sliding toward an open drain."

"Sarah," he said, squeezing her forearm with affection and concern, "you'll be fine."

She didn't feel fine. She felt so tense she thought she was going to explode. Instead, her words exploded in another harsh whisper: "Who would have believed it? Who*ever* would have believed it? My greatest dream has become my worst nightmare!" She swallowed. She was embarrassed to sense her eyes welling up with tears. "It's...it's almost unbearable..."

And the tour guide droned on: "...East Room parquet floor which had to be replaced in 1977 because the twenty-five million visitors who walked on it since the White House has been open to tours, simply wore..."

Steve stopped her, turned her toward him. "So, you never write another book," he shrugged. "You won a Pulitzer Prize, Sarah. No one can ever take that away, ever."

Sarah was shaking her head. "But what will they say?" A humorless laugh escaped her lips. "What they're saying right *now*, I suppose. She's a one-shot. She got lucky."

Steve's expression was pained. "Honey. It took you five years to write that wonderful novel. They can't expect another in just a *year*."

"Then I shouldn't have taken that advance, should I? Or signed that damn contract."

Which just yesterday, in New York City, she had done, at the urging of her agent and her editor and her publisher and, yes, even her husband.

Her smirk was as humorless as the laugh. "I have to strike while the iron's hot, they say. When the first book's out in paperback next year, I'll need the 'follow-up.'"

"I suppose timing is important," Steve allowed.

"Get another book out before I'm forgotten, they say. Can you imagine? My reputation has a *time* limit. And that advance, so much money. How can I live up to it? What if they're disappointed? What if I can't deliver?"

Perhaps her whispering wasn't a whisper, anymore. Was it Sarah's imagination, or was there irritation now, in the tour guide's droning tone: "...exquisite cabinet made by local cabinetmaker Edwin Green in 1849 for William Henry Harrison, the ninth President of the United States. Harrison was the first President to die in the White House, just a month into his term. He caught a cold at his inauguration, riding a white stallion down Pennsylvania Avenue in a blizzard, without a hat or coat..."

Sarah gripped her husband's arm. "Steve, I want to leave. I feel sick."

"You're just having another anxiety attack," he said, trying to reassure her but sounding patronizing. "Did you bring your medication?"

She put a palm to her forehead and felt herself weaving in place. "I'm so tired...so very, very tired. I...I have to lie down."

"Just lean on me," he said, and she did. Then suddenly, Steve's voice seemed far away, as if in an echo chamber, and fading, fading: "...Sarah? Sarah? Sarah! What's wrong? Someone! *Somebody!* Get a doctor! Oh, my God. Oh, my God. No...no..."

Sarah opened her eyes, waking from a deep sleep, a sleep more restful than any she'd experienced in years. Her body felt loose, like a rubber band. The fainting, she supposed, had relaxed even the muscles in her face.

Her eyes tried to focus, as she lay on the floor, staring upward at a large, bright, white object that floated above her.

An angel? The white light at the end of a tunnel? She felt panic rising in her like negative adrenalin. Had she not fainted, but...*died?*

The object began to clarify itself, turning into the massive crystal and gold-candled chandelier of the White House Green Room.

"Just be still," said a gentle, baritone voice. "Don't try to move, my dear, because you won't be able to."

He was right. Though she could "feel" her arms and legs, she couldn't budge them. Only her eyes moved. Had she had a stroke, as well?

"You will be fine in a few minutes, you'll see," the male voice said. A face leaned over her. Old, distinguished, yet delicate, with thin eyebrows over deep-set dark eyes, a long slender nose, full lips. Silver, wavy hair cascaded over a high forehead.

He must be a White House attendant, she thought, in his old-fashioned heavy dark wool suit and starched white shirt. Was this nostalgic attire part of the tour?

In any case, this was clearly someone who'd been around the White House for a long, long time.

She struggled again to sit up but couldn't. She tried to speak but wasn't able. Panic, once again, engulfed her, like freezing water, making her instantly alert, and afraid.

"There, there, my dear, do lie still," came a woman's soothing, British-accented voice. "It does take a little while to recover. It certainly did with me."

And then a female face gazed down at Sarah.

This woman was perhaps in her late forties or early fifties. Dark brown curls peeked out from underneath a large white scarf-tied straw hat. Her eyebrows were penciled on over heavily made up eyes. And on either side of her red bee-stung lips were round pink circles of rouge, which hung on her face like little balloons. The top of the woman's dress (for that's all that Sarah could see) appeared to be made of thin material, like foulard or crepe, with delicate satin ribbons trimming the scooped neck. A strange outfit, she thought, for such a cold autumn day. Why would a grown woman dress up like a Gibson Girl-esque doll?

Sarah could now open her mouth, but she still could not speak.

Then a young boy appeared at Sarah's other side. He wore a navy cap and a brown jacket with knickers and knee socks and would have been a formal looking little gentleman if the clothing had not been, essentially, rags. The boy knelt down and looked at her curiously from a cherubic, dirt-rouged face, as if studying a bug on the floor.

"She winned her a *prize*, did ya hear it?" the boy said excitedly to the others. "But what's a pula...a pula...?"

"A *Pulitzer* Prize," smiled the elderly man. "That's a very distinguished honor, not a stuffed toy from knocking down milk bottles at the fair, lad." He nodded sagely, beaming at Sarah. "We're lucky indeed to have this woman among us."

The young boy's face turned into a pout. "Well, *I* winned a prize once," he said almost defiantly, directing his comment to the elderly man. "At the Century of Progress. It was a..."

"We *know*," a new male voice interrupted. "You've told us a million times, kid!"

A young bearded man with long stringy brown hair, in a tie-dyed t-shirt and scruffy jeans and scruffier sandals stood next to the kneeling boy, a hand on the little boy's shoulder, and said, "But the Prez is right - the Pulitzer Prize is no toy."

What a strange group of people, Sarah thought. She certainly didn't remember seeing them on the tour. If these were VIPS, then the circus must be in town.

And where was Steve? Had he gone to get help?

Suddenly her body twitched, and life coursed through her veins like electricity through a conduit.

She struggled to sit up on the green-and-gold oriental rug, and the young boy grabbed her by the arm to help her.

"Where's my husband?" Sarah managed to rasp. She looked around, side to side, too quickly, the opulent, ornately decorated Green Room only adding to her dizziness. She placed one hand to her temple. "Where's Steve?"

"He's next door in the Blue Room, Sarah," the woman answered. "Am I taking a liberty by calling you Sarah? We're going to be such great friends, after all, and, at any rate, I'm afraid we overheard you and your husband speaking, and..."

Sarah smacked her hand against the carpeted floor with such a *whump*, it startled the little group. "What the hell is this about?" she demanded. "Who are you people?"

The cupie-doll woman turned her gaze away, as if Sarah had slapped her. "We only brought you in here to...recover."

On wobbly legs, Sarah got to her feet, the young boy again assisting her. She thanked him.

Then, firmly, she said, "I must see my husband," and took a few tentative steps toward the closed mahogany door of the Green Room, which led to the Blue Room.

But the woman stepped in front of Sarah, putting her hands on Sarah's shoulders, saying quietly, imploringly, "Please don't, Sarah...if I may call you Sarah. I implore you not to open that door. It will only...break your heart."

These people were straining her patience, but most of all, fear was creeping back under her skin. "*What* will break my heart?" she asked.

The cupie-doll shook her head, and her curls, lifting a gently lecturing finger. "I speak from experience, my dear. There's nothing you can do. Nothing you can say now that your dear husband will hear."

"What do you mean?" Sarah asked, fighting back terror. "Is something the matter with Steve?"

The eyes in the woman's painted face were filled with pity.

"Please, tell me!" Sarah cried.

"I'll tell ya!" the little boy blurted. "There ain't

nothin' wrong with your husband, lady. It's you! You're down with a serious case of *dead,* din'cha figure that out yet? Jeez!"

Sarah stared numbly at the boy.

Dead? She wasn't dead. She was anything but dead; she felt fine. As a matter of fact, she couldn't remember ever feeling better. Was the child out of his mind?

The hippie grabbed the little boy's arm. "*Le*-roy," he said, drawing the boy's name out to unintentionally comic effect, "I ought to *clobber* you, man!"

"Yes, Leroy," the painted lady said, in a mildly scolding tone, "that was most *rude* of you. I thought we agreed to bring her over...gradually."

"Horsefeathers!" The boy wrenched himself out of the hippie's grasp. "You chowderheads were gonna let her get away!"

"Quiet, *everyone!*" the old man bellowed, but authoritatively. "It this any way for my *Cabinet* to behave?"

His *what?* What did furniture have to do with anything? Were they *all* completely out of their minds? Was the queen of hearts awaiting in the hallway, to lop off her head?

"Look," Sarah said, smiling, sincerely she hoped, patting the air with her palms, "it's been very nice to meet you, all of you, *whoever* you are, and I appreciate your help and concern, but I really must go now, and find my husband."

She backed away from the strange little group, toward the closed mahogany door.

"We must not try to stop her," the old man instructed.

"But...she's gonna *see*," the boy whined.

"We, better than most, know the value of passing along pertinent information."

The little group began to nod at one another.

Oh-kay, Sarah thought, and turned and moved quickly toward the door and opened it. The sooner she got out of this Mad Tea Party, the better...

She moved down the hallway to the room next door, the oval Blue Room, its door open, revealing paramedics frantically laboring over a body sprawled on the gleaming parquet floor.

Her body.

"I can't get a pulse!" one paramedic shouted.

"She's decompensating!" yelled another.

Steve, slumped in a gilded chair nearby, the thinning patch at the crown in his nest of wheat-colored hair showing, was weeping into his cupped hands.

Sarah, wide-eyed with shock, backed up into the Green Room, shutting the door slowly, and leaned up against it. Poor Steve. Poor Steve, so grief stricken. The sight of him, it...it broke her heart.

Sarah's eyes flooded with tears and she, too, wept uncontrollably into her hands. How could she be dead, she thought, when she felt so alive, when her tears felt so wet against her fingers?

After a moment, when she'd composed herself, Sarah addressed the others who stood half-circled together at the center of the room, a collective look of sympathy on their faces. "Who *are* you?"

"Leroy," the elderly gentleman instructed the boy, "let us help Sarah over to the couch. And then let us all take a seat, shall we?"

The elderly man and the boy, one on her either

arm, escorted Sarah to the green-and-white candy-striped couch, and she sat, hands folded almost
primly in her lap. The old man took a place next to her
on the couch. The doll woman perched on the edge of
a gilded straight back chair to left of Sarah, while the
hippie sat in a matching chair to Sarah's right. The
boy plopped down on the carpet between the couch
and a gleaming Duncan Phyfe coffee table.

And a very happy un-birthday to me, Sarah thought.

The old man patted Sarah's hand. "I know this is
quite a shock to you, my dear. Allow me to try to clear
things up a bit." He paused, then announced, "My
name is Harrison."

Sarah looked at him blankly. The others gathered
around her exchanged little telling expressions, lifted
eyebrows, rolling eyes.

The old man's mouth twitched with suppressed
irritation.

"My name is Harrison," he repeated. "William
Henry Harrison."

As if he'd said Bond, James Bond.

"I'm sorry..." Sarah said with a two-handed shrug.

The old man's face reddened. "William Henry
Harrison!" he erupted. The little group around him
ducked their heads as if a chunk of flying lava might
strike them. "*The ninth President of the United States!*"

Sarah looked at him, astounded. "I don't believe
it," she whispered.

He smoothed his coat, returned himself to dignity.
"But it's quite true, my dear. I died here, in the White
House on April 4, 1841, and have resided within these
walls, ever since." He gestured to the others. "And
this is my Cabinet. I'll allow them to introduce them-

selves - they earned the privilege."

The painted lady leaned forward in her chair. "My name is Prudence Bentley," she said in her lovely British accent. "My dear late husband and I left England on holiday to visit relatives in the 'Colonies.' This was in 1898, mind you." She paused, then went on. "One day, we took a tour of the White House. We were in the Vermeil Room, back then it was used for billiards, when, *plop* - I simply dropped dead."

She touched her ample bosom.

"It was my heart, I do believe. In any instance, the next thing I knew, I was waking up here in the Green Room, and there was President Harrison! At first, I was as confused, as disoriented, as you are, my dear, but eventually I came to understand what a rare honor had been bestowed upon me. Within hours he had appointed me his Attorney General!"

She giggled, touching her cupie lips.

"Can you imagine, dear Sarah? A Brit like me? But, then, by now I've been here long enough to have become an American citizen."

Sarah's mouth was open, but no words were coming out.

"Me next!" the young boy cried. He thrust a thumb at his tattered chest. "Leroy Jordan's the name. Pleased to meetcha. I used to live in this shantytown and that one, so this pile of white lumber sure is a lot better. Me and my Pop and Ma and the brother, we started out in Chicago, then hopped a freight to D.C., where we heard they had a better class of Hooverville. Don't you believe it! Anyway, one day in..." He stopped and looked up at President Harrison. "When was it, again?"

"1933," the President offered.

"Yeah, yeah, 1933! I keep forgettin'. Anyway, I was out panhandlin' and it was cold as a witch's... well, anyway, it was cold, see? And I seen this line going into the White House, so me not bein' one to stand on ceremony, I cut right in. The coppers seen me and blew their whistles and startin' in chasin' me up to the second floor. I grabbed this vase, to sell later, you know, and run back to the stairs, and the bulls grab me. We scuffle, and I was just gettin' away from 'em, when, whoopsy daisy, over the railin' I go."

"Oh, dear," Sarah said.

"Only when I land, I land *hard*, and I'm still awake, see, only I know I'm a goner because my neck was twisted all funny. I mean, I can see the ceilin', but my stomach's under me. But you know what?" He grinned, snapped his fingers. "I get up anyway! And turn my head back around straight, and I'll be darned if there is President Harrison, gesturin' to me follow him up the steps past all them people with the long faces, and 'fore you know it, he's askin' me if I'd like to be in his Cabinet..." Leroy laughed. "I thought he meant shut up in a wooden box, but then he explained it to me, and said I'd be in charge of the Post Office."

Sarah smiled. So, Leroy had been in charge of the mail since the thirties; that explained a lot.

"Guess that leaves me," the hippie said, looking at Sarah with intense eyes. "I'm James Kafer, maybe you've heard of me."

Sarah shook her head, no.

"I was a protester during the Vietnam war," he explained. The eyes above the thatch of beard glittered hopefully. "I'm sure you read about it. Saw it on the tube? The guy who went over the White House wall with a bomb strapped to his chest?"

"Oh, yes," she said slowly, the memory stirring. "I was only a little girl at the time, but I do remember. You...blew yourself up."

An odd look came over James' face. "Well...it didn't come off exactly like I planned."

"Best laid plans," she said with a sympathetic *tch tch*. Then she asked, "And, so, James, what are you? In the Cabinet, I mean."

He seemed a little embarrassed. "Secretary of War."

She had to laugh.

"I think it's pretty cool," James said, not at all defensive, in fact smiling. "Because you can damn well be sure *I'll* ever get us into another Vietnam."

"Does the word Bosnia ring a bell?" Sarah asked.

The room fell silent.

President Harrison turned more toward Sarah on the couch.

"And what about you, my dear?" he asked. "Please tell us of yourself."

"Well," she said slowly, "let's see, now. My name is Sarah Hays. I'm thirty-five. I mean, I *was* thirty-five."

"And always will be, my dear," Mrs. Bentley said.

"Yes. Well, I suppose, I will be." Were these the last hallucinations of a brain dying of oxygen deprivation, she wondered? What else could she do, but ride with the delusion? It was the closest thing to reality she had.

"My husband's name is Steve," Sarah said. "A wonderful man. We teach...taught...together at a small college in Indiana." She paused, fighting back tears.

"Go on, my dear," President Harrison said gently.

Sarah swallowed. "My greatest accomplishment, I guess, was writing a book, a novel, that won a Pulitzer Prize. But you seem to know that."

James nodded. "We overheard you talking."

"I gathered as much," Sarah said.

"What's so special about the book?" Leroy asked.

Sarah looked down at the boy. "It's about growing up on a ranch in Montana and learning to deal with mental illness in the family." She stared down at her hands in her lap. "It's kind of the story of my life. That's why, it was the only story I had to tell, or ever would tell." The room fell silent once again.

Then James said, with a touch of sadness, "Well, you're one of us, now."

She looked at him sharply. "But just what exactly are you?" she asked.

"'We,'" James corrected.

"Fine," she said. "We. So, are we...ghosts? Is this heaven, or hell, or purgatory, or something I ate? I mean, I understand we all died here in the White House, beginning with President Harrison, from a cold."

Suddenly, she'd remembered the tour guide's speech, hoping the President would appreciate that she indeed did know something about him, after all.

But President Harrison slammed one fist on the coffee table, though the heavy silver urn there didn't budge, although Sarah jumped like she'd sat on a thorn.

"It wasn't a *cold*, damn it!" the elderly man shouted. "It was pneumonia. Pneu-*monia*! Why do those confounded tour guides keep reinforcing that falsehood?"

He rose from the couch, stalking to the center of

the room, hands behind his back, head shaking side to side, fuming.

"Now you've done it, lady," Leroy whispered up at her.

"When those tour guides show *Jefferson's* portrait," Harrison growled, pacing, "do they say he died of diarrhea? No. That wouldn't be dignified. But it's perfectly acceptable to make light of William Henry Harrison, who died from a 'cold' after just twenty-eight days in office."

Mrs. Bentley shifted uncomfortably in her chair. "Oh, dear," she murmured, "here we go now."

"Fasten your seat belt, babe," James whispered. "We're goin' on an ego trip."

Harrison raised a hand in the air and pointed to the heavens with one saber-like finger. "Do they mention my illustrious career? My victory at Tipicanoe? My governorship of the Louisiana Territory? No, no, *I'm* just a man who died of a *cold.* And what of my heritage? Do they speak of that? Do they even *know* of it? My father was one of the signers of the Declaration of Independence, and my grandson became the twenty-third President of the United States. But *William Henry* Harrison? He's just a man who died of a cold."

"We know your worth, Mr. President," said James, obviously hoping to placate the older man.

"But what of the world? What of my country?" Harrison asked, spreading both arms wide, palms open. "Don't you see," he said, pleadingly, now looking just at Sarah. "I have accepted that I will never get my due, but I have *not* and will *never* accept not getting my *chance,* not being allowed the time to make my mark on history."

He raised his chin; a tiny smile etched his lips.

"That's why I'm here. Why I'm *still* here. And that's why, making the best of what fate has given me, I've assembled this Cabinet." He gazed at her fondly, his eyes glittering. "And you, Sarah, you will be Secretary of State, and will do a *fine* job, I'm sure."

Sarah felt as though she'd been struck a blow.

Finally, she stood from the couch.

"Mr. President," she said quietly, "with all due respect, and believe me I'm flattered to be asked, I don't want to be Secretary of State. And I don't want to spend my eternity playing this game."

"*Game?*" the President repeated as if he hadn't heard her correctly. "My dear, perhaps you don't understand. This is no game, no simple pastime for departed souls, like cosmic croquet or celestial chess. I..." He looked at the others in the room whose eyes were riveted on him. "...*we* have been *running* this country for over one hundred and fifty years!"

Sarah blinked. Then she sat back down on the couch. "What do you mean, exactly?" she asked, feeling numb again.

"Just how have you been running the country?"

Mrs. Bentley leaned toward her, whispering conspiratorially. "We talk to them at night, mostly. Or when they daydream. Whenever they are susceptible, vulnerable, in their pensive moments."

"*Who?*" Sarah asked.

"Why, my dear," Harrison said, arching an eyebrow. "Who else? Those *other* Presidents."

Sarah gulped.

"Yeah," added Leroy, "when they're asleep is best, 'cause it don't work as good when they're awake."

James nodded. "And some need a lot more talking to than others, you dig?"

Sarah was amazed. "Are you saying that you have influenced decisions made in the White House by various Presidents?"

Leroy chortled. "You hit the nail smack on the head, lady!"

President Harrison, in the center of the room, hands clasped behind his back, puffed out his chest. "*Directing* would be a more appropriate word, I believe," he said.

"I'm sorry," Sarah said, "but I don't believe it. For the sake of argument, let's say you're real, you're ghosts, and you're really haunting the White House..."

"We hardly view it as 'haunting'" Harrison said, somewhat huffily.

"Fine," Sarah said. "How do you know you're really impacting anything? That anything you're whispering into these ears is registering?"

Mrs. Bentley directed her comment to Harrison. "Mr. President, why not give her an example?"

"Splendid idea," he pronounced. And he returned to the couch and sat next to Sarah.

"During President Cleveland's administration," he began, "there happened to be..."

James cleared his throat. "Excuse me for interrupting, man...Mr. President. But can I also make a suggestion? Why not use an example from Sarah's own lifetime? I'm not sure she's really into Grover Cleveland's administration."

Harrison nodded. "Another good idea." He winked at Sarah. "You see how wonderfully my Cabinet works together? Now..." He settled himself further on the couch. "...you were born in...?"

"Nineteen Sixty-One," Sarah said.

Harrison pressed his hands together, tenting his fingers, prayer-like. "Kennedy," he said softly. Then, as if gazing into a crystal ball, he began to speak: "October 1962. Kennedy was up all night, which was a problem, mind you. He frequently worked throughout the night. The man would simply *not* go to bed!"

"Unless there was a good-lookin' lady in it," Leroy smirked.

"Leroy!" Harrison said. "Respect! The men who work within these walls are as human as we once were, as susceptible to human frailties."

"Like pneumonia," Leroy said, nodding.

Harrison studied the boy, looking for sarcasm. Leroy just smiled his smudgy-cheeked cherubic smile.

The President harumphed, and continued: "At any rate, near dawn, Kennedy fell asleep in the chair in the Oval Office and I said to him, 'President Kennedy, Khrushchev is just a man like you, just as scared as you. Why don't you simply pick up the phone and *call* him, to avert this impending tragedy?' The next morning, Kennedy had a secret phone line installed directly to Khrushchev at the Kremlin, and that began the series of talks which ended the Cuban missile crisis."

"Uh-huh," Sarah said skeptically. "So, we have you to thank for that."

Harrison smiled.

"Jack Kennedy couldn't have made that leap without you."

Harrison shook his head, gently, no.

"But you couldn't warn him about Dallas, I suppose."

Harrison frowned. "We cannot foresee the future, my dear."

"What about Nixon, then?" she asked. "You didn't do such a hot job, there. That Watergate burglary, was that your brainstorm, guys?"

"His downfall was not our doing," President Harrison said, "but his own. However," he added, "we did hurry his impeachment along a bit."

"How?" Sarah asked.

Mrs. Bentley giggled. "How do you think 'Deep-Throat' got *his* information?"

"Really," Sarah said, still far from convinced.

James shifted in his chair. "Now, President Ford was a real problem," he said.

"You didn't like him?" asked Sarah.

"The old boy just wouldn't listen," Mrs. Bentley explained. "A more mule-headed man I've never met!"

President Harrison nodded. "He had to go."

"So, what did you do?" Sarah asked innocently.

"Let me tell!" Leroy said gleefully. "Let *me* tell!" The boy, seated on the floor in front of Sarah, was waving his hand wildly, like a kid in a classroom surprised he knew the answer.

"Very well, Leroy," President Harrison said. "You may elucidate."

"Well," the boy began, "it was about this time we discovered we could *move* things, see? Not very far, though, and not very fast. Not like in the movie, about that girl who got blood dumped on her on prom night? I watched that on TV with Amy Carter one time."

"*Carrie* you mean?" Sarah said. The film was one of her childhood favorites.

"That's the one, sister," the boy burbled. "We can't

throw knives like that, sure wish we could. Anyhow, like President Harrison here says, that guy Ford was no good. He didn't want to do *nothin'* we said. Like the time I told him to start watchin' *Star Trek*. But, no, he had to watch boring *golf*..."

"Leroy, dear," Mrs. Bentley interjected, "please get on with the story."

"Okay, okay, I'm gettin' to it," the boy said. He looked at Sarah with big brown cartoon-bunny eyes. "Remember that time Ford had the press conference in the Oval Office? An' everybody but God was there? Me an' James, we moved that bozo's chair out from the desk just as he started to sit down, an' *whump*, right on the floor he went, right smack on his behind!"

The boy howled with glee, and Sarah couldn't help laughing herself.

"And remember the state dinner with Brezhnev?" James asked with a one-sided smile. "It was in all the papers. We got under the table and tied Ford's shoe laces together, it took us an hour, all of us, with all our concentration, and when he stood up, he tripped and grabbed onto the tablecloth, man, what a mess! All that expensive bone china and everything."

Sarah laughed again. "Well, what about the time Ford fell down the steps coming off Air Force One? Surely you weren't responsible for that, were you?"

"No, Sarah," President Harrison said. "As you may have surmised, we cannot leave the grounds of the White House. I believe the man became so unhinged from what happened around here, that he began to do things to himself. Ford began to truly believe he was clumsy."

"What about Reagan?" Sarah wondered. "What

did you think of him?"

"His first term was adequate," Harrison admitted. "The man didn't always do what we wanted, but I think he listened."

"Anyway, he got them jellybeans like I asked him," Leroy reminded the President. The boy sighed. "Too bad we can't *eat* anything..."

"But," Harrison pressed on, "sometime during Reagan's second term, we would talk to him at night, and he would seem to understand, but in the morning, he'd have forgotten everything we'd said."

Mrs. Bentley nodded. "That's when we started whispering in *Nancy's* ear."

"It was the same way with Clinton," James added. "But for a different reason, of course. Clinton would go to bed exhausted and sleep so deep it was just *easier* from the start to talk to Hillary."

"That explains a few things," Sarah smiled.

President Harrison took one of Sarah's hands in his, which was surprisingly warm for a dead man. "And now, my dear Sarah, with you in our Cabinet as Attorney General, I know we'll be able to handle this present administration. You lived as a part of this generation, your insights will be invaluable..."

Sarah gently removed her hand. "Mr. President," she said softly, "I'm sorry, but I don't want to be Attorney General."

Harrison's eyes opened wide; he seemed astonished, stunned - and hurt.

"I'm sorry, sir," she said, "but I don't *want* to stay here. And something tells me, I don't have to. Isn't that correct?"

Harrison lowered his gaze and nodded. "Yes, you

have a choice, my dear - as we all had a choice - but please consider this, by joining us you would, like the rest us, be acting in the best interests of this country."

"I don't think so," Sarah said, shaking her head. "I just don't agree with you, Mr. President, or with your approach. With all due respect, sir, you are meddling."

Indignation poured out of Harrison, like steam. "I was duly elected President of these United States."

"Yes, you were, a very long time ago, by people who are as dead...deader...than you, Mr. President. Now, you're interfering with the decisions of others, the way a mother often interferes with the decisions of a grown child."

"But this country is an infant!" Harrison said. "Unable to make the right decisions without us. Come! Where's your sense of adventure, woman?"

Now Sarah took his hand in hers. She looked in his eyes, which were moist. "I'm sorry your Presidency was cut short and you weren't able to show the world what a wonderful leader you would have been."

The eyes of the dignified, very proud President Harrison began filling with tears.

"You have served long, and proudly. Don't you think it's time, finally, to step down?"

A tiny tear trickled down the old man's cheek.

"Don't you see," Sarah continued softly, yet urgently, "that you are becoming increasingly dangerous, trapped in here with only limited information?"

Desperation edged the old man's voice. "But with your contemporary knowledge, my dear..."

"Very soon my point of view would become as dated, as irrelevant, as your own. And nobody elected me to be *anything*."

Harrison said nothing.

"All your decisions haven't been correct, have they?" Sarah asked, but it was more like a statement than a question.

Leroy snorted. "Ha! Why don't cha ask Mrs. Bentley about the teapot dough."

Mrs. Bentley bristled. "The Teapot Dome wasn't all my fault," she huffed. "Maybe I did give President Harding some questionable advice, but I can't be blamed for the entire affair!" She pointed an accusing finger at James. "Maybe *you'd* like to explain your role in the Iran-Contra matter!"

James leaned forward in his chair. "You know I'm against covert activities," he said testily. "But, man, that Ollie North dude would *not* listen! So, I just had to do the best that I could."

Silence permeated the room.

"Look," Sarah finally said, "what I'm trying to say is that maybe it's time to move on. To whatever, wherever, that is. Why don't you try leave running the country to the living, and seek new office, on some higher plane?"

Harrison lowered his eyes.

Sarah stood. "Come now, Mr. President," she said with a tiny smile, "where's your sense of adventure?"

And she walked away from them, across the thick oriental carpet to the heavy mahogany door. She turned for one last look at the thoughtful little group. "Please consider what I've said," she said.

Her last glimpse of them was a forlorn cluster of fading shadows, Leroy's hand lifted in a sad tiny wave.

She opened the door.

"Oh, my God," she said, amazed as she stepped

into the hall to where she could peer in through the
open door of the Blue Room, "they're still working
on me. They're still *working* on me!"

Sarah turn back to the others, but they were gone,
the room now distorting, as if she were looking
through someone else's much-too-strong glasses.

An overwhelming tiredness came over her, just as
it had before, and she sank to her knees, swallowed
up by the floor.

A year and a half later, Sarah and her husband returned for another tour of the White House. An
unusual honor, being invited for a second VIP tour;
but considering that Sarah's previous tour had been
interrupted, the President, a big fan of hers, had insisted the invitation be made.

And she of course accepted. This time, her state of
mind was calm, she was happily at the midway point
of the writing of her second novel (and third book),
and she and Steve walked hand-in-hand, again at the
rear of the group, but this time paying close attention
to the guide's words.

"...exquisite cabinet made by local cabinetmaker
Edwin Green in 1849 for William Henry Harrison.
Harrison was the first President to die in the White
House, just a month into his term. He died of viral
pneumonia, and his passing was a great loss to the
country. There's been a renewed interest in this past
year, in William Henry Harrison. The pictorial book
displayed on the coffee table, written by Pulitzer
Prize-winning author Sarah Hays, depicts some lit-
tle-known facts about this fascinating President. Now,
next door, in the Green Room..."

SWEET DREAMS, NORMA JEANE

Barbara Collins

He hid in the recess of a doorway, a tall, thin young man with a thatch of wild, sandy hair that sprang from his head like leaves on a palm tree. His face was pale, pockmarked, his brown eyes intent, as he stared across the boulevard at the elegant, white stone apartment building on East 57th Street.

It was a hot July day in 1961 and even though the sun was concealed behind the high Manhattan buildings, there was little relief from the heat. A bead of sweat ran from the young man's forehead down the side of his cheek, but he wasn't uncomfortable. He was used to waiting for her.

Every afternoon was the same. At about four-thirty a cab would pull up in front of number 444 (where she now lived alone in apartment 13E, having recently divorced her playwright husband) and the driver would honk. And wait. And curse, and honk again. And just when it seemed the cabby was about to leave, *she* would come out, a vision of loveliness, wearing a beige skirt and blouse, or orange slacks and top, or a blue polka-dot dress but, always, the same white scarf covering that silky platinum hair, and black sunglasses shading those luminous blue eyes.

Quickly, she would climb into the back seat of the cab, removing her sunglasses, and when the driver turned to snarl at his inconsiderate passenger, his eyes would bug out in disbelief, and mouth drop open as his lips formed her name: *Marilyn Monroe!*

And they would drive off, her apologizing profusely for keeping him waiting and him gushing boyishly about seeing all her movies.

But this afternoon would be different. This afternoon the young man was not standing in his usual spot, which was on the sidewalk in front of her building, where day after day she ignored him. Yes, today would be different, he thought, he hoped, as he watched from across the street.

A cab pulled up. The driver, a big man, almost obese, with a face like a catcher's mitt, honked his horn. And waited. And cursed. And just as he looked ready to give up, the door to the apartment building opened and Marilyn came out.

The young man across the street in the doorway leaned forward excitedly, because she had on an outfit he had never seen her in before, a tight yellow dress with a plunging neckline and matching high heels.

Like butter sizzling on the hot cement, she wiggled toward the waiting cab. She opened the back door, and her head disappeared from view as she ducked down to enter the car. Then suddenly, her head reappeared as she backed out of the cab and turned slowly to look at the spot where the young man had stood, week after week, but not today.

She took a few halting high-heeled steps toward that spot, and removing her sunglasses, looked up the sidewalk toward Lexington, and down the sidewalk to the East River, her face a combination of puzzlement and worry.

The young man could almost read her mind.

I wonder where that kid is? I hope nothing's wrong.

And the young man smiled.

She returned to the cab and got in back. And the taxi drove off, its driver now having recognized her, yakking away, a big grin on his face.

But Marilyn wasn't paying any attention to *him*. No, she was looking over her shoulder, out the back window of the cab, at the place on the sidewalk where the young man should have been.

The following afternoon the young man stood in a downpour on the sidewalk in front of Marilyn's apartment, his sandy hair matted to his head, his white Ban-lon shirt and tan Chino pants, soaked and clinging to his body.

It wasn't that he didn't have an umbrella. It was just that he knew he'd be more pathetic without one.

But he was a little surprised, and pleasantly so, when the door to the building opened and Marilyn came out. The taxi wasn't due for another ten minutes.

She was wearing a beige raincoat, cinched at her waist (he'd seen it before), but missing were the white scarf and sunglasses. Her right hand held an umbrella.

The young man's heart thumped wildly as she came toward him, and then her face, that lovely, lovely face, was just inches away.

He held his breath.

"For God's sake!" she snapped, "Don't you have an umbrella?"

He couldn't tell whether she was mad-*mad*, or mad-*concerned*. But it didn't matter, she was talking to him!

She thrust the umbrella, a black one with a wooden curved handle, at him, and he took it, thrilled to be holding something she owned, yet wondering which husband the umbrella had originally belonged to.

"I want you to stop coming here," she said sternly, then added, as if it would deter him, "I'm not worth it." The rain, hitting her face, made it seem like she was crying.

He opened the umbrella, and gallantly covered her. There was an awkward silence.

Then Marilyn's eyes softened, and her voice became a mere whisper as she asked, "Where were you yesterday?"

He faked a cough. "Sick."

"And you're out here in the rain today?"

The taxi pulled up.

"You should be at home in bed!" she scolded. "Where do you live?"

"Ninety-third and Lexington."

Her eyes lit up. "That's where I'm going," she said brightly. "You can ride along."

"Thank you."

"What's your name?"

"Johnny."

"Johnny..." She repeated the name slowly, her eyes now getting a far-away look.

He knew she was thinking of a long-ago lover. He

even knew which one.

"Well, Johnny," she sighed, gesturing to the cab, "get in."

And they climbed in the back seat of the car.

She told the cabby Lexington and 93rd, but would he mind very much if they stopped for a moment at the little park just ahead?

The driver, a handsome, dark Italian man, answered he'd be glad to drive Marilyn Monroe to hell and back, if that's what she wanted.

And she laughed, a musical giggle, almost a squeal, as the cab pulled away from the curb.

At the end of 57th, just a half a block away, was a pocket park facing the East River. Not big enough for playground toys, but a nice place to sit, and watch the boats sail by, which Marilyn did a lot.

The cab stopped.

Marilyn, sitting on the left side of the young man, leaned across him, putting the fingertips of her hand (and she had such spectacular hands, long fingers with platinum colored nails) on the foggy window, moving those fingers back and forth in the wetness so that she could see out.

She was close to him, so very, very close, that he could feel the electricity coming off her voluptuous body, and see the fine hairs on her flawless face, like fuzz on a ripened peach, and smell the intoxicating scent of her perfume, Chanel No. 5.

He stared at her throat. It was so white, so soft and supple, speckled here and there with cute little moles.

"They're not there," Marilyn said disappointedly. She pulled away from the window and sat back with a sigh.

"You can go on," she told the driver.

They rode in silence, rain pattering on the top of the car, fingers on a drumhead. Then the young man said, "How do you know those boys aren't taking your money and selling the pigeons to the meat market?"

Her eyes went wide with surprise, then narrowed with annoyance.

Quickly he tried to recover. "I mean, I'm just asking," he said apologetically. "I'd hate to think you were being fooled."

"They promised me," she said flatly, "and I believe them."

"Okay," he sighed. "But I think you're too trusting."

They rode in strained silence.

As they approached Lexington and 93rd, the young man, seeing his time with Marilyn was running out, said, "About you going down to the Bowrey. You may have been able to do that five years ago, but it's too dangerous now. And besides, what good does it do?"

Marilyn turned to him, her eyes flashing, clearly irritated. "I don't see how that's any of your business!" she said, annunciating each word, lips moving like no other lips could.

The cab came to a stop.

"This is where *you* get out," she said icily. Boy, he thought, *she* sure was in a rotten mood!

She paid the driver, over-tipping him, and climbed out of the cab. The young man followed her on to the street.

He grabbed her arm.

"I know where you're going," he said. "I know who you're seeing."

Shocked, she wrenched out of his grasp, and backed up a few steps.

"He's *bad,* Marilyn!" the young man said desperately. "Please, I beg you, don't go to him!"

"Stay *away* from me!" she shouted. And she turned and ran down the street, toward the big brown building where she went every afternoon at four-thirty.

Crestfallen, the young man stared after her. He had worked so hard to meet her, to warn her...and in a matter of minutes it had deteriorated to this! What could he do to make her believe him? How could he reach her?

"Norma Jeane!" he called out.

She stopped in her tracks, one hand on the door handle of the apartment building she was about to enter.

"Norma Jeane," he repeated, softer, "please... be careful."

She stood frozen for a moment, then without looking back, opened the door and disappeared inside.

Marilyn was upset, shaking, as she entered the lobby of the building.

As usual she avoided the elevator and took the stairs; she liked to arrive out of breath, flushed and radiant, it was one of her tricks.

But she was *already* out of breath and flushed, though certainly not radiant, thanks to that Johnny! There was something very weird and very sad about that kid.

Her legs trembled as she climbed the stairs. Just who did he think he was, anyway? What gave him the right to say just anything to her, of any nature, like it wouldn't hurt her feelings, as if it were happening to her clothing?

And how dare he give her advice on who she should or shouldn't be seeing? Acting like he was a friend. Not that some fans didn't eventually become friends, but she had neither the desire nor the energy to make any new ones. Especially when the fans were becoming more and more aggressive, taking one bite out of her after another.

And Johnny was *wrong* about those two teenage boys in the park, because she could see them from her apartment window, letting the birds go.

It all started one day last month when she sat on a bench in the little park, watching them catching pigeons in a net and putting the poor creatures in cages. When she asked the boys why they were doing that, they said a meat market paid them fifty cents for each one. So, she offered to match the meat market's price, if they promised to let the birds go. Now she met the boys every couple of days or so and paid for the pigeons they caught.

But Johnny was *right* about the Bowery. She shuddered, as she climbed the stairs, thinking about what *could* have happened to her last week, when she went down there in her usual, black-wigged disguise, if that policeman hadn't come to her rescue. The policeman said someone called the precinct, and told them what she was doing, handing out money to "bums," otherwise, the cop wouldn't have been there to save her from that knife-wielding nut.

Could the anonymous caller have been her new "friend," Johnny?

Manhattan was changing. She could feel it moving

restlessly under her feet, shifting in a frightening way. She had the ability to sense this; the way she could walk into a room full of people and tell right away who was an orphan.

The city was beginning to scare her, because in it she saw much of herself. It was as if she and Manhattan were becoming one, on the verge of a nervous breakdown and unable to sleep at night.

Marilyn rang the buzzer of apartment 6A.

Almost immediately the door opened and a large man, in a black suit with vest and tie, filled its frame. He was somewhere between fifty and sixty years old, bespectacled, with dark hair and neatly trimmed beard.

To her, he looked like a more handsome Abraham Lincoln. And a little like her ex-husband.

He ushered her in, and she took off her raincoat, revealing a sleeveless blue polka-dot dress. He hung the coat up in a closet, and together they walked down a short, narrow hallway to the living room dominated by Victorian furniture.

The thick, dark drapes were closed, and the only light came from candles flickering on the fireplace mantel. A stereo provided a soothing whisper of classical music.

She turned to face the man.

"Can we please just skip the psychoanalysis today, Doctor Hilgenfeldt," she pleaded, "and get right to the injection?"

He looked down at her, over the top of his glasses. "Bad night, my dear?" he asked, concerned.

"I didn't sleep a wink," she answered wearily. "Sometimes I wonder what the night time is for. It almost doesn't exist for me. It all seems like one long, long horrible day."

She turned away from him, now, hugging herself as if she were cold. "And I'm building up such a tolerance to the Nembutal. I have to keep taking more and more. I'm just afraid one of these days..." She didn't finish the sentence.

"Yes, yes," he nodded. "This is not good."

They entered his office, a dimly lit room with a leather psychiatrist's couch, a large mahogany desk littered with papers, and a bookcase crammed with medical journals. In one corner was a glass cabinet where the doctor kept his drugs. On the wall next to the cabinet, hung a picture of Sigmund Freud; the stern Freud frowned toward the drugs, as if giving his opinion of them.

Marilyn lay down on the couch.

The doctor crossed the room to the cabinet.

"I'm moving back to Hollywood next week," she told him.

Busy getting the injection ready, the doctor stopped and turned to look at her.

"Are you sure this is wise?" he asked, his voice sharp as the needle. "We have made such progress together..."

"Yes, well," she said apologetically, "I'm sorry, but I have no choice. I owe those bastards at Fox one last picture."

The doctor approached Marilyn, syringe in one hand, needle pointed up, and loomed over her.

"I was wondering," she said, looking up at him, searching his face, "if you could recommend another psychiatrist for me?"

He thought for a moment. "Yes," he answered slowly, "I know someone I think you'd like in Beverly Hills."

Marilyn partially rose from the couch, supporting herself with both elbows. "It's not a *woman,* is it?" she asked bitterly.

Her previous psychiatrist, a female, locked her up just six months ago in a New York loony bin. If it hadn't been for Joe, thank God for Joe, flying up from Florida, threatening to tear the place apart brick by brick, she *never* would have gotten out.

"No, my dear," the doctor said calmingly, "this is a man." Then he added, gesturing toward the picture of Freud, "As a matter of fact, he told me that he was once psychoanalyzed by Sigmund Freud."

Marilyn, a real Freud fan, liked that, and smiled, and lay back on the couch.

"I'm giving you a higher dosage," the doctor explained, rubbing an alcohol-soaked cotton ball on her arm. "I think you could use a little more rest."

She nodded, closing her eyes, sighing in anticipation of the drug.

The needle entered her creamy white flesh.

What Marilyn liked about the Brevital was the quickness of it – one second, she was awake and miserable, the next she was plunged into a cool pool of nothingness, void of exhausting and debilitating dreams. It was a deep, peaceful sleep that only a patient on an operating table, or a stiff on a morgue slab, was lucky enough to enjoy.

But as Marilyn slowly came out of the darkness, she thought she was having a dream, or rather, a *nightmare,* for she felt as if she were suffocating; there was a terrible weight on her body. And a hand on her dress, caressing one breast. Then a mouth began kissing her neck.

Willing herself to swim up, up, to break the surface of that cool pool of nothingness, she realized, to her horror, that the person on top of her was Doctor Hilgenfeldt!

She squirmed and tried to throw him off, but he was heavy, and she was so weak from the drug.

How sad, Marilyn thought, *if only he'd asked nicely, I would have gladly...*

But now the doctor was no different than all the other men who used and betrayed her.

She screamed.

And Johnny was there pulling him off of her, and throwing the doctor across the room with such force that the man crashed into the medicine cabinet, smashing it, glass shards flying, drugs spilling out on to the floor, as he crumpled bleeding, one hand reaching out to the wall for support, taking the picture of Freud down with him. Marilyn, on the edge of the couch, shrieked, both hands to her cheeks, terrified of what she sensed the young man might do next, as he approached the doctor, who was sprawled on the floor.

Because Johnny looked different, larger, not thin and frail, skin even whiter, eyes somehow slanted, nearly yellow in color, lips curled back showing sharp white teeth.

The young man moved closer, a wild animal coming in for the kill.

Marilyn jumped off of the couch, thrusting one hand toward him, fingers spread wide. "No, Johnny, no!"

She grabbed the young man's arm. It was ice cold. "He didn't hurt me," she sobbed, tugging at that arm. "Please, let's just go."

She repeated her plea, instinctively, until the strange look went out of Johnny's eyes, and color returned to his face. Maybe she'd imagined the seeming transformation; maybe the drug had distorted her perceptions...

"Only for you," was all the young man said. "Only for you."

And with a parting look of hatred at the slumped, semiconscious doctor, Johnny put an arm around Marilyn and walked her out of the room.

They sat in the dark on one of the benches in the pocket park. The rain had turned to drizzle. Out on the East River, a boat sailed forlornly by in the mist.

"I'm not going to press any charges," Marilyn said in a small voice. "I don't want the publicity."

The young man looked at her. She was no longer the glamorous Marilyn Monroe he had ridden with earlier in the cab. The rain, and her tears, had washed all the make-up away, and along with it, that artificial woman, revealing just a frightened, vulnerable girl, who, to him, was even more intoxicatingly beautiful than the movie star image.

"He'll never bother you again," the young man told her.

Or any other woman. The young man would see to that. He'd return some night soon, to the doctor's apartment, gaining entrance in another form, and finish him off. The doctor would not, however, walk the night with the others. He was not worthy. He would be, instead, simply another physician who sadly abused and over-indulged and, consequently, overdosed on his own drugs.

Marilyn, however, *was* worthy; tonight, soon, very soon, he would bestow her this gift of death, that was life...

Marilyn turned to the young man. "How did you know about Doctor Hilgenfeldt?" she asked.

"Do you mean, how did I know you were seeing him? Or how did I know he was a fiend?"

"Both."

"I followed you, when you first went to see him... then checked him out." The young man gestured with one hand. "There'd been a few complaints by female patients, which nothing ever came of. He either paid them off or had connections.

Marilyn looked startled, which he assumed was in response to the revelation about the doctor's unethical behavior, but then she said indignantly, "You've been spying on me!"

"Well...yes," he said.

She stared at him.

"Look," he sighed, gesturing with both hands. "I'll level with you. I wasn't really sick yesterday, I don't live on Lexington and 93rd, and my name isn't Johnny."

He wasn't sure how she'd take that, but he wasn't prepared for what happened next.

She slapped his face.

It stung, and he closed his eyes for a minute and let the rain take the hurt out.

Then he said softly, "Okay, I deserved that. But if someone you'd never met approached you on the street and said your shrink was a rapist, would you have believed it?"

She looked away from him.

"Well? Would you have?"

"No."

"See? I was just trying to protect you."

She looked back at him. "*Why?*" she asked defiantly.

He was silent for a moment, then said, "Because of something you did."

"And what was that?" she asked, not so defiantly.

He gazed out at the river, its surface choppy and murky. "It was almost a year ago," he said. "You'd been playing here in the park one evening with a girl who had polio, remember?"

"Susie. Mrs. Jensen's granddaughter. She was visiting from Ohio."

"The old woman came to take her home because a storm was coming..."

Marilyn nodded. "A really bad one."

"Yet still you sat, while the wind howled, and the rain poured..."

"I was thinking, 'My marriage is over.'"

"Suddenly, lightning struck that tree." The young man pointed to the large oak, nearby; an ugly gash in the bark, a gaping wound, ran down the trunk to its roots.

Marilyn turned to him excitedly. "That was the most incredible thing!" she said in a breathless little girl voice. "I was sitting with one foot on the ground, like this..." She crossed one leg over the other, to show him."...and when the lightning came shooting out of the bottom of that tree, and skittered across the grass in front of my foot, it actually blew out a hole in my shoe!"

She smiled, wiggling one foot, then she frowned.

"But then I saw the bat, there on the ground," she continued. "It must have been hanging from a branch, when the lightning struck. At first, I thought it was dead, but when I got closer, I could see its little breast moving in and out..."

"And you picked it up and took it home."

She nodded. "Did you know," she said, turning her body even more toward his, putting one arm on the back of the bench, "that bats can't see very well, but the reason they don't go bumping into everything is because they make this little squeaking noise, humans almost can't hear it, and the noise echoes off even the smallest thing, and bounces back and tells them something's there." She smiled. "You know, sonar, *before* sonar." Her eyes lit up. "Hey! Do you suppose that's where they got the idea from?"

He smiled. How he loved her. How he would love being with her forever...

"And did you know," she went on, "that most bats are really very sweet creatures and can be kept as pets?" She put one beautifully manicured finger to her lips, bit on it, then gestured outward with the finger. "The only problem is, though, they eat a lot of insects. You have to feed them an awful lot of bugs."

Which she got for him, rooting around in the park after dark, with those same manicured fingers.

Marilyn sat back on the bench. "After I let the bat go, I found out it wasn't the kind of bat usually found in the United States. It was a *vampire bat*, from South America! They suck blood, you know. I read it in a book."

"Really?"

She looked at him. "Now *how* do you suppose it got way up here?"

He shrugged. "It happens."

"I guess it could have bit me."

He leaned toward her. "Would that have been so bad?" he whispered, lips almost brushing her throat. "If it was a vampire bat, you could live forever."

She was silent for a moment, then said softly, "To live forever...what an awful thought."

He looked at her curiously, "Living forever doesn't appeal to you?"

She shook her head. "Maybe on celluloid. But for me, the *real* me, not the r-e-e-l me, the only thing that makes life worth living is knowing that someday it will end."

"But I don't understand..."

"The fact that I'm famous gives me a feeling of happiness," she explained, "but it's only temporary. It's like caviar. Caviar is nice, but to have caviar every day at every meal, forever..."

She stood up and looked down at him.

"I live for my work and for the few people I can count on, but one day my fame will be over and I will say 'goodbye fame; I have had you, and I always knew you were fickle.' And it will be a relief to be done." She smiled sadly. "Don't you see?"

Still seated on the bench, he looked up at her. "I guess bats *are* blind, in more ways than one."

She held out one hand. "Walk me home?"

They strolled slowly down 57th street, arm in arm. The rain let up, and the clouds parted, revealing a brilliant moon, which reflected in the puddles on the sidewalk. But the mirror images in the puddles were only of Marilyn.

She would have made a lousy vampire. Compassion was a bad trait for a child of the night, as he knew all too well.

They stopped in front of her building. She turned to him.

"Goodnight, Johnny. Sweet Dreams. Wish me the same?"

"Goodnight, Marilyn," he said. "Sweet dreams." Then he added, "But my name really isn't Johnny."

"That's okay," she said with a half-smile, half-smirk. "My name really isn't Marilyn."

He watched her walk to the door of her building, where she stopped and looked back.

"Hey!" she said gaily. "Did you hear the one about the vampire who bit Marilyn Monroe?"

"No." He smiled.

"The poor fella died of a drug overdose!" And she laughed, that musical laugh. But it caught in her throat.

She blew him a mocking movie-star kiss.

And then she was gone.

QUARRY'S LUCK

A Quarry Story
Max Allan Collins

Once upon a time, I killed people for a living.

Now, as I sit in my living quarters looking out at Sylvan Lake, its gently rippling gray-blue surface alive with sunlight, the scent and sight of pines soothing me, I seldom think of those years. With the exception of the occasional memoirs I've penned, I have never been very reflective. What's done is done. What's over is over.

But occasionally someone or something I see stirs a memory. In the summer, when Sylvan Lodge (of which I've been manager for several years now) is hopping with guests, I now and then see a cute blue-eyed blonde college girl, and I think of Linda, my late wife. I'd retired from the contract murder profession, lounging on a cottage on a lake not unlike this one, when my past had come looking for me and Linda became a casualty.

What I'd learned from that was two things: the past is not something disconnected from the present; you can't write off old debts or old enemies (whereas, oddly, friends you can completely forget); and not to enter into long-term relationships.

Linda hadn't been a very smart human being, but she was pleasant company and she loved me, and I wouldn't want to cause somebody like her to die again. You know, an innocent.

After all, when I was taking contracts through the man I knew as the Broker, I was dispatching the guilty. I had no idea what these people were guilty of, but it stood to reason that they were guilty of something, or somebody wouldn't have decided they should be dead.

A paid assassin isn't a killer, really. He's a weapon. Someone has already decided someone else is going to die, before the paid assassin is even in the picture, let alone on the scene. A paid assassin is no more a killer than a nine-millimeter automatic or a bludgeon. Somebody has to pick up a weapon, to use it.

Anyway, that was my rationalization back in the seventies, when I was a human weapon for hire. I never took pleasure from the job, just money. And when the time came, I got out of it.

So, a few years ago, after Linda's death, and after I killed the fuckers responsible, I did not allow myself to get pulled back into that profession. I was too old, too tired, my reflexes were not all that good. A friend I ran into, by chance, needed my only other expertise. I had operated a small resort in Wisconsin with Linda, and I now manage Sylvan Lodge.

Something I saw recently, something quite outrageous really, even considering that I have in my time witnessed human behavior of the vilest sort, stirred a distant memory.

The indoor swimming pool with hot tub is a short jog across the road from my two-room apartment in the central lodge building (don't feel sorry for me: it's a bedroom and spacious living room with kitchenette, plus two baths, with a deck looking out on my storybook view of the lake). We close the pool room at ten p.m., and sometimes I take the keys over and open the place up for a solitary midnight swim.

I was doing that, actually, I'd finished my swim and was letting the hot tub's jet streams have at my chronically sore lower back, when somebody came knocking at the glass doors.

It was a male figure, portly, and a female figure, slender, shapely, both wrapped in towels. That was all I could see of them through the glass; the lights were off outside.

Sighing, I climbed out of the hot tub, wrapped a towel around myself, and unlocked the glass door and slid it open just enough to deal with these two.

"We want a swim!" the man said. He was probably fifty-five, with a booze-mottled face and a brown toupee that squatted on his round head like a slumbering gopher.

Next to him, the blonde of twenty-something, with huge blue eyes and huge, big boobs (her towel, thankfully, was tied around her waist), stood almost behind the man. She looked meek, even embarrassed.

"Mr. Davis," I said, cordial enough, "it's after hours."

"Fuck that! *You're* in here, aren't you?"

"I'm the manager. I sneak a little time in for my-self, after closing, after the guests have had their fun."

He put his hand on my bare chest. "Well, *we're* guests, and *we* want to have some fun, too!"

His breath was ninety proof.

I removed his hand. Bending the fingers back a little in the process.

He winced, and started to say something, but I said, "I'm sorry. It's the lodge policy. My apologies to you and your wife."

Bloodshot eyes widened in the face, and he began to say something, but stopped short. He tucked his tail between his legs (and his towel), and took the girl by the arm, roughly, saying, "Come on, baby. We don't need this horseshit."

The blonde looked back at me and gave me a crinkly little chagrined grin, and I smiled back at her, locked the glass door, and climbed back in the hot tub to cool off.

"Asshole," I said. It echoed in the high-ceilinged steamy room. "Fucking asshole!" I said louder, just because I could, and the echo was enjoyable.

He hadn't tucked towel 'tween his legs because I'd bent his fingers back. He'd done it because I mentioned his wife, who we both knew the little blonde bimbo wasn't.

That was because (and here's the outrageous part) he'd been here last month, to this very same resort, with another very attractive blonde, but one about forty, maybe forty-five, who was indeed, and in fact, his lawful wedded wife.

We had guys who came to Sylvan Lodge with their families; we had guys who came with just their wives;

and we had guys who came with what used to be called in olden times their mistresses. But we seldom had a son of a bitch so fucking bold as to bring his wife one week, and his mistress the next, to the same goddamn motel, which is what Sylvan Lodge, after all, let's face it, is a glorified version of.

As I enjoyed the jet stream on my low back, I smiled and then frowned, as the memory stirred. Christ, I'd forgotten about that! You'd think that Sylvan Lodge itself would've jogged my memory. But it hadn't.

Even though the memory in question was of one of my earliest jobs, which took place at a resort not terribly unlike this one...

We met off Interstate 80, at a truck stop outside of the Quad Cities. It was late, almost midnight, a hot, muggy June night; my black T-shirt was sticking to me. My blue jeans, too.

The Broker had taken a booth in back. The restaurant wasn't particularly busy, except for an area designated for truckers. But it had the war-zone look of a rush hour just past. It was a blindingly white but not terribly clean-looking place and the jukebox, wailing "I Shot the Sheriff" at the moment, combatted the clatter of dishes being bused.

Sitting with the Broker was an oval-faced, bright-eyed kid of about twenty-three (which at the time was about my age, too) who wore a Doobie Brothers t-shirt and had shoulder-length brown hair. Mine was cut short, not soldier-cut, but businessman short.

"Quarry," the Broker said, in his melodious baritone; he gestured with an open hand. "How good to see you. Sit down." His smile was faint under the wispy mustache, but there was a fatherly air to his manner.

He was trying to look casual in a yellow Ban-lon shirt and golf slacks; he had white, styled hair and a long face that managed to look both fleshy and largely unlined. He was a solid-looking man, fairly tall; he looked like a captain of industry, which he was in a way. I took him for fifty, but that was just a guess.

"This is Adam," the Broker said.

"How are you doin', man?" Adam said, and grinned, and half-rose. He seemed a little nervous, and in the process, before I'd even had a chance to decide whether to take the hand he offered or not, overturned a salt shaker, which sent him into a minor tizzy.

"Damn!" Adam said, forgetting about the handshake. "I hate fuckin' bad luck!" He tossed some salt over each shoulder, then grinned at me and said, "I'm afraid I'm one superstitious motherfucker."

"Well, you know what Stevie Wonder says," I said.

He squinted. "No, what?"

Sucker.

"Nothing," I said, sliding in.

A twentyish waitress with a nice shape, a hair net and two pounds of acne took my order, which was for a Coke; the Broker already had coffee and the kid a bottle of Mountain Dew and a glass.

When she went away, I said, "Well, Broker. Got some work for me? I drove hundreds of miles in a fucking gas shortage, so you sure as shit better have."

Adam seemed a little stunned to hear the Broker spoken to so disrespectfully, but the Broker was used to my attitude and merely smiled and patted the air with a benedictory palm.

"I wouldn't waste your time otherwise, Quarry. This will pay handsomely. Ten thousand for the two of you."

Five-grand was good money; three was pretty standard. Money was worth more then. You could buy a Snickers bar for ten cents. Or was it fifteen? I forget.

But I was still a little irritated.

"The two of us?" I said. "Adam, here, isn't my better half on this one, is he?"

"Yes, he is," the Broker said. He had his hands folded now, prayerfully. His baritone was calming. Or was meant to be.

Adam was frowning, playing nervously with a silver skull ring on the little finger of his left hand. "I don't like your fuckin' attitude, man..."

The way he tried to work menace into his voice would have been amusing if I'd given a shit.

"I don't like your fuckin' hippie hair," I said.

"What?" He leaned forward, furious, and knocked his

water glass over. It spun on its side and fell off my edge of the booth and we heard it shatter. A few eyes looked our way.

Adam's tiny bright eyes were wide. "Fuck," he said.

"Seven years bad luck, dipshit," I said.

"That's just mirrors!"

"I think it's any kind of glass. Isn't that right, Broker?"

The Broker was frowning a little. "Quarry..." He sounded so disappointed in me.

"Hair like that attracts attention," I said. "You go in for a hit, you got to be the invisible man."

"These days everybody wears their hair like this,"

the kid said defensively.

"In Greenwich Village, maybe. But in America, if you want to disappear, you look like a businessman or a college student."

That made him laugh. "You ever see a college student lately, asshole?"

"I mean the kind who belongs to a fraternity. You want to go around killing people, you need to look clean-cut."

Adam's mouth had dropped open; he had crooked lower teeth. He pointed at me with a thumb and turned to look at Broker, indignant. "Is this guy for real?"

"Yes indeed," the Broker said. "He's also the best active agent I have."

By "active," Broker meant (in his own personal jargon) that I was the half of a hit team that took out the target; the "passive" half was the lookout person, the back-up.

"And he's right," the Broker said, "about your hair."

"Far as that's concerned," I said, "we look pretty goddamn conspicuous right here, me looking collegiate, you looking like the prez of a country club, and junior here like a roadshow Mick Jagger."

Adam looked half-bewildered, half-outraged.

"You may have a point," the Broker allowed me.

"On the other hand," I said, "people probably think we're fags waiting for a fourth."

"You're unbelievable," Adam said, shaking his greasy Beatle mop. "I don't want to work with this son of a bitch."

"Stay calm," the Broker said. "I'm not proposing a partnership, not unless this should happen to work out beyond all of our wildest expectations."

"I tend to agree with Adam, here," I said. "We're not made for each other."

"The question is," the Broker said, "are you made for ten thousand dollars?"

Adam and I thought about that.

"I have a job that needs to go down, very soon," he said, "and very quickly. You're the only two men available right now. And I know neither of you wants to disappoint me."

Half of ten grand did sound good to me. I had a lake-front lot in Wisconsin where I could put up this nifty little A-frame prefab, if I could put a few more thousand together.

"I'm in," I said, "if he cuts his hair."

The Broker looked at Adam, who scowled and nodded.

"You're both going to like this," the Broker said, sitting forward, withdrawing a travel brochure from his back pocket.

"A resort?" I asked.

"Near Chicago. A wooded area. There's a man-made lake, two indoor swimming pools and one out-door, an 'old town' gift shop area, several restaurants, bowling alley, tennis courts, horse-back riding..."

"If they have archery," I said, "maybe we could arrange a little accident."

That made the Broker chuckle. "You're not far off the mark. We need either an accident, or a robbery. It's an insurance situation."

Broker would tell us no more than that: part of his function was to shield the client from us, and us from the client, for that matter. He was sort of a combina-tion agent and buffer; he could tell us only this much:

the target was going down so that someone could collect insurance. The double indemnity kind that comes from accidental death, and of course getting killed by thieves counts in that regard.

"This is him," Broker said, carefully showing us a photograph of a thin, handsome, tanned man of possibly sixty with black hair that was probably dyed. He wore dark sunglasses and tennis togs and had an arm around a dark-haired woman of about forty, a tanned slim busty woman also in dark glasses and tennis togs.

"Who's the babe?" Adam said.

"The wife," the Broker said.

The client.

"The client?" Adam asked.

"I didn't say that," Broker said edgily, "and you mustn't ask stupid questions. Your target is this man, Baxter Bennedict."

"I hope his wife isn't named Bunny," I said.

The Broker chuckled again, but Adam didn't see the joke.

"Close. Her name is Bernice, actually."

I groaned. "One more 'B' and I'll kill 'em *both*, for free."

The Broker took out a silver cigarette case. "Actually, that's going to be one of the...delicate aspects of this job."

"How so?" I asked.

He offered me a cigarette from the case, and I waved it off; he offered one to Adam, and he took it.

The Broker said, "They'll be on vacation. Together, at the Wistful Wagon Lodge. She's not to be harmed. You must wait and watch until you can get him alone."

"And then make it look like an accident," I said.

"Or a robbery. Correct." The Broker struck a match, lighted his cigarette. He tried to light Adam's, but Adam gestured no, frantically.

"Two on a match," he said. Then got a lighter out and lit himself up.

"Two on a match?" I asked.

"Haven't you ever heard that?" the kid asked, almost wild-eyed. "Two on a match. It's unlucky!"

"*Three* on a match is unlucky," I said.

Adam squinted at me. "Are you superstitious, too?"

I looked hard at Broker, who merely shrugged.

"I gotta pee," the kid said suddenly, and had the Broker let him slide out. Standing, he wasn't very big, probably five seven. Skinny. His jeans were tattered.

When we were alone, I said, "What are you doing, hooking me up with that dumb-ass jerk?"

"Give him a chance. He was in Vietnam. Like you. He's not completely inexperienced."

"Most of the guys I knew in Vietnam were stoned twenty-four hours a day. That's not what I'm looking for in a partner."

"He's just a little green. You'll season him."

"I'll ice him if he fucks up. Understood?"

The Broker shrugged. "Understood."

When Adam came back, Broker let him in and said, "The hardest part is, you have a window of only four days."

"That's bad," I said, frowning. "I like to maintain a surveillance, get a pattern down..."

Broker shrugged again. "It's a different situation. They're on vacation. They won't have much of a pattern."

"Great."

Now the Broker frowned. "Why in hell do you think it pays so well? Think of it as hazardous duty pay."

Adam sneered and said, "What's the matter, Quarry? Didn't you never take no fuckin' risks?"

"I think I'm about to," I said.

"It'll go well," the Broker said.

"Knock on wood," the kid said, and rapped on the table.

"That's Formica," I said.

The Wistful Wagon Lodge sprawled out over numerous wooded acres, just off the outskirts of Wistful Vista, Illinois. According to the Broker's brochure, back in the late '40s, the hamlet had taken the name of Fibber McGee and Molly's fictional hometown for purposes of attracting tourists; apparently one of the secondary stars of the radio show had been born nearby. This marketing ploy had been just in time for television making radio passé, and the little farm community's only remaining sign of having at all successfully tapped into the tourist trade was the Wistful Wagon Lodge itself.

A cobblestone drive wound through the scattering of log cabins, and several larger buildings, including the main lodge where the check-in and restaurants were, were similarly rustic structures, but of gray weathered wood. Trees clustered everywhere, turning warm sunlight into cool pools of shade; wood-burned signs showed the way to this building or that path, and decorative wagon wheels, often with flower beds in and around them, were scattered about as if some long-ago pioneer mishap had been beautified by nature and time. Of course, that wasn't the case, this was the hokey hand of man.

We arrived separately, Adam and I, each having reserved rooms in advance, each paying cash up front upon registration, no credit cards. We each had log-cabin cottages, not terribly close to one another.

As the back-up and surveillance man, Adam went in early. The target and his wife were taking a long weekend, arriving Thursday, leaving Monday. I didn't arrive until Saturday morning.

I went to Adam's cabin and knocked but got no answer. Which just meant he was trailing Mr. and Mrs. Target around the grounds. After I dropped my stuff off at my own cabin, I wandered, trying to get the general layout of the place, checking out the lodge itself, where about half of the rooms were, as well as two restaurants. Everything had a pine smell, which was partially the many trees, and partially Pine Sol. Wistful Wagon was Hollywood rustic - there was a dated quality about it, from the cowboy/cowgirl attire of the waiters and waitresses in the Wistful Chuck-wagon Cafe to the wood and leather furnishings to the barnwood-framed Remington prints.

I got myself some lunch and traded smiles with a giggly tableful of college girls who were on a weekend scouting expedition of their own. *Good*, I thought. *If I can connect with one of them tonight, that'll provide a nice cover.*

As I was finishing up, my cowgirl waitress, a curly-haired blonde pushing thirty who was pretty cute her-self, said, "Looks like you might get lucky tonight."

She was refilling my coffee cup.

"With them or with you?" I asked.

She had big washed-out blue eyes and heavy eye make-up, more '60s than '70s. She was wearing a 1950s style cowboy hat cinched under her chin. "I'm not supposed to fraternize with the guests."

"How did you know I was a fraternity man?"

She laughed a little; her chin crinkled. Her face was kind of round and she was a little pudgy, nicely so in the bosom.

"Wild stab," she said. "Anyway, there's an open dance in the ballroom. Of the Wagontrain Dining Room? Country swing band. You'll like it."

"You inviting me?"

"No," she said; she narrowed her eyes and cocked her head, her expression one of mild scolding. "Those little girls'll be there, and plenty of others. You won't have any trouble finding what you want."

"I bet I will."

"Why's that?"

"I was hoping for a girl wearing cowboy boots like yours."

"Oh, there'll be girls in cowboys boots there tonight."

"I meant, just cowboy boots."

She laughed at that and shook her head; under her Dale Evans hat, her blonde curls bounced off her shoulders.

She went away and let me finish my coffee, and I smiled at the college girls some more, but when I paid for my check, at the register, it was my plump little cowgirl again.

"I work late tonight," she said.

"How late?"

"I get off at midnight," she said.

"That's only the first time," I said.

"First time what?"

"That you'll get off tonight."

She liked that. Times were different, then. The only way you could die from fucking was if a husband or boyfriend caught you at it. She told me where to meet her, later.

I strolled back up a winding path to my cabin. A few groups of college girls and college guys, not paired off together yet, were buzzing around. Some couples in their twenties up into their sixties were walking, often hand-in-hand, around the sun-dappled, lushly shaded grounds. The sound of a gentle breeze in the trees made a faint shimmering music. Getting laid here was no trick.

I got my swim trunks on and grabbed a towel and headed for the nearest pool, which was the outdoor one. That's where I found Adam.

He did look like a college frat rat, with his shorter hair. His skinny pale body reddening. He was sitting in a deck chair, sipping a Coke, in sunglasses and racing trunks, chatting with a couple of bikinied college cuties, also in sunglasses.

"Bill?" I said.

"Jim?" he said, taking off his sunglasses to get a better look at me. He grinned, extended his hand. I took it, shook it, as he stood. "I haven't seen you since spring break!"

We'd agreed to be old high-school buddies from Peoria who had gone to separate colleges. I was attending the University of Iowa; he was at Michigan. We avoided using Illinois schools because Illinois kids were who we'd most likely run into here.

Adam introduced me to the girls; I don't remember their names, but one was a busty brunette Veronica, the other a flat-chested blonde Betty. The sound of splashing and running screaming kids – though this was a couple's hideaway, there was a share of families here, as well – kept the conversation to a blessed minimum. The girls were nursing majors. We were engineering majors. We all liked Credence Clearwater. We all hoped Nixon would get the book thrown at him. We were all going to the dance tonight.

Across the way, Baxter Bennedict was sitting in a deck chair under an umbrella reading *Jaws*. Every page or so, he'd sip his martini; every ten pages or so, he'd wave a waitress in cowgirl vest and white plastic hot pants over for another one. His wife was swimming, her dark arms cutting the water like knives. It seemed methodical, an exercise work-out in the midst of a pool filled with water babes of various ages.

When she pulled herself out of the water, her suit a stark, startling white against her almost burned black skin, she revealed a slender, rather tall figure, tight ass, high, full breasts. Her rather lined leathery face was the only tip-off to her age, and that had the blessing of a model's beauty to get it by.

She pulled off a white swim cap and unfurled a mane of dark, blond-tipped hair. Toweling herself off, she bent to kiss her husband on the cheek, but he only scowled at her. She stretched out on her colorful beach towel beside him, to further blacken herself.

"Ooo," said Veronica. "What's that ring?"

"That's my lucky ring," Adam said.

That fucking skull ring of his! Had he been dumb enough to wear that? Yes.

"Bought that at a Grateful Dead concert, didn't you, Bill?" I asked.

"Uh, yeah," he said.

"Ick," said Betty. "I don't like the Dead. Their hair is greasy. They're so...druggie."

"Drugs aren't so bad," Veronica said boldly, thrusting out her admirably thrust-worthy bosom.

"Bill and I had our wild days back in high school," I said. "You shoulda seen our hair, down to our asses, right Bill?"

"Right."

"But we don't do that anymore," I said. "Kinda put that behind us."

"Well I for one don't approve of drugs," Betty said.

"Don't blame you," I said.

"Except for grass, of course," she said.

"Of course."

"And coke. Scientific studies prove coke isn't bad for you."

"Well, you're in nursing," I said. "You'd know."

We made informal dates with the girls for the dance, and I wandered off with "Bill" to his cabin.

"The skull ring was a nice touch," I said.

He frowned at me. "Fuck you, it's my lucky ring!"

A black gardener on a rider mower rumbled by us.

"Now we're really in trouble," I said.

He looked genuinely concerned. "What do you mean?"

"A black cat crossed our path."

In Adam's cabin, I sat on the brown, fake-leather sofa while he sat on the nubby yellow bedspread and spread his hands.

"They actually do have a sorta pattern," he said,

"vacation or not."

Adam had arrived on Wednesday, the Bennedicts had arrived Thursday around two p.m., which was check-in time.

"They drink and swim all afternoon," Adam said, "and they go dining and dancing, and drinking, in the evening."

"What about mornings?"

"Tennis. He doesn't start drinking till lunch."

"Doesn't she drink?"

"Not as much. He's an asshole. We're doing the world a favor, here."

"How do you mean?"

He shrugged. He looked very different in his short hair. "He's kind of abusive. He don't yell at her, but just looking at them, you can see him glaring at her all the time, real ugly. Saying things that hurt her."

"She doesn't stand up to him?"

He shook his head, no. "They're very one-sided arguments. He either sits there and ignores her or he's giving her foul looks and it looks like he's chewing her out or something."

"Sounds like a sweet guy."

"After the drinking and dining and dancing, they head to the bar. Both nights so far, she's gone off to bed around eleven and he's stayed and shut the joint down."

"Good. That means he's alone when he walks back to their cabin."

Adam nodded. "But this place is crawlin' with people."

"Not at two in the morning. Most of these people are sleeping or fucking by then."

"Maybe so. He's got a fancy watch, some heavy gold jewelry."

"Well that's very good. Now we got ourselves a motive."

"But she's the one with jewels." He whistled. "You should see the rocks hanging off that dame."

"Well, we aren't interested in those."

"What about the stuff you steal off him? Just toss it somewhere?"

"Hell no! Broker'll have it fenced for us. A little extra dough for our trouble."

He grinned. "Great. This is easy money. Vacation with pay."

"Don't ever think that. Don't ever let your guard down."

"I know that," he said defensively.

"It's unlucky to think that way," I said, and knocked on wood. Real wood.

We met up with Betty and Veronica at the dance; I took Betty because Adam was into knockers and Veronica had them. Betty was pleasant company, but I wasn't listening to her babble. I was keeping an eye on the Bennedicts, who were seated at a corner table under a Buffalo head.

He really was an asshole. You could tell, by the way he sneered at her and spit sentences out at her, that he'd spent a lifetime, or at least a marriage, making her miserable. His hatred for her was something you could see as well as sense, like steam over asphalt. She was taking it placidly. Cool as Cher while Sonny prattled on.

But I had a hunch she usually took it more personally. Right now, she could be placid. She knew the son of a bitch was going to die this weekend.

"Did you ever do Lauderdale?" Betty was saying. "I got so drunk there..."

The band was playing "Crazy" and a decent girl singer was doing a respectable Patsy Cline. What a great song.

I said, "I won a chug-a-lug contest at Boonie's in '72."

Betty was impressed. "Were you even in college then?"

"No. I had a hell of a fake I.D., though."

"Bitchen!"

Around eleven, the band took a break, and we walked the girls to their cabins, hand in hand, like high school sweethearts. Gas lanterns on poles scorched the night orangely; a half-moon threw some silvery light on us, too. Adam disappeared around the side of the cabin with Veronica and I stood and watched Betty beam at me and rock girlishly on her heels. She smelled of perfume and beer, which mingled with the scent of pines; it was more pleasant than it sounds.

She was making with the dimples. "You're so nice."

"Well thanks."

"And I'm a good judge of character."

"I bet you are."

Then she put her arms around me and pressed her slim frame to me and put her tongue half-way down my throat.

She pulled herself away and smiled coquettishly and said, "That's all you get tonight. See you tomorrow."

As if on cue, Veronica appeared with her lipstick

mussed up and her sweater askew.

"Good night, boys," Veronica said, and they slipped inside, giggling like the schoolgirls they were.

"Fuck," Adam said, scowling. "All I got was a little bare tit."

"Not so little."

"I thought I was gonna get laid."

I shrugged. "Instead you got screwed."

We walked. We passed a cabin that was getting some remodeling and repairs. I'd noticed it earlier. A ladder was leaned up against the side, for some re-roofing. Adam made a wide circle around the ladder. I walked under it just to watch him squirm.

When I fell back in step with him, he said, "You gonna do the hit tonight?"

"No."

"Bar closes at midnight on Sundays. Gonna do it then?"

"Yes."

He sighed. "Good."

We walked, and it was the place where one path went toward my cabin, and another toward his.

"Well," he said, "maybe I'll get lucky tomorrow night."

"No pick-ups the night of the hit. I need back-up more than either of us needs an alibi, or an easy fuck, either."

"Oh. Of course. You're right. Sorry. 'Night."

"'Night, Bill."

Then I went back and picked up the waitress cowgirl and took her to my cabin. She had some dope in her purse, and I smoked a little with her, just to be nice, and apologized for not having a rubber, and she said, Don't sweat it, pardner, I'm on the pill, and she rode me in her cowboy boots until my dick said yahoo.

The next morning, I had breakfast in the cafe with Adam and he seemed preoccupied as I ate my scrambled eggs and bacon, and he poked at his French toast.

"Bill," I said. "What's wrong?"

"I'm worried."

"What about?"

We were seated in a rough-wood booth and had plenty of privacy; we kept our voices down. Our conversation, after all, wasn't really proper breakfast conversation.

"I don't think you should hit him like that."

"Like what?"

He frowned. "On his way back to his cabin after the bar closes."

"Oh? Why?"

"He might not be drunk enough. Bar closes early Sunday night, remember?"

"Jesus," I said. "The fucker starts drinking at noon. What more do you want?"

"But there could be people around."

"At midnight?"

"It's a resort. People get romantic at resorts. Moonlight strolls..."

"You got a better idea?"

He nodded. "Do it in his room. Take the wife's jewels and it's a robbery got out of hand. In and out. No fuss, no muss."

"Are you high? What about the wife?"

"She won't be there."

"What are you talking about?"

He started gesturing, earnestly. "She gets worried about him, see. It's midnight, and she goes looking for him. While she's gone, he gets back, flops on the bed, you come in, bing bang boom."

I just looked at him. "Are you psychic now? How do we know she'll do that?"

He swallowed; took a nibble at a forkful of syrup-dripping French toast. Smiled kind of nervously.

"She told me so," he said.

We were walking now. The sun was filtering through the trees and birds were chirping and the sounds of children laughing wafted through the air.

"Are you fucking nuts? Making contact with the client?"

"Quarry, she contacted me! I swear!"

"Then *she's* fucking nuts. Jesus!" I sat on a bench by a flower bed. "It's off. I'm calling the Broker. It's over."

"Listen to me! Listen. She was waiting for me at my cabin last night. After we struck out with the college girls? She was fuckin' waitin' for me! She told me she knew who I was."

"How did she know that?"

"She said she saw me watching them. She figured it out. She guessed."

"And, of course, you confirmed her suspicions."

He swallowed. "Yeah."

"You dumb-ass dickhead. Who said it first?"

"Who said what first?"

"Who mentioned 'killing.' Who mentioned 'murder.'"

His cheek twitched. "Well...me, I guess. She kept

saying she knew why I was here. And then she said, *I'm* why you're here. I hired you."

"And you copped to it. God. I'm on the next bus."

"Quarry! Listen...this is better this way. This is much better."

"What did she do, fuck you?"

He blanched, looked at his feet.

"Oh God," I said. "You *did* get lucky last night. Fuck. You fucked the client. Did you tell her there were two of us?"

"No."

"She's seen us together."

"I told her you're just a guy I latched onto here to look less conspicuous."

"Did she buy it?"

"Why shouldn't she? I say we scrap Plan A and move to Plan B. It's better."

"Plan B being...?"

"Quarry, she's going to leave the door unlocked. She'll wait for him to get back from the bar, and when he's asleep, she'll unlock the door, go out and pretend to be looking for him, and come back and find him dead, and her jewels gone. Help police, I been robbed, my husband's been shot. You know."

"She's being pretty fucking helpful, you ask me."

His face clenched like a fist. "The bastard has beat her for years. And he's got a girlfriend a third his age. He's been threatening to divorce her, and since they signed a pre-marital agreement, she gets jack shit, if they divorce. The bastard."

"Quite a sob story."

"I told you: we're doing the world a favor. And now she's doing us one. Why shoot him right out in the open, when we can walk in his room and do it? You got to stick this out, Quarry. Shit, man, it's five grand a piece, and change!"

I thought about it.

"Quarry?"

I'd been thinking a long time.

"Okay," I said. "Give her the high sign. We'll do it her way."

The Bar W Bar was a cozy rustic room decorated with framed photos of movie cowboys from Ken Maynard to John Wayne, from Audie Murphy to the Man with No Name. On a brown mock-leather stool up at the bar, Baxter Bennedict sat, a thin handsome drunk in a pale blue polyester sportcoat and pale yellow Ban-lon sport shirt, gulping martinis and telling anyone who'd listen his sad story.

I didn't sit near enough to be part of the conversation, but I could hear him.

"Milking me fucking dry," he was saying. "You'd think with sixteen goddamn locations, I'd be sitting pretty. I was the first guy in the Chicago area to offer a paint job under thirty dollars, $29.95! That's a good fucking deal, isn't it?"

The bartender, a young fellow in a buckskin vest, polishing a glass, nodded sympathetically.

"Now this competition. Killing me. What the fuck kind of paint job can you get for $19.99? Will you answer me that one? And now that bitch has the nerve..."

Now he was muttering. The bartender began to move away, but Baxter started in again.

"She wants me to sell! My life's work. Started from nothing. And she wants me to sell! Pitiful fucking money they offered. Pitiful..."

"Last call, Mr. Bennedict," the bartender said. Then he repeated it, louder, without the "Mr. Bennedict." The place was only moderately busy. A few couples. A solitary drinker or two. The Wistful Wagon Lodge had emptied out, largely, this afternoon, even Betty and Veronica were gone. Sunday. People had to go to work tomorrow. Except, of course, for those who owned their own businesses, like Baxter here.

Or had unusual professions, like mine.

I waited until the slender figure had stumbled half-way home before I approached him. No one was around. The nearest cabin was dark.

"Mr. Bennedict," I said.

"Yeah?" He turned, trying to focus his bleary eyes.

"I couldn't help but hear what you said. I think I have a solution for your problems."

"Yeah?" He grinned. "And what the hell would that be?"

He walked, on the unsteadiest of legs, up to me.

I showed him the nine-millimeter with its bulky sound suppresser. It probably looked like a ray gun to him.

"Fuck! What is this, a fucking hold-up?"

"Yes. Keep your voice down or it'll turn into a fucking homicide. Got me?"

That turned him sober. "Got you. What do you want?"

"What do you think? Your watch and your rings."

He smirked disgustedly and removed them; handed them over.

"Now your sport coat."

"My what?"

"Your sport coat. I just can't get enough polyester."

He snorted a laugh. "You're out of your gourd, pal."

He slipped off the sport coat and handed it out toward me with two fingers; he was weaving a little, smirking drunkenly.

I took the coat with my left hand, and the silenced nine-millimeter went *thup thup thup*; three small, brilliant blossoms of red appeared on his light-yellow Ban-lon. He was dead before he had time to think about it.

I dragged his body behind a clump of trees and left him there, his worries behind him.

I watched from behind a tree as Bernice Bennedict slipped out of their cabin; she was wearing a dark halter top and dark slacks that almost blended with her burnt-black skin, making a wraith of her. She had a big white handbag on a shoulder strap. She was so dark the white bag seemed to float in space as she headed toward the lodge.

Only she stopped and found her own tree to duck behind.

I smiled to myself.

Then, wearing the pale blue polyester sport coat, I entered their cabin, through the door she'd left open. The room was completely dark, but for some minor filtering in of light through curtained windows. Quickly, I arranged some pillows under sheets and covers, to create the impression of a person in the bed.

And I called Adam's cabin.

"Hey, Bill," I said. "It's Jim."

His voice was breathless. "Is it done?"

"No. I got cornered coming out of the bar by that

waitress I was out with last night. She latched onto me – she's in my john."

"What, are you in your room?"

"Yeah. I saw Bennedict leave the bar at midnight, and his wife passed us, heading for the lodge, just minutes ago. You've got a clear shot at him."

"What? Me? I'm the fucking lookout!"

"Tonight's the night and we go to Plan C."

"I didn't know there was a Plan C."

"Listen, asshole, it was you who wanted to switch plans. You've got a piece, don't you?"

"Of course..."

"Well you're elected. Go!"

And I hung up.

I stood in the doorway of the bathroom, which faced the bed. I sure as hell didn't turn any lights on, although my left hand hovered by the switch. The nine-millimeter with the silencer was heavy in my right hand. But I didn't mind.

Adam came in quickly and didn't do too bad a job of it, four silenced slugs. He should have checked the body - it never occurred to him he'd just slaughtered a bunch of pillows; but if somebody had been in that bed, they'd have been dead.

He went to the dresser where he knew the jewels would be and was picking up the jewelry box when the door opened and she came in, the little revolver already in her hand.

Before she could fire, I turned on the bathroom light and said, "If I don't hear the gun hit the floor immediately, you're fucking dead."

She was just a black shape, except for the white handbag, but I saw the flash of silver as the gun bounced to the carpeted floor.

"What...?" Adam was saying. It was too dark to see any expression, but he was obviously as confused as he was spooked.

"Shut the door, lady," I said, "and turn on the lights."

She did.

She really was a beautiful woman, or had been, dark eyes and scarlet-painted mouth in that finely carved model's face, but it was just a leathery mask to me.

"What..." Adam said. He looked shocked as hell, which made sense; the gun was in his waistband, the jewelry box in his hands.

"You didn't know there were two of us, did you, Mrs. Bennedict?"

She was sneering faintly; she shook her head, no.

"You see, kid," I told Adam, "she wanted her husband hit, but she wanted the hitman dead, too. Cleaner. Tidier. Right?"

"Fuck you," she said.

"I'm not much for sloppy seconds, thanks. Bet you got a nice legal license for that little purse pea-shooter of yours, don't you? Perfect protection for when you stumble in on an intruder who's just killed your loving husband. Who *is* dead, by the way. Somebody'll run across him in the morning, probably."

"You bitch!" Adam said. He raised his own gun, which was a .380 Browning with a home-made suppresser.

"Don't you know it's bad luck to kill a woman?" I said.

She was frozen, one eye twitching.

Adam was trembling. He swallowed; nodded.

"Okay," he said, lowering the gun. "Okay."

"Go," I told him.

She stepped aside as he slipped out the door, shutting it behind him.

"Thank you," she said, and I shot her twice in the chest.

I slipped the bulky silenced automatic in my waistband; grabbed the jewel box off the dresser.

"I make my own luck," I told her, but she didn't hear me, as I stepped over her.

I never worked with Adam again. I think he was disturbed, when he read the papers and realized I'd iced the woman after all. Maybe he got out of the business. Or maybe he wound up dead in a ditch, his lucky skull ring still on his little finger. Broker never said, and I was never interested enough to ask.

Now, years later, lounging in the hot tub at Sylvan Lodge, I look back on my actions and wonder how I could have ever been so young, and so rash.

Killing the woman was understandable. She'd double-crossed us; she would've killed us both without batting a false lash.

But sleeping with that cowgirl waitress, on the job. Smoking dope. Not using a rubber.

I was really pushing my luck that time.

DALLIANCE AT SUNNYDALE
Barbara Collins

Henry hated Sunnydale. He wished he'd never let his wife of fifty-seven years talk him in to moving there.

But Bernice had tricked him, by calling Sunnydale a "retirement community," and "assisted living apartments."

Bull-crap. No matter what new-fangled names it went by these days, Sunnydale was still a nursing home, the last stop on the way to the grave, and a place Henry swore he'd never end up.

At the time, however, when Bernice approached Henry with a brochure printed on slick paper that showed large comfortable apartments, a cheerfully decorated dining room displaying delectable foods, and an attractive (especially the females) staff looking dedicated and eager to serve them, it seemed like a good idea. Bernice had rheumatoid arthritis and he was recovering from a stroke. Neither could climb the stairs anymore or do anything but the simplest of household tasks. So, they sold their rambling house in the city and took up residence in the country.

But Sunnydale was not so sunny, Henry soon discovered. It was a dreary, sprawling, one-floor institution stuck out in the middle of nowhere, where no one came to visit, not even their grown children.

And who could blame them?

Bernice, on the other hand, loved Sunnydale. She told him many times how happy she was, content to live out her dying days there.

Henry only felt miserable.

And lonely.

As he shuffled out of the solitude of his tiny bedroom (they each had their own) and into the miniscule living room, he glanced at his wife, who was seated in the only recliner, her swollen legs up. She was wearing an old cotton house dress and matted, furry slippers. Her white hair, long ago blonde and shoulder-length, was cut mannishly short, its texture as coarse as the slippers. Her face, once beautiful, was now a pasty, lumpy thing, eyes two shriveled-up raisins disappearing into rising dough.

Despite her dilapidated appearance, however, he still did love Bernice, in a way. After all, at his age, he was no prize either; he could stand to lose a good fifty pounds. But at least he tried to stay well-groomed, although his wife never seemed to notice.

Today, Bernice was doing what she did every day: watching a cable channel called "TLC."

Once, Henry asked her what the initials stood for, and she told him it either meant The Learning Channel or Tender Loving Care, she wasn't sure.

He said *he* could use a little tender loving care, but she didn't hear him. Or pretended not to.

With some difficulty, Henry got his walker, which was stored in the entryway of their living quarters.

He paused and looked back at his wife.

"I'm going now," he said.

She nodded slightly, her eyes glued to the set, not interested in where he was headed.

Of course, how far could that be?

Henry's shoulders slumped, and he steered the walker, its small wheels squeaking, out their open front door and into the hallway.

He couldn't understand why anybody would find a show like that, about some strangers who come into your house and rearrange the furniture, the least bit entertaining. What if you didn't like it? Or the other program his wife watched, about disfigured children getting their faces fixed. The other day, Bernice insisted on telling him all about some boy who was born with only one eye. Henry was happy the little fella got another eyeball, but did he have to hear the gruesome details of the operation at dinnertime when he was trying to eat oyster stew?

Then there was another show Bernice liked, about birthing babies. Talk about embarrassing! He asked his wife why she cared about such things at her age, especially when she'd had three children herself, and she looked at him as if he had mush for brains, and snapped, "Well, I didn't actually *see* what happened down there, now did I?"

Henry thought, *why would you want to?* When *that* show came on (which was now) he made himself scarce.

Henry pushed the walker slowly along the scuffed-up corridor, dragging his left leg, which hadn't recovered from the stroke yet. Tediously, he passed more rooms belonging to other residents; sometimes he could hear muffled cries behind the closed doors of the really sick ones.

He shuffled by the dining room, where a nauseating conglomeration of smells wafted out, telling him that another "delectable" dinner was under way in the kitchen. As Henry went by the nurse's station, two unattractive broads (that's how he thought of them) in stained white smocks, one as fat as the other was thin, were having an argument over the dosage a patient *should* have received that morning. The two women didn't seem to notice him.

Somewhat winded, Henry finally reached the apex of the outrageously expensive retirement community called Sunnydale, the recreation center.

Here, amid plastic flowers and uncomfortable furniture, those who could make it to the gray-painted room could watch even more TV, or exercise their feeble minds by playing the tattered board games, or put together puzzles without all their pieces.

On this dreary afternoon, only a few residents were in the RC.

A man Henry knew as Fritz sat in his wheelchair in a corner watching a football game on a small wall-mounted television set. The old gent's wife, Henry forgot her name, was probably watching the same channel as Bernice, forcing Fritz to flee.

In the center of the room, two other men, Edgar and Vernon, both widowers (the former had Lupus, the latter a bad ticker) were having a rollicking game of checkers. They looked like embalmed corpses.

There was one female in the room.

Margaret.

She had been incarcerated at Sunnydale about six months ago. A petite, slender widow, Margaret was about as good-looking as they came at her age, which he guessed to be around eighty. (He had heard from Bernice, who was always catty about other women, that poor Margaret had been barren, and no children would ever visit her, as if theirs did.)

The trim widow had been friendly to Henry, but pretty much stayed in her apartment, cooking her own meals (smart lady) instead of partaking in the "sumptuous" food provided by Sunnydale's non-hair-net-wearing cooking staff.

Margaret was setting up the Scrabble board on a card table in the corner of the room opposite the blaring television. She noticed Henry and smiled invitingly, showing lovely white teeth.

Henry felt a jolt of electricity shoot up his spine from his loins, and he made a beeline toward her as fast as his bum leg and squeaky walker would let him.

"Hello, Henry," Margaret said warmly, gazing up at him with velvety blue eyes that twinkled like stars in a midnight sky.

The board game with its many alphabet pieces was spread out on the table before her like a tribal wooden offering.

"Margaret," he replied with a slight nod of his head.

"Oh, please...call me Maggie."

"All right, then. Maggie."

She certainly was a looker, with soft silver hair

done up in a French twist.

"Would you like to play with me?" she asked with an impish smile on painted Betty-Boop lips.

What a humdinger!

"Okay," Henry said. He set his walker alongside the table next to her three-pronged cane and lowered himself into a folding chair.

"Do you remember how to...do it?" she asked, cocking her head coyishly to look at him.

Was the woman talking about Scrabble or something more suggestive? Or was his love-starved mind working overtime?

He decided to feel her out. "It has been a while," he said, carefully choosing his words, "but I think it'll come back to me."

"If you do it with me it will," she responded. Then asked, "Were you any good at it?"

Now he was sure she was flirting with him, the little minx.

Across the room, the TV erupted as someone made a touchdown.

Henry made his own forward pass, hoping to score. "Well, Maggie," he said slyly, "how good I am at it depends on my partner."

She seemed to find his answer amusing; a smile tickled her cupie-doll mouth.

"I think, Henry," Maggie replied, "I'd like to find out just how good you are."

She divided up the alphabet pieces, and announced, "You go first."

Henry studied his wooden squares, and after a moment, spelled out the word ROMANCE, in the center of the board.

Maggie immediately used the "E" from his word and went upward to make CUDDLE.

Then he took a "D" and spelled DALLY.

As their supply of letters dwindled, the words got more risqué, and they giggled like two kids discovering their body parts were different.

So, Henry was surprised when Maggie suddenly announced that she wanted to quit. And she reached out and disturbed all the pieces.

He thought they were having fun. Had he gone too far and offended her?

As Maggie stood and retrieved her three-footed cane, a disappointed Henry struggled to his feet.

"I'm going back to my room," she told him.

"Okay."

"That's room one-ten."

"Uh-huh."

"Maybe you'd like to visit me sometime. Say, tonight after midnight?"

She gave him a wicked wink, leaving a shocked Henry standing, in more ways than one.

At a little before midnight, Henry was in the cramped bathroom of his so-called apartment.

Bernice was next door in her bedroom, sound asleep. He could hear her through the thin wall, snoring to beat the band.

He'd just taken a shower, and shaved, and was rooting around in the medicine cabinet trying to find a bottle of cologne that he remembered one of the children had given him a few years ago for his birthday.

He finally located the bottle, still in its wrapper, beneath the bathroom sink. He opened the lid and sniffed. The cologne smelled okay, so he dabbed a little behind his ears.

Then Henry put the toilet seat down and sat and removed the tags on a new jogging outfit (Christmas; another of his children) which he'd never felt compelled to wear – he couldn't exactly go jogging.

Dressed, he returned to the mirror for a final inspection, feeling as giddy as he had on his first date, when he took a girl (not Bernice) smooching at a drive-in.

Satisfied with his appearance (he thought he looked more like seventy-three than eighty-three) Henry shut off the bathroom light. Holding onto the wall in the dark, dragging his left foot, he slowly made his way to the front door where his hotrod of a walker awaited him.

The walker looked a little beat-up; there were dings in the chrome, and the tread on the wheels was worn. He made a mental note to buy a newer model, one that went faster.

Quietly, cautiously, he opened the door and peered out into the hallway.

The dimly lit corridor was empty. Henry knew from past insomniac nights that the nurse on duty, the thin one, would be taking a cigarette break about now. He would have to shake a leg (and a bum one at that) to get to Maggie's room in the opposite corridor, before the broad got back.

Henry cursed his paralyzed limb, and the squeaking wheels of the walker. With every step, the hallway seemed to stretch on farther and farther, and he wondered if he should give up and turn back.

But the thought of spending time alone with the lovely Maggie spurred him on.

If you're not going to work, he told his left leg, *at least stay out of my way!*

A man on a mission, Henry was moving quicker now than he ever believed he could.

He passed the dining room, then the empty nurse's station on his right, and finally the recreation center on his left. He was entering the opposite corridor, when a voice boomed behind him, nearly giving poor Henry a heart attack.

"Hey, pops! Where do you think you're going?"

Clutching the walker, Henry turned his head to see Leroy, the security guard, approach. Big and burly and about as dim as the hall lighting, Leroy usually slept the night away in the staff's room.

Henry's squeaky wheels must have awakened him.

"I said," Leroy repeated, "where do you think you're going?"

"My apartment?"

Leroy smirked. "Which is? Or do you even know, old man?"

Henry counted on Leroy not knowing.

"Uh...one ten."

"Well, all right then, let's get going." The guard grabbed Henry roughly by one arm, propelling him and his walker along.

"Now stay in there," Leroy warned, depositing Henry in front of Maggie's door. "Or I'll report you." He poked Henry's chest. "Get it?"

"Got it," Henry replied with a smile as Leroy turned on his heels.

Henry opened the door and guided his walker inside.

The living room was pitch black and very quiet.

He frowned. Shouldn't there be a lamp on?

He had pictured Maggie, on his long journey down the corridor, waiting for him seductively on the couch, music playing softly from somewhere.

He felt foolish. Had he misunderstood her invitation? As his eyes grew accustomed to the darkness, he noticed a flickering of light coming from the open doorway of the single bedroom. It seemed to beckon him.

Excitement replaced apprehension, and Henry parked his walker next to Maggie's three-pronged cane in the entryway.

Carefully, he headed toward the shaft of light, but immediately bumped into an end table.

"Henry?" a feeble voice called out from the bedroom.

"Yes. It's me."

He moved forward again more cautiously, and at last arrived at the open door.

Maggie was in bed, propped up by several plump pillows; she was wearing a pink nightgown with lace trim, her shoulder-length silver hair caressing her shoulders.

A lavender colored candle burned on the nightstand, emitting a scent of lilacs. Maggie looked lovely in its soft, flickering light.

Henry stood awkwardly in the doorway, a nervous bridegroom on his wedding night.

"Come here," Maggie said with a reassuring smile. "You must be tired." She patted the bedspread next to her.

He approached and tentatively sat on the bed.

She leaned toward him and gently pushed him

back against the pillows, then snuggled up to him. They stayed that way for a while, Maggie with her head on his shoulder, Henry on his back, one arm around her, watching the shadow of the candle's flame lick the ceiling.

Henry closed his eyes, enjoying the warmth of her body and the fresh smell of her hair.

He might have fallen asleep, he wasn't sure, but the next thing Henry felt was Maggie's soft small hand beneath his jogging shirt, massaging his chest. Then her hand moved slowly downward, and he stiffened, yes, in more ways than one.

She began to caress his manhood, and Henry moaned with pleasure.

Then she tugged his slacks down and when she took him into her warm, wet mouth, Henry gasped.

He couldn't believe what was happening!

Once, when he turned fifty, he begged Bernice to do such a thing, and she grudgingly agreed. But after a few minutes, Henry asked her to stop.

Too much teeth.

Now Maggie stopped.

Henry lifted on his elbows to give Maggie an appreciative smile; it was more than he had hoped for, and he was thankful for however brief she serviced him.

But to his surprise (and delight!) Maggie turned away, then set her dentures on the nightstand, and returning to pleasing Henry, even better than before.

Henry lay back in ecstasy. No teeth at all!

Later, entwined in each other's arms, Henry said, "Our lovemaking was a little one-sided tonight, my darling."

She kissed his cheek. "Giving you pleasure, Henry, gives me pleasure. That's all I care about."

Henry smiled broadly.

Why couldn't all women be like Maggie?

By the end of the week, Henry could scoot down to Maggie's room (with the help of a brand-new walker) in half the amount of time it took him that first night. And to his amazement, his left leg was responding to all the exercise; he could even lead with it a little.

Maggie, he discovered on their second night together, had retained a nice firm body, breasts soft and round and hardly droopy at all. Oh, sure, there was some sagging here and there, a little tummy, some varicose veins...but who cared? She was a goddess compared to Bernice, who was becoming a growing problem in his mind with each passing day. He wished he was married to Maggie, instead.

While Maggie seemed to enjoy a bit of tomfoolery, she preferred to give Henry oral sex.

Who was he to argue?

On their eighth night together, however, he found Maggie sobbing in her bedroom. By the light of the lavender candle, she showed him a letter from her attorney that said her funds were depleted and she would have to leave the nursing home by the end of the month.

Seated on the edge of the bed, Henry held her until she had quieted down.

"I won't let you go," he said firmly.

"You have no choice," she sniffled. "I have no one...no other funds..."

"Hell, I'll pay for your room here."

Maggie shook her head, silver hair moving in gentle arches. "Your family would never allow it."

He realized that Maggie was right. His children handled their estate, paid all the bills. They would never understand his feelings for another woman.

"Oh, Henry," Maggie moaned, "just when I've found true love." She began to cry again. "What will become of me?"

Henry clutched her tighter. "I'll think of something."

"But what?"

He kissed her tear-stained cheek. "I'll divorce Bernice and marry you, my sweet."

Maggie pulled away from him.

"Then how much money will you have?" she asked. "Enough for Bernice, *and* you and me?"

Henry thought about that. "No," he admitted, lowering his head. "There's barely enough for her and me."

"But...if she was gone..."

Henry straightened. "What do you mean?"

"I mean...I meant...*when* she is gone," Maggie said, moving closer, putting her arms around Henry, "would there be enough money for you and me?"

Henry nodded numbly.

Maggie sighed. "Well, maybe something will happen to her...before the month is out."

"Yes," he said, her words sinking in, taking root. "You never know..."

Maggie smiled and wiped away her tears. Then she made love to him on the bed.

The next day, while Bernice was watching TV, Henry stayed in his bedroom, thinking of ways she could "accidentally" pass away.

He lay on the bed, hands behind his head, elbows splayed out, his mind racing with possibilities.

The first idea that came to Henry was that his wife could expire from taking too much of her rheumatoid arthritis medication. The staff at Sunnydale was always making stupid mistakes when it came to administering the resident's prescriptions, and an accidental overdose could easily be blamed on them. But unfortunately, he realized, Bernice took charge of her own medicine, rather than pay the extra cost of having a nurse tend to her daily.

It would seem highly unlikely his wife would make such a blunder on her own.

And even if she did happen to take too much medication, how much would be enough to kill her? The last thing Henry wanted was for Bernice to become a comatose vegetable, needing round the clock care, running through their money even faster.

Henry stared at the ceiling.

What if, he thought, she fell in the tub, cracked her head, and drowned? He could probably make that happen. But then, Bernice always took a shower, sitting on a silly little stool, while she sponged herself off.

If he whacked her from behind with, say, his heavy orthopedic shoe, someone might question why the drain was closed allowing the tub to fill up.

Henry sighed; this wasn't going to be easy.

By mid-evening, when he still hadn't come up with a plan, a frustrated Henry went into his wife's bedroom to say good-night to her as he usually did.

She was asleep already, on her back, snoring loudly, laboredly.

He thought, *Someone should put her out of her misery,* and that was when the solution came to him.

Henry remembered that movie about a nuthouse where one of the inmates suffocated Jack Nicholson with a pillow because Nicholson had part of his brain taken away.

It occurred to Henry that Bernice had only half of a brain these days. She was no good to anyone, not him or even herself. She was just a decomposing body taking up space.

And hadn't she told him she wanted to stay at Sunnydale until her dying day? He would give Bernice her wish.

Henry took the extra pillow on the bed, placed it over his wife's face, and pressed down firmly.

She struggled a bit. But Henry was strong, and after a few minutes her body went limp.

He kept the pillow in place for a while longer, just to be sure. Then he removed it.

Her face had already turned blue.

He checked for a pulse in her neck and found none.

Satisfied that she was gone, Henry turned her over so that she was face-down into one of the pillows, making it look like she had smothered in her sleep.

In the morning, he would discover her body, and react with the appropriate sadness, though no such emotion touched him even remotely now.

He left the bedroom, closing the door behind him.

Was it so wrong to want a little bit of happiness in the waning years of his life?

Henry didn't think so.

Maggie lit the scented candle on the nightstand. It was a little before midnight and she expected Henry to be along soon. She fluffed up the pillows and lay back in bed, pulling the white sheet up modestly around her nude body.

Maggie was proud of her figure. She weighed nearly the same at age eighty-one that she had at eighteen, a trim ninety-five pounds. What other woman her age could boast such a thing who wasn't dying of some disease or other?

She was happy that Henry found her attractive and wanted to marry her. She desperately needed someone to take care of her, now that financial ruin was at hand.

Henry just had to come through for her. Otherwise, she would be moved to the county home, which was little more than a snake pit.

Before Henry, Maggie had tried to attract some of the other men at Sunnydale, easier prey because they were already widowers; but none of them could be lured by sex. Edgar was afraid that he might have a heart attack; Vernon, she found out after nearly dislocating her jaw, was impotent.

But Henry, oh Henry...*he* was interested in sex. (She, herself, had been dead down there since menopause.)

Maggie didn't mind giving Henry, or any man, sex, as long as it led somewhere. After she hooked Henry, however, she would soon put a stop to his active libido.

Maggie heard him out in the living room, and after a moment, he appeared in the doorway.

Even by the faint light of the candle, she could see that his face was flushed.

"Henry? What is it?"

He came to the bed and gathered her in his arms.

"Maggie, will you marry me?" he asked, his breath coming in quick, sharp spurts.

"You know I would, Henry," she told him, caressing his face with one hand, "if you were free."

He smiled conspiratorially. "I *am* free, my darling."

"You...you mean...?"

"Yes. She's dead."

"But...but how?"

"It would be better if you didn't know the details," he replied.

Maggie nodded slowly. "Yes, I agree."

She had already thought about what she would do if things went awry. After all, she never asked Henry directly to kill his wife. He came to that decision on his own.

Maggie would tell the authorities that he had become obsessed with her, like in one of those cable TV movies, and came to her room and forced her to have sex. If she told anyone, he'd said, he would kill her.

Anyway, some such story.

Henry kissed her full on the mouth, his tongue tickling hers, and she pretended to respond.

When their lips parted, she asked sweetly, "Would you like me to...?" Her hand slipped inside his pants.

"No. Tonight, I want to make love to you."

"All right, Henry." She would provide the appropriate oooh's and aaah's this time.

Henry mounted her, and she moaned accordingly.

But she was so tight and dry that intercourse was painful. And Henry was so damn heavy!

That was why she preferred giving him head (what

a disgusting way of putting it), which was no more bothersome than sucking on a big thumb until some tiny bit of goo oozed out, that she couldn't taste now-adays, anyway.

She used the time to think about other, more pleasant things, like what her life would be like with money.

Henry was grinding away on top off her, working himself up into a sweat. Each thrust seemed to knock the wind out of Maggie, and she lay still, hoping the end would come soon.

Then at last it came, Henry shuddered and collapsed.

"Henry? Could you please get off?" she said, finding it difficult to speak. "You're hurting me."

But Henry didn't move, remaining sprawled on top of her.

Maggie was sure he was dead, and panic set in. She struggled to get out from under him. But he was too heavy for her small, frail body, pinning her down like a big fallen tree.

Her breathing became short and labored. She could not cry out. She felt soon that her lungs would collapse under the crush of Henry's lifeless body.

With her last orgasmic breaths, Maggie watched the candle's white flame flickering on the bedroom ceiling, shadows dancing there, swaying romantically.

LOVE NEST
Barbara Collins and Max Allan Collins

The name's Sam Knight, and if you never heard of me, don't worry about it, you will. At least, if my daughter Becky, and don't *you* ever call her that, has her way.

And Becky usually gets her way.

Sure, I've done a few jobs over the years that caught some press attention, the most sordid of which was a wife-killed-husband-for-his-money number that got me written up in *People*. But what the hell kind of gauge is that? That article drummed up more crank phone calls than business.

But to hear Becky, Rebecca, talk, you'd think I was Mike Hammer. And let me tell you, there are differences between me and Mike Hammer. First, I've fired a gun, on the job, a grand total of twice. Never killed a man in my life, a proud record I hope to maintain.

Second, Mike Hammer gets laid once in a while.

Becky's my only child. I wanted a son, and it looks like I finally got my wish: my little girl has grown up into a goddamn businessman.

Not that I'm not proud of her, and not that I'm not relieved she got her brains from her mother. The only thing she got from me was some college money, and you don't want to know what those fancy-ass degrees of hers cost me.

We'd never been too close, which is my fault, no question. So, I was surprised when she showed up on my doorstep last Christmas after being fired from that company she worked for in Minneapolis. I was proud of her, though, for not putting up with those conniving bastards.

They had tried to get her to use information culled from one client to the advantage of another, better-paying client.

"That's not my idea of ethics," she had said grandly.

"In my game," I told her, nodding, "you treat a client like a priest treats a confessor."

She seemed to like the sound of that as much as I liked the sound of a word like "ethics" coming from her.

Anyway, we sat around the kitchen table, me mostly keeping my mouth shut, her yakking, trying to figure out what she was going to do...

She kept mentioning needing a product, something she could use her experience, her know-how, to market herself. I bobbed my head up and down, like I knew what the hell she was talking about but was just trying to give her a little support. Little late for me to act like a father, but I guess till the final whistle blows, you're still in the game.

Then she had looked at me with her mother's big brown eyes, and said that I'd never realized my full potential, never taken advantage of my reputation. That I could be that "product" she was looking for.

"Is that what I am to you?" I asked her. "A potential 'product'? A Popiel Pocket Fisherman for the '90s?"

That stopped her cold; she didn't say a word, but the look on her face was so damn pitiful.

I'd slapped her once, when she was little, for some terrible infraction, like spilling a soft drink or dropping a jam-covered spoon. She hadn't cried. What was she, ten? She'd just looked at me quaveringly with a hurt that had nothing to do with pain.

I had never hit her again, no matter how deeply drowning in my cups I was.

But now here she was, all grown up, giving me that same quaveringly hurt look.

Maybe I saw this as a shot at reconciliation. A chance to be there for her, when I hadn't been while she was growing up, when I was too busy working and drinking and running around on her mother. She was out of the house by the time I cleaned up my act. At least her mother, God rest her soul, had a few good years with a sober, faithful husband.

But as a father to the little girl she'd been, and to this would-be big businesswoman she'd grown up into, I stunk.

So, before the whistle blew, I figured I better go along with her, and her half-baked scheme. Only I was underestimating my daughter; her scheme was fully baked, all right.

Six months ago, I closed the office over on Sixth and University where I'd been for twenty years, and we moved into a pretentious marble tombstone of a building downtown, where the rent is about equal to my total billings last year.

But I'll be damned if we aren't making a go of it.

She hired a secretary, a heavy-set woman with no sense of humor and the face of Ernest Borgnine (I had interviewed just the right blonde for the job, but Becky said overweight women were often prejudiced against), and a computer nerd, and two inexperienced minority graduates from Drake University. All of whom, including Ms. Borgnine, are doing a hell of a job.

Becky knows how to run a business, all right. But she doesn't know jack shit about the detective game.

Me, I'm mostly a figurehead, putting in a cameo appearance each day before hitting the rubber-chicken circuit. Otherwise, you can find me at Barney's Pub, watching ESPN on the big screen, pretending an O'Doul's is a real beer.

My big bitch with Becky is this snobbish attitude she has about who our clientele should be, not wanting to "deal with trivial matters."

"People don't come to private detectives for 'trivial' reasons," I said.

"We don't want to deal with people," Becky said. "We want to deal with corporations."

Becky, like most liberals, has great compassion for the masses and complete contempt for individual human beings.

I thought it was time she learned what our business was really about, flesh-and-blood people with problems that need solving, not bottom lines or high profiles or market shares.

So, yesterday, after I'd come back from Barney's to discover she was out getting a perm, I took just the sort of case she would have turned her turned-up nose at.

The sort of case that would really curl her hair.

Rebecca Knight is the name, though it's unlikely you've ever heard of me. But it's a safe bet you've heard of Sam Knight - my father.

The Satariano case? The Hollingsworth murder trial? The Sniper of Keo Way? Any of those ring a bell?

I thought as much. After all, *People* magazine called him "the most famous real-life Sam Spade alive." Recently we've gone into business together, operating Knight and Associates out of an elegant modern marble Art-Deco building in downtown Des Moines. It's highrise and high rent, but then so is the profile it provides.

You may be thinking I'm using my father's reputation to make a name for myself. Wrong. Following in my father's flatfoot-steps was never an ambition of mine. For one thing, I wear a size six, and for another, neither Dad nor Nancy Drew was my role model.

I'm strictly a businesswoman, BA from the University of Iowa, MBA from the University of Minnesota. I held a position in marketing at a prestigious Minneapolis corporation (which shall remain nameless for legal reasons), but a year ago I resigned, I got tired of being verbally pawed by sexists and bumping up against the glass ceiling.

On a holiday visit home, I told my father I'd quit, and that what I really wanted was to go into business for myself, to be my *own* boss. I had the skills, and the background; all I needed was the right product to promote.

Imagine my surprise when Dad suggested that *he* should be the "product!"

Still, stunned as I was, I could immediately see the potential. We would capitalize on *his* reputation and *my* business skills, and turn a rundown, antiquated one-man operation into a state-of-the-art thriving investigative firm!

That was six months ago. Dad moved out of his tiny office in a distressed section of town, and we moved into our suite of offices at towering 801 Grand. I hired a receptionist, a computer whiz, a couple of top-flight young investigators.

I run the day-to-day operations. Dad's in the office a couple of hours each day, but mostly he's out in the field, or drumming up business. And I've listed him with a speaker's bureau, so he's often out giving nostalgic talks about his big cases before the Kiwanis and other business groups.

Our biggest area of disagreement (politics doesn't count) is the direction of the business. *I* feel the greatest percentage of our cases should come from the many nationally prominent insurance companies situated here in Iowa's capital city. The work is steady, clean, and lucrative.

But *he* seems to feel that just about any financially or emotionally impaired person that might wander through our doors deserves our immediate and full attention.

Which is why we're barely speaking right now.

It was the middle of the afternoon when I returned to the office after a very successful meeting with the CEO of Mutual Insurance. Coming out of our glass door was a woman with long stringy blond hair. I guessed her age to be about thirty. Her face was pretty, but hard; the kind of hard a woman gets from too much smoking or drinking or both. She wore torn cut-off jeans and a tight polka-dot top with the shoulders cut out; the outfit might have been cute on someone younger and thinner.

The woman looked right at me, yet through me, then disappeared down the hall.

Inside, I asked Evie, our receptionist, "Who was that?"

"A new client," she answered, fingers clicking on the keyboard.

"That was a *client*? Of *ours*?"

Evie stopped typing and looked up at me. "According to your father," she said, arching an eyebrow. Then she shrugged and returned to her work.

I turned and marched down the carpeted corridor to his office.

He was lying on the couch, shoes off, crossed feet in well-worn socks, a cigarette in one hand, ashes dotting the front of his not-so-white shirt, reading the sports section of the *Des Moines Register*.

"I'm back," I said, forcibly cheerful.

"Oh...ah...hello, Pumpkin," my father said. He sat up on the couch, ashes and newspapers falling to the floor.

Pumpkin? He never calls me that.

I narrowed my eyes.

He cleared his throat. "I took on a new client while

you were gone," he told me, "and..." He stopped and sniffed the air. "You get a perm again?"

"Never mind," I said irritably. "I want to hear about this client."

He gestured for me to sit next to him on the couch, but I remained standing.

"Look," he explained, "I just couldn't turn the poor kid down..."

"Poor is right. And she hasn't been a 'kid' since *Mary Tyler Moore* wasn't a rerun."

His eyes flared, a hint of the rage he could summon that I remembered all too well from childhood. He was doing his best to keep it in check when he said, "Damnit, Becky, when are you going to realize this business isn't just about money?"

"Okay. Fine. Just please tell me this isn't a marital surveillance job."

He began putting on his shoes, brown Florsheim wingtips. "The folder's on the desk with a picture of the husband," he said.

I sighed. "Well, it's your time."

He was standing now, reaching for his coat on the back of the couch. "She insisted the surveillance start tonight," he went on, "and, unfortunately, you've got me speaking to some damn PLO or PEO club this evening."

"What?" I was beginning to smell a rat, a big one in Florsheim shoes. "So, you'll cancel the talk," I suggested.

Snugging his tie, a Nichole Miller print I'd given him last Christmas, he stopped to look at me. "And disappoint a bunch of little old ladies who are dying to meet me?" he asked. "Now how would that look?"

He paused, then added. "Word'll get around your 'product' is unreliable."

He was making me furious. I said, "Then put one of the other investigators on the surveillance!"

My father shook his head. "They're both working overtime on that embezzlement case that goes to court next week, *you* know that." His expression turned conciliatory, and he patted my shoulder. "Everything you'll need is in the folder."

"But..."

"See you tomorrow, Pumpkin," he smiled, going out the door, doing that magic trick every card-carrying parent can perform so well.

"*Da - ad!*" I whined, turning me back into a five-year-old.

I was not happy, hiding in my car in the parking lot of a country-western bar on Euclid. Still in my jacket and skirt from work, I was feeling grungy, even if they were Armani.

It was almost midnight, and the bar, Heartthrob, had stayed busy all evening, the tuneless, twanging music from inside leeching out every time someone entered or left the dilapidated building, men and women of all shapes and sizes in country-style apparel that seemed more like costumes than clothing, looking for a little laughter, a little love, a little lust...

Tired, I leaned back against the headrest and closed my eyes. In my mind I could see the photo "our" client had given us of her husband and herself.

His name was Lyle. He was tall, muscular, confident, with sandy hair and a charismatic, if smirky, grin. The wife's name was Mary, and she was smiling at him, obviously in love, one arm around his waist, a little too tight, as if she instinctively knew how hard it would be holding onto this one. Still, if the picture had appeared in a tabloid, the caption would have read, *In happier times.*

But I wondered if there really had been any happier times for her, or simply the illusion of it, because she'd always been afraid of losing him to someone taller, thinner, prettier...

I opened my eyes, and he was standing just outside the door to the bar, kissing the neck of a woman who looked a lot like his wife.

Only taller, thinner, prettier.

I shrank behind the wheel of my Buick, an unwilling, embarrassed voyeur, as the two pawed at each other, doing a drunken mating dance, like some kind of new country two-step, until suddenly he grabbed her roughly by the hand and pulled her toward his truck.

They got in the cab of the black Chevy, and I was wondering if they were going to stay in there all night, when he started the engine and pulled out of the parking lot.

I followed him, as I had earlier when he'd gotten off work at Kafer Welding Company.

We were traveling east on Euclid, when he moved into an outer lane to catch interstate 35 going north. I groaned. Couldn't they settle for a motel in the city?

A few miles on the other side of Ankeny, a small community north of Des Moines, the truck turned off onto a secondary road and headed east. We'd been driving for an endless half an hour.

Ten minutes later, he swerved onto a gravel road

and I ate his dust for another five, when suddenly the dust vanished and along with it, the truck.

I panicked and slammed on my brakes, stopping in the middle of the road; everything ahead was dark and still. Driving forward again, I passed a small clapboard farmhouse that sat near the road on my left, and saw the Chevy parked down the short dirt lane. I went on by. About a mile further on the gravel road, I turned around and doubled back, headlights out.

Slowly, I pulled up alongside the mailbox on the road in front of the farm house, which was partially obstructed from view by a thin row of scraggly pines.

There was no name on the box, just numbers.

I turned off the car and got out a small steno pad and pen from the glove compartment and wrote the address down, then recorded the county road numbers we'd taken, so I could remember how to get back to Des Moines. It was getting stuffy in the car, so I hit the button and eased my window down.

A cool night breeze wafted in, instantly revitalizing me from my sleepy state. I looked through the rustling pines toward the house. A front room light was on. The back was dark.

I was sure, in the morning, I'd find out the house was rented by Lyle. *A safe, easy love nest to bring his dates,* I thought.

My hand was on the ignition key when I heard a loud thump from the direction of the house. The noise was more than a door slamming. Like a piece of furniture being over-turned.

I sat still. The sounds of whispering pines and squeaking bugs returned, and my hand went back to the ignition key.

Before I could turn it, a muffled scream shattered the solitude.

I froze. It was a woman, and she was *not* crying out in ecstasy...

I didn't know what to do; unlike my father, I don't carry a firearm. All I had was a flashlight in the glove compartment, and I grabbed it as a feeble form of protection and slid silently out of the Buick.

A three-quarter moon hung in the sky, showing me the way as I hurried down the dirt lane. Approaching the side of the house I could see that the back bedroom window was open, flashes of white lace curtains fluttering against the screen in the breeze. The room itself was dark.

Looking inside, I didn't dare use the flashlight. I could make out, from light from another room, a bed with its rumpled sheets, a dresser, and an overturned nightstand, with the lamp on its side on the floor.

My attention was drawn to noises now coming from somewhere else in the house: a man's angry voice. Presumably, my client's husband...

I moved along the clapboard to a side front window. It was closed, shade drawn, but there was light behind it. The sides of the cheap, plastic shade had curled from exposure to the sun and heat, and that allowed me to peek inside.

She was tied in a wooden chair, in the kitchen, hands behind her back, wearing just panties and a bra, head hung, blonde hair covering her face.

He was standing before her, in jeans sans shirt, yelling, shaking a butcher knife at the woman. I couldn't hear what he was saying, but I didn't have to be a trained lip-reader to make out his mouth forming words like "bitch" and "whore."

I stepped back from the window, mouth hanging open. This was more than a simple one-night stand. This was a guy with a real attitude problem. And this was a special kind of love nest, the kind with bodies buried in the basement. I glanced toward my Buick, thinking of the car phone, but by the time help could get here it would be too late.

Retracing my steps to the bedroom window, I pushed on the old screen and it popped inward, onto the floor, and I hitched my skirt up and climbed in. I moved through the dark bedroom, toward the light of the kitchen, then down a short narrow hallway, hugging the wall.

Lyle was still shouting at her, but now pacing back and forth.

"Who the *fuck* do you think you are!" he yelled; knife gripped in one hand. Beyond him I could see the poor woman, motionless, head hung, apparently unconscious.

Lyle halted in front of her, his back to the hallway. "I have to decide what to do with you," he growled.

I had already decided what to do with him. I lurched forward and slugged Lyle on the side of his head with my flashlight as hard as I could.

He stiffened, and for one horrifying moment I thought he might just rub his skull, turn, and look at me with a scowl; but then his legs went out from under him, the knife tumbling from his hand, and he went down, rattling the floor boards, and lay still.

I let out a big quavering breath of air I'd been holding for the past few minutes. My knees were knocking, but I ran to the woman and untied her hands, which were bound with the western blouse I'd seen her in earlier.

She moaned a little, and lifted her head, and her face was swollen and bruised.

"Who...who are you?" she asked.

I told her I was a private investigator hired to follow the jerk who just tried to kill her.

"Oh" was all she said.

After finding a dish towel on the kitchen counter, I went over to the unconscious Lyle, got on my knees, and began tying his hands behind his back with the cloth. I was wondering what to use to bind his legs, when out of the corner of my eye I saw the woman rise out of the chair and stoop to pick up the knife.

Maybe it was her somnolent state, which I had attributed to shock, or maybe it was the look in her eyes, cold and so very dead, but the hair on the back of my neck stood up.

Still on my knees by the fallen Lyle, I sat back on my haunches.

She approached me slowly with the knife in one hand, held down by her side.

"I'm grateful you saved me," she said, with a small, haunted smile, "but I'm afraid I don't have any choice..."

Now, the blade in her hand went up, poised over her head, and I pushed off with my legs as the knife came swishing down, glinting in the kitchen light, and I lunged with both of my hands at her arm, twisting it around her back. And three hundred and twenty dollars of karate lessons went out the window as I threw myself on her, bringing her down on the floor, lying on top of the woman like I was a beached whale, my

fingernails digging into her wrist, feeling the weapon
come loose in her hand.

I didn't know why she said what she'd said, or did
what she'd done, and I wasn't about to discuss it. I had
the knife now, and I grabbed the western blouse that
had been discarded nearby and tied her hands behind
her back with it again. She lay sobbing on the floor.

There wasn't a phone, so I went out the front
door and hurried down the short dirt lane to use
the one in my car.

A figure stepped out of the darkness.

I shrieked and jumped a mile.

"I've already called the police," my father said.

I stared at him.

"How long have you been here?" I demanded.

"A while."

My mouth fell open. "And you did *nothing?!*"

"You handled yourself just fine," he said.

"I could have been *killed!*" I screamed at him.
"Why didn't you *help* me?"

He put both hands on my shoulders and looked me
right in the eye. "Because I won't always be there to
help you, Pumpkin," he said softly.

And I leaned my head against his chest and wept.

Sam Knight's the name, though you've probably never heard of me. But I'll bet you've heard of *Rebecca*
Knight, my daughter.

People magazine said Becky was "fearless, in the
face of a female mass murderer," and that she was "a
new breed of woman detective, with brains, brawn
and beauty." Now, that's some kind of gauge!

Just why "The Cut-Throat Cowgirl," so dubbed

by the media, felt the need to lure men to her rented farmhouse and slit their throats is beyond me. That's for the shrinks to discover. But you can bet ol' Lyle will think twice before picking up another female.

Becky's head's gotten a little big lately, with all the publicity. So what. Let her have her moment. I haven't had the heart to tell her I was in the hallway with my gun that night.

I'm proud of my daughter.

And when she reads this, she'll finally know.

AMAZING GRACE
Max Allan Collins

Grace Rushmore, at eighty, seemed aptly named to those who knew her well. She surely did move with an easy grace; years ago, when she and husband Lem were courting, her dancing particularly suited her name, her movements as fluid as a gentle stream, as lovely as she wasn't.

But those who only knew Grace in her later years, which had begun really around age forty, saw a skinny, sunken-cheeked old woman right out of Grant Wood's *American Gothic*, her countenance severe, her words rare, and perhaps the most graceful things about her, to those who knew her from a distance, was how uncomplainingly hard she worked, how well she had raised the four children who survived (of the ten she'd carried), and how nobly she'd tolerated Lem and his reprobate ways.

In 1909, when Lem had come calling, she already

looked like the old maid she seemed destined to become. Lemuel Richard Rushmore had been tall and handsome, tall enough that her bony, lanky frame next to him didn't seem so odd, though he was much too good-looking for her, people had whispered from the start. But no one was surprised by the union, nonetheless.

After all, Grace's father was Jonathan Holding, one of the most prosperous farmers in Polk County, Iowa, and Lem's bad reputation had preceded him. Like Grace, Lem was thirty and unmarried. He had been arrested for stealing horses three times and convicted once, doing a year in the county jail, a sentence her Baptist father considered unduly lenient. Lem was a rounder, it was said, a man married only to drink but whose good looks and easy charm had brought him plenty of female affection, unmarried and married alike.

But what a smile Lem had. He was fun, and he was funny, and he wouldn't hurt a fly. People just *liked* him. Even Papa had come to be fond of him, particularly after Lem sat in the parlor, hat in hands, and promised he had changed his ways and wanted only to settle down, have a family, and work hard. He'd never farmed but was eager to learn.

They had married in 1910, and now it was 1960. Fifty years had passed that had only felt like one hundred. Not all of it was bad, though. Lem was kind to her, in his way. Brought her flowers on birthdays and anniversaries, though not always on the days themselves. He was good to her children, giving them candy and winning their love, and leaving the spanking to her. She never was as loved by her offspring as Lem was.

His looks had left him by his fifties. His hair had long since turned white and his handsome face became a bucket-headed exaggeration of itself, like something a State Fair caricature artist drew. The tall frame grew a pot belly – beer will do that, and a lot of beer will *really* do that – and his nose spread and reddened.

He never did pitch in at the farm in any way. Sort of pretended to for a while, but not for long. Instead he hung out in the pool rooms of nearby Des Moines and at various saloons and houses of ill repute. After their tenth child died, Lem never bothered trying to have relations with her. She was relieved, because he had bouts of what he called "the French disease," which had played a role in all those miscarriages, the doctors said.

In these fifty years, rewards had been few and far between for Grace. But Lem was pleasant, even kind, called her "Sweet Thing" even now. Just like when they sat on her papa's front porch in the swing and he held her hand and smiled at her. The smile was still nice, thanks to those fancy dentures she'd bought him.

The farm was run by others, since Papa died during the second war and money was coming in. Not as much as Lem would have liked, and he had encouraged Grace to use her skills in the kitchen to bring in a little more.

She, in particular, had a sweet touch. She could have been a professional baker, Lem always said. They ought to sell the farm and buy a bakery in town and she could whip up those sweet delights, as he put it. Her specialty, what she was best known for, was wedding cakes. She had taken a course in town on decorating, uncovering a natural artistic knack for it, and the golden lemon-touched wedding cake with the delicious cream-cheese frosting was her claim to Polk County fame.

Some people said the only time she smiled was when a bride-to-be and her mother came to pick up their special cake, with its towering tiers, perfectly spaced and arranged like some castle in the sky. The happy clients would *oooh* and *aaah* and a tiny smile would etch itself on Grace's grooved, deep-cheeked face.

She knew this because girl friends at church (girls in their seventies and eighties like her) would tease her about it.

"You should smile *more*, Gracie," they'd say.

"You're so pretty when you smile," they'd lie.

But what did she have to smile about?

Really, though, when she thought about it, she had plenty to smile about. Four lovely children, grown and successful, Robert and Lucas and Jennifer and Beth, all married, generating twelve grandchildren and two great grandchildren so far. Not a bum in the batch. No carousers. No loose women.

When she thought about this in church, which she frequently did (Lem accompanying her on Christmas and Easter only), she knew that her brood turning out so well was a miracle.

And she would bow her head and thank God.

Only her oldest, Beth, lived in the area. The others would be coming from hither and yon. That was so very exciting, contemplating it. Not in many years had the entire clan been under one roof. Each little family had its own Christmas traditions, though her kids always made sure one of them brought their family to the big old farmhouse to spend a few days at the holidays with Grandma and Grandpa. Great Grandma and Great Grandpa now, for the two little tykes of Beth's daughters.

Grace sat in the big cupboard-lined kitchen with Beth, who at forty-eight was quite attractive, if a little heavy, her features echoing her father's, before dissipation. She dressed rather severely, a black and gray suit with pink and gray pillbox hat today, since as a third-grade teacher flashy apparel was not appropriate. They drank hot tea and shared the frosted sugar cookies Grace usually only made at the holidays. This was just September, though, and the Golden Anniversary celebration was the closest thing to a holiday coming up.

In two weeks.

"Where's Pop?" Beth asked.

"At his job."

Lately, Lem had been bartending part-time in a little town nearby.

Beth's expression tightened. "I don't suppose there's any chance...nothing."

"What, dear?"

She sighed, summoned a smile. "Is there any chance we might keep him sober at the festivities?"

Grace lifted an eyebrow. "Doubtful. The punch won't be spiked, *that* much, I can promise you."

Her daughter glanced away, thoughtfully. "Maybe I could talk to him."

"Welcome to try."

Beth smiled. "You know, Lucy and Sam love Pop

to death."

"He's always been good with kids."

"Well, he's always *been* one, hasn't he?" She shook her head. "Mother, how have you managed it?"

"A day at a time."

"Well, of course, but...you've worked so *hard*." Beth paused. "That's something I wanted to talk to you about."

"What is, dear?"

She sat forward. "Jenny and Bob's Martha and Luke's Aggie and I...we all want to pitch in. We want to make the meal. No, no objections! You tell us what you want to have and just turn the kitchen over to us."

Grace was shaking her head. "Won't hear of it."

"No! Now, listen to me, you stubborn old girl. This is going to be *your day*. You have *earned* it! You let us in here, in your precious kitchen, and we'll wait on you and show you that the good cookin' you've demonstrated all these years was catching. We are darn *good* at it, too, thanks to you!"

Grace smiled a little. She could smile. A little. She said, "All right. I want ham and turkey and you'll use my stuffing recipe."

"Of course. You bet."

"Mashed potatoes, brown gravy, green beans *and* creamed corn. Corn muffins."

"Way ahead of you."

Grace raised a finger. "But one thing, *I'll* do the cake. It's my specialty. It's what I'm known for. I'll have it ready before I turn this torture chamber over to you girls. Understood?"

Beth was smiling, nodding. "Understood."

Grace cleaned the old house, every nook, every cranny. No one was staying with them; all her children with their families either went to a motel or bunked in with Beth who had a big, nice house in Des Moines. After all, the old homestead was terribly rundown, Grace knew, nothing she could do about it. But just the same, every bedroom would be spic and span.

For the three days before the 50th celebration, she cleaned like a woman possessed, washing windows, mopping floors, bending here, on tippy toes there, as graceful as the young woman she'd been, dancing. She hadn't been this happy in years. She barely noticed that Lem hadn't been around for three days. Not that such a thing was unusual. Benders, he called them. And he was taking penicillin, so that meant the houses of ill repute again.

Eighty years old and still a rounder.

She didn't get worried till the afternoon before the Big Day. She had spent all morning working on the cake, and it was a masterpiece, towering, tall, white with frosting filigree, guarding the secret of the moist, yellow cake within. Five tiers! The top tier a small cake for her and Lem to share.

She called every saloon she knew of, starting with the one where he sometimes worked. Then the pool halls. Finally, her children. Jenny and her husband and kids were already in Des Moines, with Beth. Nobody had seen Lem, but Jenny and Beth said they'd be over.

Beth, in a navy-blue suit with white trim, and Jenny, in a more colorful yellow and green frock, did not mention their father at first. Instead they gaped at the magnificent cake and clapped and laughed and sang their mother's praises. They were sincere enough, but still, she thought, trying too hard.

The cake was on the table like a confectionary centerpiece her well-honed cake knife at the ready; but her girls would have to settle for cookies and tea. The women sat at one end of the kitchen table, chattering about who was coming – *everyone!* – and how wonderful tomorrow would be.

Grace said, "I want to ask you something."

"Sure," Jenny said.

"Of course," Beth said.

Her face went to one daughter, then the other. "Why do love your father more?"

"What?" they both said, smiling in horror.

Both her girls leaned forward and put their hands on hers and looked at her intently, searching for tears that weren't there.

"Oh, Mother, don't be silly," Jenny said. "We love you *equally*."

Beth said nothing.

"It never felt that way," Grace said.

Silence took the room, leaving nothing but the fragrance left over from baking that cake.

Finally, Beth sighed. "We *did* love him more."

Jenny frowned at her sister.

"When we were children," Beth added.

Jenny said nothing.

"He was easy to love," Beth went on, sighing, shaking her head. "He was a big ol' teddy bear. He gave us nickels and candy and hugs. He took us to the movies while you were slaving over a hot stove. He was a wonderful father when we were six or eight or even eleven. You were the disciplinarian. *Of course,* we loved him more."

Jenny, understanding, said, "When we got older, we knew who to love. We knew who was worthy. Mom, we'll always love Daddy. He's a great big kid. But you were everything to us...even when we...even when we didn't know it."

Their mother smiled a little. Yes, she did. Nodded.

Then Grace said, "The grandkids love him, too. I think I just *scare* them."

Beth smirked. "Why *wouldn't* they love him? He's one of them."

The girls laughed. Grace kept the smile going.

"Mom," Jenny said, clutching Grace's hand, "it's been a long haul, but you made it. Don't spoil your day by thinking about the, uh...well the bad things. The hard parts. No marriage is perfect. Think about the houseful of kids of all ages who will be here to celebrate you and everything you've done for us."

They talked about other things for a while. Jenny's boy Jimmy, 11, watched too much TV (*Maverick* was his favorite), and her older girl, Kathy, 16, wore too much make-up and hair spray (a Breck girl). Beth's grandkids, Sam and Lucy, seven and five respectively, were a pistol and a little lady, respectively.

At the door, Beth said, "He'll show up. He won't miss this."

"He wouldn't do that to you," Jenny said.

But they all knew he might. Maybe not intentionally, but a drunk out on a drunk? Who knew what he might do?

Her husband stumbled in before midnight, barely able to walk. His clothes were a mess, an unmade bed with a souse in it. His lips were thick and loose. Always seemed liver-lipped when he got really drunk.

Somehow, she walked him in and got him to the downstairs bathroom with its shower fixture. Helping him out of his shoes to step into the tub, fully clothed, was tricky. She got the spray going in his face and he drowned standing up for a while but came around somewhat. Enough to strip himself out of his clothes with only a little assistance.

Naked, he was an even bigger baby. Not much hair on him, except that white butch on his skull. Pink like the pigs Papa used to slaughter. She had a bathrobe for him. Got him into it. Walked him up the stairs and into his bedroom. They hadn't slept in the same room for years.

"Sweet thing," he said, and plopped on top of the bed covers. Clumsily he got his dentures out and dropped them into the waiting glass on the bed stand, *plink, plink.* "Sweet thing..."

Then he was snoring.

That was when she decided.

When the whole family was gathered, and all the well wishes and speeches were over, she would tell them. She would tell *him.*

"I want a divorce," she would say. Then she would stand and point at him like God almighty at the world's worst sinner and say, "And I want you out of this house, Lemuel Richard Rushmore, right this minute."

She looked down at the big pink baby in the bathrobe, snoring, his lips flapping over the tooth-lessness, and clenched her fists and promised herself she would tell him.

Tell them all.

And then the day was everything Grace had dreamed it would be.

After all these years, finally *her* day.

Her girls and the wives of her boys indeed cooked a wonderful dinner, after which Grace's cake was the sensation of the entire event. She served it up herself, and Beth spirited away the top little tier for the hostess and host to share later. Lem had two big pieces but Grace held back, making sure everyone else got however much of the sweet, wonderful stuff as they wanted. Then it was gone.

The younger kiddies were running around, having fun exploring the big old house, while the older ones were bored, Grace knew. She showed them to the den where the small black-and-white TV would have to do. The grown-ups danced to some old 78's and even she and Lem cut a rug to "By the Light of the Silvery Moon." Everyone's eyes were big and some teared up when they saw how light on their feet the old couple was.

That was when she softened. She might still throw the old scallywag out, but not today. That would be cruel. That might ruin everyone else's good time.

But she did harden again some, when she saw Lem pouring liquid from a flask into his cup of punch. Five times, she saw that. Still, it only seemed to make Lem more jovial. He had never been a really nasty drunk. That much you could say for him.

And it was fun to watch him caper with the children. The kiddies squealed with laughter, just loving the attention of the big white-haired teddy bear.

Finally, the husband and wife, the Golden Anniversary couple, sat in high-backed chairs with windows behind them streaming sunshine while everybody brought them presents and said kind words. Almost everything Grace received was a kitchen item, green bean slicer, a hand-held ice crusher, pots, pans, and a dishwasher that everybody had pitched in on, rolled out by the boys with a big golden ribbon around it (it would be installed later). This got applause. As for Lem, he got tobacco for his pipe, a fancy pool cue, a sweater, a joke book, a few other things. Not as much as Grace. He was half-recipient of the dishwasher, after all.

A day that had begun around eleven o'clock was over by sundown, and everyone took their leave. Lem disappeared off somewhere and Grace went to the door and saw everyone out. Thanked each one, squeezed their hands, giving all of them smiles wider than they'd ever seen from her.

She stood on the front stoop and waved and smiled some more as each vehicle drove off, hands big and small waving back at her from car windows, smiles everywhere, then fading with what was left of the sun.

A more perfect day she could not imagine.

All that remained was to have a piece of her white-frosted masterpiece.

In the kitchen, Lem was sitting in his undershirt and suspenders having one last bite of the small final tier of the Golden Anniversary cake. He had eaten every bit. Every morsel. She sat beside him, and he looked at her with frosting and crumbs on his thick smiling lips and she picked up the cake knife and thrust it into his eye.

He sat there with his mouth open, some semi-masticated cake within, the handle of the knife sticking straight out, then toppled to the floor. She looked over at the sink where her children had piled the dirty dishes that would not wait for the installation of the new dishwasher.

But she would clean up later. In the morning.

For now, she stepped over her husband and went upstairs to her bed and Bible.

Lemon Layer Cake (family size)

Cake:
3 cups sifted all-purpose flour
1 Tbl. baking powder
½ tsp. salt
1 cup butter, softened
1 and 3/4 cups sugar
4 large eggs
2 tsp. vanilla extract
1 cup buttermilk
1 Tbl. lemon zest, heaping
1/3 cup lemon juice

Frosting:
1 cup butter, softened
8 ounces cream cheese, brick-style and softened
5 cups powdered sugar
2 Tbl. lemon juice
1 tsp. vanilla extract
pinch of salt

Cake Directions:
With an electric mixer, cream the butter and sugar together in a large bowl until smooth. Add the eggs and vanilla and beat until smooth. In a separate bowl combine the flour, baking powder, and salt. Add the dry ingredients into the wet mixture. Add

the buttermilk, lemon zest, and lemon juice and mix on low until there are no lumps. The batter will be a little thick. Pour batter evenly into three round greased 9-inch pans. Bake at 350 degrees for 20 to 25 minutes depending upon your oven. When done, let cool completely.

Frosting Directions: In a large bowl, beat the butter until creamy. Add the cream cheese and beat until smooth. Add the powdered sugar, lemon juice, vanilla, and pinch of salt and continue mixing until creamy. If frosting is too thin, add more powdered sugar; if too thick, add more lemon juice.

Assembly: Using a sharp knife, slice a thin layer off the top of each cake to make a flat surface. Place one cake on a cake stand, and evenly cover the top with about 1 cup of the frosting. Place second cake on top of the first, and cover with another cup of frosting, repeat for the third cake, this time covering all sides of the cake. Refrigerate for half and hour before slicing. *Bon appetit!*

TRAILER TRASHED

Barbra Collins

Tanya—nineteen, blonde, petite, and pretty—sat at a gray Formica table in the tiny kitchen of her mobile home and poured whiskey into a Wile E. Coyote glass. She took a swig, then almost choked on an involuntary sob. So far, the Southern Comfort hadn't given her much comfort.

Jake, her husband of two years, padded in from the single back bedroom, wearing faded NASCAR boxer shorts, his brown hair flattened where his head had hit the pillow. He was fairly handsome when cleaned up, but had gotten too thin for Tanya's liking, unloading heavy boxes at his Wal-Mart job. He took one look at her and groaned. "Ahhh, hon, you're not *cryin'* again..."

That only made the tears flow harder.

"It's that stupid MTV program, ain't it?"

Tanya, sniffing snot, managed to snap, "It *ain't* stupid!" Then she added in a pitiful voice, "You

know bein' on that show meant the world to me."
And Tanya broke down again.

He said indifferently, "Well, get over it. Them guys
didn't want us. Move on."

But she couldn't. "I don't know why Sheila and
Rick got picked for the *Trailer Marvelous Makeover Show*," she sobbed. "I'm *way* prettier than her,
and you're better-lookin' than that doofus." Tanya
slammed a small fist on the table. "She's *fat,* and
he's a *drunk!*"

"Darlin', it ain't the *people* they was after...it's the
trailer. Sheila and Rick got a double-wide... Besides,
those Hollywood types probably thought by them
pictures you sent that our place looks just fine. We
didn't *need* no damn makeover."

"Didn't *need no* makeover!" she shouted. "Just *look*
at this place!"

He spread both hands defensively. "What?"

She jumped from her chair, hands fluttering. "This
stuff ain't even *ours!* We didn't pick it out, some stupid
strangers did! It come with the repossessed trailer."

"So? It's ours now."

"So, I want nice things, Jake...things that don't have
pee stains from somebody *else's* pit bull, not ours."

He sighed. "I don't have time for this...I gotta go to
work. Where's my lunch?" She gestured dismissively
toward the Dale Earnhardt lunch box on the counter,
where a stale peanut-butter sandwich and an overripe
banana languished inside.

"Okay. Thanks, sugar." He lingered, wearing a
goofy smile.

Tanya thought, *If he's waitin' for a goodbye kiss,
he can forget it.* She went over to the sink and pre-

tended to be busy.

After a while, the flimsy aluminum screen door banged shut.

Tanya, fresh tears welling in her eyes, watched out the dirty kitchen window as her husband climbed into his pickup truck, then left in a cloud of dust.

She crossed over to the other small kitchen window and peered out. At the end of the gravel road of Happy Trails Trailer Court she could see the *Trailer Marvelous* film crew's long, shiny, old-school Airstream camper parked near Sheila and Rick's large mobile home; the camper had arrived a few hours ago, and people wearing Tee-shirts with the show's logo were scurrying back and forth between the two, getting ready for tomorrow's shoot.

Tanya felt sick to her stomach, like she had to throw up a bad fast-food meal.

The kitchen wall phone rang. She wiped her eyes with her fingertips, then answered it.

"Tanya!" The voice on the other end was breathless with excitement. "Do ya see 'em?"

"Yes, I see 'em," Tanya said flatly.

"I wish me and Rick didn't have to go bowlin' tonight so I could stay round and watch . . . but I guess they're gonna be leaving here soon, anyways—just checkin' the place out today, before comin' back first thing in the morning to shoot."

Wish they would shoot you, Tanya thought.

"Tanya?"

"Yeah."

"You're comin' to the Big Expose when they're done decoratin', aren't ya? They want all the neighbors to see the unveiling, right along with us. It'll be a riot!"

Tanya said sullenly, "I dunno."

"You'll get to be on TV!"

Yeah, in the background, she thought, but said, "Maybe I'll be there."

"Okay. Well...I'll let ya go," Sheila said, sounding hurt, and hung up.

With a dejected sigh, Tanya took a few steps into her narrow living quarters and plopped down on the sagging sofa. All the crying and turmoil had made her exhausted.

She'd closed her eyes for only a minute when there came a sharp knock at the door.

"Jesus Christ," Tanya muttered, getting up. "Why don't people just leave me the hell alone?"

"What!" she snarled, flinging the screen door wide. Then both hands flew to her mouth, covering a gasp.

Standing on her very own portable steps were Bart Brooks, host of *Trailer Marvelous,* and the show's star designer, Johnny Hardy!

"Oh, ma God!" Tanya squealed. "I don't believe it!"

Had they come personally to ask her to attend the Big Expose? If so, she'd swallow her pride and attend.

"Is this the home of Tanya and Jake?" Bart asked politely.

The former country-western star was tall, clean-shaven, and cute as a hound dog...but his clothes were *weird:* striped yellow golf shirt, plaid hat, wing-tip brown shoes. Like that old geezer her grandmother (bless her soul) used to be so crazy about—the one who smoked a pipe and sang "Ba-ba-ba-ba-boo" (but younger, of course!).

"Yes...yes!" Tanya sputtered. "This is them...I mean, we is us."

Johnny asked, "May we come in?"

The show's designer, decked out in torn blue jeans and a heavy-metal Tee-shirt, was a hunk, with streaked blond hair and cool dragon tattoos on both arms. Johnny was the kind of guy she would just love to pick her up at the Lonely Bull Tavern some night Jake was working late shift.

Barely able to contain her excitement, Tanya stepped aside.

"The kitchen is best," she suggested as the TV stars hesitated just inside. "The couch ain't so hot, as you might notice."

Spotting the whiskey bottle left on the table, Tanya dashed ahead of them, grabbed it, and stashed the booze in one of the lower cupboard drawers that worked. She didn't want them thinking *she* was a damn lush, like Rick. The men pulled out worn vinyl chairs.

"Can I get you something to drink?" she offered. "We got Sam's Cola."

Bart grinned easily and said, "Some of that Southern Comfort would be nice."

"Ditto." Johnny smiled.

Tanya smiled back shyly and retrieved the bottle, along with three glasses. Then she joined them at the table.

Bart began slowly. "As you know, we're supposed to film up the road tomorrow at Sheila and Rick's..."

Tanya, pouring the drinks, nodded. "...and I have to say, between you and me and the lamppost..." He paused while Tanya handed him a glass.

"Lamppost?" she asked. "We don't got none. Wish we did 'cause it gets awful dark out here at night."

The two men exchanged glances and laughed. And Tanya laughed. It always amazed her how funny she could be sometimes, like she was some kind of comedy-club genius.

Bart looked down at his glass, swirled the whiskey. "What I'm trying to say is we're beginning to think we made a mistake in picking those two for the show."

"Really!" It came out too happy, so Tanya tried again. "Really?"

Johnny belted back his drink and set the glass down with a clank. "Yeah, *big mistake*. I mean, what audience is gonna care if some jerk with a porky wife gets a shelf made to put his beer-can collection on?"

Bart leaned forward, interjecting, "But a sexy little gal like you could help ratings."

Tanya felt herself blush.

Johnny smirked. "Which are in the toilet right now."

Tanya frowned, said, "But I thought the show was popular. All my friends watch it."

Bart sighed. "We're up against *Extreme Full Body Tattoo Bikers' Mud Wrestling* this season, and our slice of the pie just got smaller."

She wasn't sure what pie had to do with it, but Tanya wanted to help if she could. If the program got dropped, she'd lose a lot of good decorating tips, like making a picture frame out of macaroni (but she wished they would have had the common sense to say not to cook it!). She dared to ask, "If you don't want Sheila and Rick, why don't you come here to our place?"

Bart sighed. "Darlin' we'd sure love to...but unfortunately, the producers have already signed a contract with them."

"So?" she said. "Why can't you sign another one with me?"

Johnny said, "Because Sheila and Rick would sue us."

Tanya asked, "Can they do that?"

Bart replied, "Oh, yeah. And *that* kind of publicity we don't need."

Tanya thought hard but couldn't come up with a solution. Finally, she asked despairingly, "Then what *can* we do?"

The men, drinks finished, stood. Bart said, "Pray for a miracle, I guess."

"What kind of miracle?" asked Tanya.

Bart laughed humorously. "Like maybe a tornado or earthquake hits... Or a fire breaks out over there and we can cancel with them and film over here."

Johnny had stepped into the living area and was surveying it, hands on hips. "Ya know," he said, "this place really has possibilities."

Tanya was at his side. "Like what?"

The designer spread an arm out, fingers splayed. "Like maybe a leopard-covered contour chair over there..."

Tanya squealed, "Could it have heat and vibrate?"

"...and in that corner, one of those hanging cages with cherubs... You know what I'm talking about? Where liquid beads slide down the wires while it plays 'You Light Up My Life'?"

"I've always *wanted* one of those!" She stuck out her lower lip. "But we could never afford it. Jake won't let me work 'cause men keep hittin' on me. He just wants a damn housewife."

Bart said, "Well, you'd have fifteen-thousand dollars to play with."

Tanya smiled. That's what each featured trailer owner got to spend on redecorating. Practically a fortune! Her mind began to whirl.

Then she frowned. But the kind of "miracle" Bart mentioned didn't seem likely to happen between now and tomorrow morning. She'd never even *heard* of an earthquake around these parts ... and it wasn't tornado season yet. As far as a fire breaking out at Sheila and Rick's trailer, what were the chances of that?

At the dented screen door, Bart said, "Well, thanks for the drink. You should know that you and Jake were our second choice, but you should've been our *first.*"

Tanya managed a weak smile. "I guess second just ain't good enough."

Johnny, at the bottom of the steps, turned to Tanya, framed in the doorway, "I don't know...look at what happens if Miss America gets dethroned..."

"What?"

He shrugged. "The runner-up steps in."

The two men climbed into a black Mercedes and, with gravel crunching under its wheels, drove off.

Tanya watched until the dust dissipated, then went to find the gas can.

A cool night breeze flapped the American flag that hung on a short pole attached to Tanya's mobile home as she slipped outside and down the steps, gas can in hand.

She had seen Sheila and Rick drive by her trailer earlier in their rusted-out Camry, happy grins on their faces—which would soon be wiped off, she had thought. Jake's shift at Wal-Mart had already ended, but Tanya could always count on him going out for beers with his lowlife friends and not coming home for hours.

Dressed in black sweats, Tanya crept confidently along the back sides of the trailer homes, making her way slowly toward Sheila and Rick's. Occasionally, a mangy cat hissed, or a penned-up dog growled, stopping Tanya in her tracks; but that was nothing out of the ordinary, so no one looked out.

With only a distant yard light to guide her, Tanya searched quickly among the short weeds by the steps of the double-wide for the spare key Sheila kept hidden in a piece of fake rubber dog poop Tanya had once given her friend for a Christmas present.

Finally, Tanya spotted it, reached down, and picked up the brown swirled thingie, which looked real in the dark. It squished in her hand. Yuck! It *was* real! Disgusted, she wiped her gooey hand on the weeds and tried again...this time with better results.

Inside the trailer—they'd had tacos for dinner— Tanya set the gas can down and risked turning on a small table lamp made out of an armadillo. She'd never torched a place before and didn't know where to start. The fire should look like it broke out naturally (helped along with the gas, of course). Tanya looked toward the kitchen area, remembering a late-night movie she'd caught about a woman who was going to lose her house to her husband and his mistress. The wife turned on all the kitchen appliances, which caused an electrical fire, then left.

Tanya went over to the kitchen, where a blender sat on the counter. Sheila had once used it to make her a really wretched margarita after Tanya got her house-arrest ankle bracelet removed. Tanya made sure that the appliance was plugged in, then tried to get it going, but the thing was broken. She crossed to the microwave, punched in ninety-nine minutes, pressed *start,* and...nothing. Busted.

With a determined sigh, Tanya returned to the living room. She stared at the couch. One time, her uncle Bob had fallen asleep with a cigarette in his hand while watching *All-Star Wrestling* and started a fire in his pants. Maybe the sofa was the best place to begin...

Carefully—because once this guy next to her at the pump had spilled gasoline all over himself, then flicked his Bic and lighted himself—Tanya sprinkled the pungent petrol all over the couch, then did the same to the ugly recliner (maybe Sheila and Rick's trailer *did* need a Marvelous Makeover).

Satisfied, Tanya stood back and surveyed her handiwork.

Now, how to start it.

This could be tricky because she had to get herself out before the fire took hold. She remembered another movie about this couple who wanted to collect some insurance money, so before they flew to Tijuana, they left a candle burning that caught the curtains on fire.

This idea seemed perfect because Sheila always had a candle or two going whenever Tanya and Jake came over, to cover the septic-tank smell.

In a drawer in the kitchen, Tanya found a small tealight, which she took back to the living room and placed on the gas-soaked couch. It should give her plenty of time to get back to her trailer. Maybe *she* could even be the one to call the fire in. Sometimes the local news played the 911 call over the disaster they were covering. Wouldn't *that* be cool!

Tanya lit the tiny candle, then picked up the gas can and left, making sure the door was relocked and the poop key put back in the weeds.

It took about a half an hour before Tanya saw flames lick at the sky. Watching from her kitchen window, she was amazed how fast the blaze spread; in a matter of minutes the whole double-wide was engulfed.

Tanya dialed 911 but was too late; somebody else had beaten her to it. Oh, well. With Sheila and Rick now out of the picture, the *Trailer Marvelous* show would be coming to her place, and she'd get to be seen on TV, which was way better than just her voice.

Six months later, Tanya's dream came true.

Latrisha, tall, slender, dressed in a cotton denim shirt and slacks, yelled, "Hey, everybody! Tanya's gonna be on!"

The other women, dressed the same, stopped playing pool and cards and gathered around the single small set in the recreation room of Joliet Women's Prison.

Latrisha patted the seat of a plastic chair directly in front of the television. "Sit here, girl! You gonna be famous...You in the pre-mirror show."

Excitedly, Tanya sat, and soon the program's title, *The World's Wackiest Criminals*, filled the screen.

When the host of the program, Bart Brooks, came on, all the women (except for Tanya, whose eyes were glued to the TV) whooped and hollered.

One the inmates said, "I thought he was on a different show."

Someone else said, "Yeah, but that went under."

Bart's face filled the screen.

"Tonight, we have a tale of jealousy and greed, a betrayal by a best friend—"

Tanya said, "She weren't my best friend," and got shushed by the other women.

"—who wanted to be on Trailer Marvelous, *our former series, so badly that she burned a contestant's home to the ground, not realizing that our film crew had set up small cameras inside and a feed was already going, capturing her entire movements."*

As Tanya watched the ten-minute footage, she heard laughs and snickers around her. And when it was over, some of the women seemed disappointed as they got up and returned to their previous activities.

Latrisha asked, "Girl, what's the matter? You don't look happy."

Tanya, still seated, said, "They was laughin' at me."

"Oh, they wasn't," Latrisha told her. "They was laughin' *with* you."

"But I weren't laughin'."

Latrisha put an arm around her. "Never you mind... they's just jealous 'cause you got on tee vee." She paused, then added, "You gonna get *respect* now around here, you'll see."

A female guard clanged the butt of her nightstick against the steel bars of the rec-room door.

"Fun's over," the woman announced, her voice

high and shrill. As the inmates pissed and moaned, the matron singled out Tanya and Latrisha, who were apart from the others. "You two ...you're on latrine duty in the morning."

Tanya, shuffling back to her cell along with Latrisha, said thoughtfully, "Ya know, I think that Bart guy knew all along I was gonna set that fire."

Latrisha gave her a wide-eyed look. "Girlfriend, that's jus' silly."

Tanya shrugged. "I dunno...why else would he have them tiny cameras going?"

Latrisha stopped her with a hand. "Honey, it don't matter...'cause millions of people saw you. You're a TV star now!"

"That's right," Tanya said firmly. "I'm a TV star. I got on TV."

"So it was worth it, girl."

"Yeah, it *was* worth it."

Tanya entered her cell. The bars slammed shut.

She was sure it was worth it.

Anyway, she was pretty sure.

WHAT'S WRONG WITH
HARLEY QUINN?

Barbara Collins and Max Allan Collins

Amanda, in a silk leopard-print dress, stood on the little balcony of a suite at the Marriott Marina gazing out at the spectacular view of San Diego Bay, the early morning sun nearly blinding, turning paddle-boats, sailboats, and the occasional military cruiser into mirages, as it shimmered off the blue water.

Beyond was Coronado Island, and the red roof peaks of the Hotel Coronado, where Marilyn Monroe once scampered on the beach while filming *Some Like It Hot,* clearly visible from Amanda's high vantage point.

Below, a long line of comic book fans the size of ants extended along the entire length of the boardwalk, having queued up for hours for something or other, this being the first full day of the San Diego Comic-con, and the reason that she and Robert and his twelve-year-old son Jayden, were staying downtown.

Amanda, slender, blonde, thirty, leaned over the

railing, breathing in deeply the cool salty fresh air, wishing she could bottle it and take it back to Omaha, where they'd left unbearably hot and humid weather.

She had been so looking forward to having the day to herself, with Robert at a business meeting in La Jolla, and Jayden taking in the convention by himself. But overnight, her plans of shopping Seaport Village, the Gaslamp district, and upscale Mission Valley mall had become threatened.

She turned away from the railing, went through the sliding glass doors, then exited the bedroom. Across the spacious living-room-with-kitchenette, she could hear Robert speaking to Jayden in the boy's room. Tentatively, she approached the open door.

Her husband was seated on the bed, stepson still in his pajamas under the covers, propped up with pillows.

"No, you *can't* go to the convention," Robert said. His steel-gray hair went well with the Brooks Brothers suit, his handsomeness not particularly reflected in his son's pouting face. "You've got the flu and a fever."

Jayden had spent the night vomiting into an ice bucket.

"Well," the boy asked desperately, "can't *you* go for me?"

"You know I can't. My meeting is important."

Her husband always knew what was important.

"Then," Jayden said, pleading now, "couldn't we stay an extra day?"

"I have another key meeting in Los Angeles tomorrow."

Jayden began to cry, choking out, "Everybody *else* gets to go off and do what *they* want, but not *me*. It's just not fair!"

"Son, life's not fair," Robert said, not coddling the boy. "It's just full of disappointments."

She wondered if that list included his second marriage to a much younger woman. A gulf between Amanda and Robert seemed ever-widening, the chief cause, his son's refusal to accept his stepmom, who he blamed for his parents' divorce. Her efforts to get along with the boy had proved fruitless.

She stepped aside as Robert came out muttering, "Next time I come alone," flashing her a dismissive glance, lumping her in with his dissatisfaction.

Her husband picked up his briefcase and, without a look back, left the suite.

Amanda entered the lion-cub's den, where the boy had covered his head with the bed sheet, making a ghost of himself.

"I'll stay with you," she heard herself say.

He flung back the sheet. "*That* makes it all better."

She risked sitting on the edge of the bed. "We could have fun watching movies, and get room service."

He screwed his face up. "*Fun*? In between puking? Is it hard work, being that dumb?"

Amanda's manicured nails dug into her palms. Still, she persisted in trying to please. "Okay...then why don't *I* go to the convention and get those things you want."

For weeks the boy had been working on an annotated map of the vendors on the convention floor, indicating which ones he would go to, and what to buy.

"*Things*?" he mocked.

"Collectibles."

"You don't even know what I'm after."

"Tell me."

His features played a symphony of sarcasm. "Pins of characters from games and anime. Lacquered pins. Limited editions."

"Just point me in the right direction."

"Oh, okay," he said, smirking. "Sure. Absolutely. First you go to Figpin. I want Batman and Robin, Thanos, Duke Caboom, and Goose...in that order. Forget Harley Quinn, I don't care about that one. Then at Udon get me pins of Okami, Chibi, Shantae, and Gatcha. Got that?"

"I will," she said, "after you give me the list you made."

Jaydon studied her. Then he reached over to the nightstand, plucked off a sheet of paper, along with the badge she'd need to get into the convention, and tossed them at her.

"Even if you get just *one* pin," he said, "I *guess* it's better than nothing."

"Thank you," she said.

Jaydon snorted. "Good luck."

Boiling, Amanda went to her bedroom, slipped on a pair of Louboutin beige pumps, picked up a Vuitton tote-bag, put on her Jimmy Choo sunglasses, and departed.

Did the boy *want* her to fail? Well, she *wouldn't!* Not when it seemed as though her entire marriage hinged on her success. Even if Jayden's attitude toward her didn't change one iota, Robert would see how hard she'd tried. And eventually, her husband would start blaming the boy, and pack him off to his mother.

On the sidewalk outside the Marriott, Amanda fell in like a piece of driftwood caught in the tidal wave of fans pouring from across the wide street and moving as one down the sidewalk toward the convention center, which was about to open, thousands of them, many dressed in costumes, "cosplay," Jayden called it. A few characters she recognized: Batman and Spiderman, Groot from *Guardians of the Galaxy*, and the Addams Family's "Thing." But the rest seemed weird apparitions, like the guy in a red jumpsuit holding huge scissors, or the girl with a large teacup and saucer on her head.

As if the tide of the throng had hit a dam, moving forward became excruciatingly slow, and Amanda got poked, prodded, pinched and stepped on. A sudden surge in the crowd signaled the multiple doors to the vast concrete convention center had opened, and whatever indignities she'd so far suffered increased, including getting her butt jabbed with a plastic sword. But there was no turning back, as she was swept along with the multitudes.

Amanda got caught up in it all in more ways than one. The excitement in the air, the electricity created by the hopes, dreams, and high expectations of thousands of fans who'd waited the whole year for Comic-Con, was as exhilarating as Neiman's summer designer sale.

No one seemed to be going in through the first set of double glass doors, and she nearly broke away to enter there, until noticing the sign above them, which read "DISABLED ONLY." Then she was being sucked down toward the next set of doors, through which fans were directed between what looked to be metal detectors, devices that authorized each badge as it was pressed against a screen. And she followed suit.

Finally, Amanda had a little breathing room, and stood getting her bearing as others rushed around her, managing not to knock her down. She was in a large lobby area, the convention floor straight ahead via another set of doors where two monitors in yellow comic-con staff t-shirts were trying valiantly to see that each person entering had a badge. Would she get stopped if they noticed the name on hers was Jayden?

But then she was in the vast high-ceilinged chamber, where no end was in sight, assaulted by sights, sounds, and smells. There was so much more on hand than just comic books; this was a world's fair of pop culture, a wall of bizarre t-shirts here, an array of video game consoles there, posters and prints of Disney and *Star Wars* images in temporary pegboard art galleries, rows of cardboard boxes brimming with games, videos and, yes, even comic books.

The noise was deafening, coming from everywhere - from competing vendors, loudspeaker announcements, and the crowd itself – like the din at the MGM Grand, but a hundred times more! The smell was a combination of fast food and body odor, cut with an occasional whiff of breath mint, as she moved shoulder-to-shoulder with these creatures in baby steps to nowhere.

If it was this bad now, what would it be like by the end of the day?

These observations were fleeting, however, Amanda keenly aware of her disadvantage as a novice, a stranger in this strange land, as she frantically searched for the aisle where the Figpin booth was located.

The floor was laid out on a grid, like the Manhattan of Robert's business trips, north/south streets wide, cross streets narrow. Those broad aisles made some progress possible.

And then there it was!

Down a cross street, a tiny booth, maybe eight feet long, where two female employees in black t-shirts emblazoned with the Figpin logo stood behind a counter, each tending to one customer, placing items into black bags.

Two customers! That's all! No big line, pushing and shoving. Hardly the big impossible deal Jayden had promised.

Sighing with relief, Amanda approached the nearest clerk after the male customer had left.

"Hi," she said.

"Help you?" the employee asked. Her name tag said Kimberly.

"Yes, please." She checked her list. "I'd like Batman and Robin, Thanos, Duke Caboom, and Goose."

Kimberly gave her a crooked smile. "*New* here?"

"First time," Amanda chirped.

"Ah-huh," she said. "Well, you have to get in the queue."

Amanda looked around. "What? Where?"

"Over there," Kimberly responded, pointing toward the end of the aisle where a male Figpin employee held a sign on a wooden stake up high that said "LINE BEGINS HERE," and behind which fans snaked out of sight.

"Oh," Amanda said, crestfallen.

The customer beside her said, "You need a card, you know." This was a cute blonde in her early twenties dressed in a short-skirted sailor outfit with "AHOY" on the white cap.

Armed with this new information, Amanda asked Kimberly, "Card?"

But the Figpin employee, losing patience with newbie Amanda, said, "You'll have to move away." Then shouted to her cohort down the aisle, "*Next!*"

Amanda stepped side and waited until AHOY had collected her bag of goodies, before asking her, "*What* did I need? I mean, I have a credit card..."

By way of an answer, AHOY produced a four-inch-by-six card depicting the character pins available, along with their price. A big black "X" had been drawn through it, so there was no chance the card could be reused.

Amanda asked, "Where do I get one of those?"

"You can't. Today's allotment has already been passed out." A weary sigh. "I had to camp out all night to get mine. But you can try again tomorrow."

Amanda shook her head. "I won't be here."

AHOY shrugged. "Sorry," she said, and slipped into the crowd, swallowed up without a burp.

Amanda stood there calculating, then wended her way down the crowded aisle along an edge of the Figpin line, where people waited patiently for their turn, cards in hand.

She walked slowly, surprised the fans were mostly millennials and older with the occasional teens. Where were the children? Wasn't this, after all, a comic book convention? The few kids she'd encountered, being dragged along by harried parents, either looked traumatized or were crying, and it was unsettling to see a small Superman or Wonder Woman in such distress.

Amanda selected a round-faced male in wire-frames wearing a Yoda t-shirt and cargo shorts.

"Hi," she said, flashing the smile that had caught Robert's attention in the bar where he'd come after a quarrel with a wife who didn't understand him. He'd said.

"Yeah?"

"Ummm...I was wondering if you'd get *me* some pins, too...I'd give you the cash, of course." She batted her natural long eyelashes at him.

"Can't do that," he said, unimpressed.

His refusal surprised her a little, even in these circumstances; she wasn't used to men turning her requests down.

"Not even," she asked, "for an up-charge?"

"It's not that, lady," he replied.

Lady!

"I can't," he went on, "because you're only allowed one of *each pin* per card."

"Oh."

"And I'm getting them all - as is everybody else." He added, "Except maybe Harley Quinn."

The one pin Jayden didn't want.

Curious, Amanda asked, "What's wrong with him?"

"Her."

"Her."

"If you don't know, I can't tell you."

She exchanged shrugs with him, then continued along the queue, noting the abundance of fans in wheelchairs.

To one such fan, a female in a green body-suit, her long red hair wig entwined with vines, her right leg in a leg brace, Amanda commented, "Must have been hard camping out all night."

The woman looked up at her in mild disgust. "I didn't. Disabled get into the convention first."

"Really?"

"Something *wrong* with that?"

"No, no...of course not," Amanda replied. "It's only right. Only fair."

When Amanda lingered, the woman said, "*What?*"

"Uhh...I was wondering, I didn't get a card, if maybe you'd be willing to sell some of your pins?"

Her eyes narrowed, lips curling. "You think just because I'm in a wheelchair I need *money*? Am I a *beggar?*" The words came like slaps.

"Oh, I didn't mean that at all!"

The woman continued, speaking louder. "You stand there in your *designer* clothes, and *expensive* jewelry and think you can take *advantage* of a *disabled* person?"

Everyone around them was looking their way.

"No...you misunderstand," Amanda said, with a nervous smile. "Sorry!"

She backed away to a respectful distance where she stood, confused, pondering what had just happened.

Had she broken some comic convention protocol?

"We're not *all* that rude," a sympathetic voice said.

Her eyes focused on an Asian guy in his mid-twenties, slim in a Godzilla t-shirt and jeans.

He went on with a smile. "But sometimes this atmosphere, y'know, gets to people."

She returned the smile. "Nice to know."

"I didn't get a card, either," he said with a shrug, then asked, "Did Figpin tell you to come back this afternoon?"

She shook her head.

"Well, they're going to pass out some more cards - not a lot, but some."

"At the booth?" she asked, gesturing in that direction.

"No. There'll be another line here." He studied her a moment. "If you promise to keep this to yourself..."

Amanda leaned close with a nod.

"...*don't* come any earlier than two, even though other people probably will, understand? They risk getting in trouble."

"...okay. Man, these fans. They really love this stuff, don't they?"

"You're not a fan, are you? It's for your kid, right?"

"Right."

His shrug indicated an acceptance of Robert's view that life wasn't fair. "Hey, not everybody in these lines are fans. Plenty are dealers, looking to sell these pins on e-bay or in their shops for big money."

"Are you a dealer?"

"No. I *do* love this stuff." He winked. "See you at two. Not before!"

She spent the next four hours in lines to snag more pins for Jayden. At Udon, Amanda scored Okami and Chibi, but they'd run out of Shantal and Gatcha. She had less luck at Ukiyo-e Heroes, landing only the Samurai Riding T-Rex. And no luck at all at Bait, where the wait had been the longest for a limited edition of a golden Dragonball Z pin; all she got for her effort was being told at the check-out counter the precious item had sold out almost immediately. A sign had been posted saying as such, if only she'd known to look.

Demoralized, dejected, Amanda trudged back to Figpin, arriving a few minutes before two, where several hundred people had already queued up.

What the hell?

Why had that Asian guy told her to come so late? Was he having a laugh at her expense? There was no way she'd get a card with all these people in front of her!

Resigned, she walked to where a Figpin staff member stood with a sign denoting the end of the line, and joined it, fuming.

And waited.

Then something began happening at the front of the queue; someone was speaking in a loud voice, though in the cacophony of the hall it got lost, anyway.

"What's going on?" she asked a guy in front of her.

"They're being punished for getting here early," he said, smiling.

Punished? In what way?

Just how that punishment would be administered became clear when the two sign-wielding staff members traded places, making the end of the line the beginning, and vice versa.

Holy switcheroo, Batman!

That Asian guy had given her good advice, after all. She did have a chance to get a card. *More* than a chance...

...until everyone at the front rushed to the back, causing a stampede, and Amanda got shoved aside so forcefully she was thrown to the floor, compelled to crawl away to safety, else get maimed by marauding feet.

She sat there wide-eyed, as suddenly the air filled with cards, fluttering down like large confetti. Whatever staff member assigned to passing them out had

283

apparently felt threatened enough to just toss the things in the air and run for cover...which only made the situation worse.

The melee was like nothing Amanda had ever witnessed, dozens upon dozens of fans scrambling after the strewn-about cards, meat thrown to starving sharks.

Had Amanda remained standing (she had no doubt) she'd have been right in there with them, joining in the feeding frenzy.

As security people in yellow shirts moved in, pulling people apart, a hand reached out to help her up.

"Are you all right?" her Asian friend asked.

"Physically," Amanda said, smoothing out her leopard-print dress.

"I tried to get you one," he said, gesturing with a card. "But I was lucky to get this."

She nodded.

Impulsively, he thrust the card toward her. "Here. You can have it."

"Really?"

"Yeah," he sighed. "Don't bother thanking me. Word is, all they have left is Harley Quinn."

She took the card, thanked him anyway, and when he had disappeared into the crowd, let it slip from her hand. She'd score no points with Jayden for a Harley Quinn.

What she needed was a drink. Something to deaden herself against the withering look her stepson was sure to bestow upon her for the few paltry pins she'd come back with.

Amanda left the convention, touching her badge on its necklace against the security screen as she went out, as others were doing. Nobody in a hurry now.

Since Fifth Avenue in the Gaslamp District was packed with bodies, she made her way over to less-crowded Sixth, walked up a few blocks, and found a nondescript hole-in-the-wall bar, where she settled at small high-top table by the front window. The mix of casual clothes and costumes going by provided something to look at, anyway. They made a mind-boggling, mind-numbing parade.

"Something?" asked a weary waitress with lots of miles on the odometer.

"Scotch and water," Amanda said. "And make it a double."

"Good choice."

The woman started off and Amanda's gazed returned to the window on the comic con world.

And then saw someone she recognized roll by.

"Never mind!" Amanda shouted at the waitress and jumped off the stool and rushed outside.

A half a block up the street was the young woman who'd maligned her, still dressed as (what she'd learned since was) the Batman villainess Poison Ivy, zipping along in her motorized wheelchair, its pouches stuffed with bags.

Amanda hurried to catch up, keeping Ivy in sight. This was a second chance to score some of those sought-after pins. Her offer to buy had been spurned earlier. But now Amanda knew this woman might be a dealer, or a fan who could use some *real* money. She wanted to get her alone to prevent another scene and avoid waving cash around on the street.

And Amanda had a good five-hundred dollars in her tote.

After a while, the woman slowed, making Amanda's

tracking easier, although as the crowd thinned some, the stalker in the leopard-print dress had to keep some bodies in between her and her prey.

At G Street, Ivy turned right, and continued on to Ninth, Tenth, and Eleventh, the landscape getting progressively rundown and less populated.

Where was the woman going?

At Eleventh, the wheelchair took a left, and by the time Amanda had turned the corner, it and its occupant had disappeared.

Frustrated, Amanda walked along, passing service stores - a dry cleaners, tat parlor, pawn shop - peering in the smudged windows to see if her quarry had gone in one.

But no Ivy.

Finally, Amanda came to a stop outside a low-end hotel, a weathered, paint-peeling, four-story affair, just a step up from a flophouse. Lodging during comic con was at a premium, and this was the kind of place a fan operating on a budget or out of desperation might settle for.

Worth a try.

Amanda went in, finding herself in a small, stuffy, unpopulated lobby, its furnishings dating back many decades. To the left, the check-in counter was vacant. To the right was a small elevator, in use, whining in protest; the floor indicator stopped at 2.

Near the elevator were exposed stairs, and Amanda bounded up them. When she'd reached the second floor, there was Ivy, at the end of the corridor, struggling to get herself and the chair through her room's door.

Ivy backed out a bit, took off her leg brace, then

stood, tossed the brace on the seat of her transport, and proceeded to drag the chair inside.

Ha.

The door was inches from closing when the pointed toe of Amanda's Louboutin's prevented it from doing so. The erect wheelchair rider gasped as Amanda pushed her way in.

"Remember me?" Amanda said.

Ivy, backing up against a sagging bed, was too startled to answer.

"Congratulations on a remarkable recovery," Amanda said, shutting the door behind her.

The wheelchair was between them.

Ivy's face reddened. "Get out or I'll call the front desk!"

"I don't think anyone's attending it right now. But go ahead. If you get anybody, I'll report your con to the con...Rhonda Riley." She was reading the name on the badge on its noose-like loop around Poison Ivy's neck. "And they'll surely ban you from ever attending again."

Amanda didn't know if they'd really do that, but it seemed likely.

"What do you want?" Ivy snarled. "Batman and Robin."

"Is *that* what this is about? It'll *cost* you."

"No, it won't. I offered you money before, but you turned it down. And I was prepared to go much higher now, till I saw what a fraud you are. Now you're just going to hand over the Caped Crusader and Boy Wonder."

The woman glared at Amanda. Her chin was trembling. Maybe she was wishing she had Poison Ivy's powers, whatever *they* were.

Then Ivy sputtered, "Okay...*fine!*"

The wheelchair still between them, Ivy began digging among sacks in the back pouch, when Amanda said, "Know what? Think I'll take 'em all," and shoved the wheelchair into her.

Ivy fell backward, stumbling, and hit her head on the pointed edge of a wooden lamp table, then slid down its leg to the floor and sat there.

"Oops," Amanda said, then went over and leaned down.

Ivy wasn't dead. Just knocked out. For a moment she felt relief, but then Amanda realized this had gone too far. That the woman would report her, not just to the con, but to the police.

So Amanda dragged her into a tiny and rather grimy bathroom, stripped her of the homemade costume and the rest of her things, hauled her up and danced her unconscious body into the bathtub shower. There she banged the woman's head on the tile wall, where a slip might have sent her, just once, but very hard. That was enough to send blood streaming down into the tub in scarlet tendrils. Amanda eased the woman down into the porcelain coffin and checked her wrist for a pulse.

Nothing. Good. Multiple blows would have been telling, and this needed to be an accident.

Amanda returned to the outer room, to the wheelchair, where she collected from the sacks only the pins (there were a lot of them), leaving behind any other stuff. She didn't need that junk and, anyway, the remaining con purchases would make it look better when the police investigated.

The pins went into her tote, along with their sacks and receipts (mostly paid by cash).

Returning to the bathroom, Amanda used a washcloth to turn on the shower - not too hot, not too cold, but just right - Ivy was past caring, but why make the authorities suspicious? For good measure, she dropped a small bar of soap next to the slumped body.

With the washcloth, Amanda wiped the doorknobs and anything else she might have touched. She wasn't entirely new to this; she had a record that Robert didn't know about. But that was another story.

The check-in desk was unattended, and the lobby empty, not a likely place for con guests to congregate; the place was as dead as Ivy. Back out on the street, Amanda made her way to the Marriott, disposing of the sacks and receipts in various receptacles along the way.

Robert was not back from his meeting yet, and she entered Jayden's bedroom where he had been playing video games on the TV, empty wrappers from the mini-bar strewn across the bed.

He snapped at her: "Why didn't you answer my texts!"

She approached the bed. "Because I was busy."

"Doing *what?*" the boy said, scowling. "I don't see any sacks."

"That's because everything's in here." She slowly took handfuls of pins from her tote and sprinkled them on the bedspread while she watched Jayden's eyes grow wide.

"Are you *kidding* me?" he exclaimed, hands sifting through, separating his pins. "You got Batman and Robin!"

"You're welcome."

He gasped. "Migod! You even snagged the special Dragonball Z!"

She had?

He went on, "The net said that one sold out really fast." He looked at her, the scowl history. "How did you do all this?"

Amanda shrugged. "Right place and right time, I guess."

"Man, I owe you. I really owe you."

She sat on the edge of the bed. "Then let's call a truce, okay? And not for just an hour, or a day, or a week...but always." She cocked her head. "Besides, you may need me next year, if we come back to the convention. I have my ways, you know."

His eyes were bright as new pennies; she hoped his new attitude would be worth more. "We'll make a killing!"

Maybe so. Poison Ivy probably wasn't the only disabled faker that would make an easy target.

Jayden stuck out a hand. "Deal."

She grasped it, and they smiled at each other.

"There's only one pin I don't want," he said, looking his loot over, selecting a woman in combat gear holding a futuristic-looking gun. "Harley Quinn."

"I know," Amanda said. "I'll take her. I think she's cool."

Amanda put the pin on her dress, next to her heart, patting it in place. "So, what's wrong with Harley Quinn?"

Maybe she'd finally get an answer.

He nodded toward the pin. "She's not dressed like a harlequin."

Amanda frowned. "And why would she be dressed like a - *oh!* Duh. *I* get it!"

Stepmother and stepson were laughing together as Robert entered the room.

"What's going on here?" her husband asked, smiling a little himself.

"Dad! Dad! Just look what Amanda got for me."

While Jayden was showing Robert the collection of pins, Amanda slipped out, leaving them alone.

Ten minutes later, Robert joined her on the balcony. Took her in his arms. "Thank you for doing that."

"I had a good time," she said.

His kiss was passionate and promised a better future.

After he'd gone, Amanda leaned on the railing, looking out at the peaceful panoramic view, where the sun was just beginning to set over the bay.

And she did have a good time, at that. A rather fun adventure, a unique experience. She felt no regret, no remorse. That terrible woman got what she deserved, didn't she?

Impersonating someone disabled. What kind of monster would do that?

A Look At:
An Eliot Ness Mystery Omnibus

A FAST-PACED, ONE-TWO PUNCH OF CRIME
AND DROP DEAD SUSPENSE.

Legendary lawman Eliot Ness goes solo… In 1929,
Eliot Ness put away Al Scarface Capone and became
the biggest living legend this side of law and order.
Now it's 1935. With The Untouchables and Prohi-
bition behind him and the Great Depression falling
darkly across the nation, Ness arrives in Cleveland to
straighten out a crooked city.

An anonymous ring of bent cops is dealing in
vice, graft, gambling and racketeering, over lorded
by a mysterious top cop known as the outside chief.
But between corrupt politicians, jealous colleagues,
a parasitic reporter and two blondes with nothing in
common, Ness has big troubles pulling the sheets off
the bed of blue vipers.

"For anybody who loves crime novels, Max Allen
Collins is the gold standard."

An Eliot Ness Mystery Omnibus includes: Dark
City, Butcher's Dozen, Bullet Proof and Murder by
The Numbers.

AVAILABLE NOW

About the Authors

MAX ALLAN COLLINS was named a Grand Master in 2017 by the Mystery Writers of America. He is a three-time winner of the Private Eye Writers of America "Shamus" award, receiving the PWA "Eye" for Life Achievement (2006) and their "Hammer" award for making a major contribution to the private eye genre with the Nathan Heller saga (2012).

His graphic novel Road to Perdition (1998) became the Academy Award-winning Tom Hanks film, followed by prose sequels and several graphic novels. His other comics credits include the syndicated strip "Dick Tracy"; "Batman"; and his own "Ms. Tree" and "Wild Dog."

His innovative Quarry novels were adapted as a 2016 TV series by Cinemax. His other suspense series include Eliot Ness, Krista Larson, Reeder and Rogers, and the "Disaster" novels. He has completed twelve "Mike Hammer" novels begun by the late Mickey Spillane; his audio novel, Mike Hammer: The Little Death with Stacy Keach, won a 2011 Audie.

For five years, he was sole licensing writer for TV's CSI: Crime Scene Investigation (and its spin-offs), writing best-selling novels, graphic novels, and video games. His tie-in books have appeared on the USA TODAY and New York Times bestseller lists, including Saving Private Ryan, Air Force One, and American Gangster.

Collins has written and directed four features and two documentaries, including the Lifetime movie "Mommy" (1996) and "Mike Hammer's Mickey Spillane" (1998); he scripted "The Expert," a 1995 HBO World Premiere and "The Last Lullaby" (2009) from his novel The Last Quarry. His Edgar-nominated play "Eliot Ness: An Untouchable Life" (2004) became a PBS special, and he has co-authored (with A. Brad Schwartz) two non-fiction books on Ness, Scarface and the Untouchable (2018) and Eliot Ness and the Mad Butcher (2020).

Collins and his wife, writer Barbara Collins, live in Iowa; as "Barbara Allan," they have collaborated on sixteen novels, including the "Trash 'n' Treasures" mysteries, Antiques Flee Market (2008) winning the Romantic Times Best Humorous Mystery Novel award of 2009. Their son Nathan has translated numerous novels into English from Japanese, as well as video games and manga.

Barbara Collins made her entrance into the mystery field as a highly respected short story writer with appearances in over a dozen top anthologies, including Murder Most Delicious, Women on the Edge, Deadly Housewives and the best-selling Cat Crimes series. She was the co-editor of (and a contributor to) the best-selling anthology Lethal Ladies, and her stories were selected for inclusion in the first three volumes of The Year's 25 Finest Crime and Mystery Stories.

As "Barbara Allan," she and her husband Max Allan Collins write the long-running "Trash 'n' Treasures" mystery series. Their Antiques Flee Market (2008) won the Romantic Times "Best Humorous Mystery Novel" award of 2009. They have also appeared under their joint byline in Ellery Queen's Mystery Magazine.

The Collins's first novel together, the Baby Boomer thriller Regeneration, was a paperback bestseller; their second collaborative novel, Bombshell – in which Marilyn Monroe saves the world from World War III – was published in hardcover to excellent reviews. Both are back in print from Thomas & Mercer under their "Barbara Allan" byline.

Two acclaimed hardcover collections of Barbara's work have been published – Too Many Tomcats and (with her husband) Murder - His and Hers, with a follow-up, Suspense – His and Hers – coming from Wolfpack, who are bringing out the previous collections as well.

Barbara also has been the production manager and/

or line producer on several of Max's independent film projects, including Mommy (1995), Mommy's Day (1997), Real Time: Siege at Lucas Street Market (2001) and Eliot Ness: An Untouchable Life (2005).

The writing duo lives in their native Muscatine, Iowa. Their son, Nathan, is a Japanese-to-English translator with numerous books, manga and video games to his credit. Barb divides her time between writing and providing Day Care for her two grand-childen, Sam and Lucy.